A PRICE TO PAY

A PRICE TO PAY

A Novel

ALEX CAPUS

Translated by
John Brownjohn

First published in German as *Der Fälscher, die Spionin und der Bombenbauer* in 2013
Copyright © Carl Hanser Verlag, Munich, 2013

First published in English in 2014 by
HAUS PUBLISHING LTD.
70 Cadogan Place, London SW1X 9AH
www.hauspublishing.com

Translation copyright © John Brownjohn, 2014

Print ISBN 978 1 908323 73 6
ebook ISBN 978 1 908323 74 3

Typeset in Garamond by MacGuru Ltd
info@macguru.org.uk

Printed and bound by TJ International Ltd, Padstow, Cornwall

A CIP catalogue for this book is available from the British Library

This book has been translated with the support of the Swiss Arts Council Pro Helvetia.

swiss arts council
pr⊃helvetia

Émile Gilliéron
1885–1939

Laura d'Oriano
1911–1943

Felix Bloch
1905–1983

1

I like the girl. It pleases me to picture her sitting in the open doorway of the rearmost carriage of the Orient Express with the glittering silver waters of Lake Zurich gliding past her. It could be early November 1924, I don't know the exact date. She is thirteen years old, a tall, thin, rather gawky girl with a small but deeply incised furrow above her nose. Her right leg is drawn up, her left dangling over the step into space. She's leaning against the door frame, swaying to the rhythm of the rails with her fair hair fluttering in the wind. For protection from the cold she clutches a woollen blanket to her chest. The notice board on the side of the carriage reads 'Constantinople-Paris', and emblazoned above it are some brass lettering and the company's emblem incorporating the royal lions of Belgium.

She is using her right hand to smoke cigarettes that quickly smoulder away in the airstream. It's not unusual for children to smoke where she comes from. Between cigarettes she sings snatches of oriental songs – Turkish lullabies, Lebanese ballads, Egyptian love songs. She wants to be a singer like her mother, but a better one. She will never enlist the help of her legs and cleavage on-stage, the way her mother does, nor will she wear a pink feather boa or be accompanied on the piano by individuals like her father, who always keeps a tumbler of brandy on top of the piano and winks and performs a glissando whenever her mother flashes her garter. She wants to be a genuine artist. She has a big, expansive feeling in her chest and will some day lend expression to it, she knows that for sure.

Her voice is still thin and hoarse, she knows that too. She can hardly hear herself as she sits on her step and sings. The wind snatches the melodies from her lips and bears them off into the turbulence behind the last carriage.

It is three days since she boarded the blue, second-class carriage in Constantinople with her parents and her four siblings. Since then she has spent many hours sitting in the open doorway. Inside the compartment with her family it's stuffy and noisy, and outside it's mild for the time of year. During those three days on her step she has sniffed the scent of Bulgarian vineyards and watched hares cavorting in the stubbly wheat fields of Vojvodina, waved to Danubian bargees who responded with blasts on their hooters, and, in the suburbs of Belgrade, Budapest, Bratislava and Vienna, glimpsed weary men in vests sitting in front of their plates in the dimly-lit kitchens of soot-stained tenement buildings.

When the wind blows the smoke from the locomotive to the right she sits in the left-hand doorway, when it veers she changes sides. Once, when a conductor shooed her back into the compartment for safety's sake, she made a show of obeying, but as soon as he'd gone she opened the door again and resumed her seat on the step.

On the third evening, shortly before Salzburg, the conductors had gone from compartment to compartment to announce an unscheduled change of route: the train would turn off after Innsbruck and skirt Germany to the south by going through Tyrol and Switzerland. Now that Franco-Belgian troops had marched into the Ruhr, it was almost impossible for the

Franco-Belgian Orient Express to follow its usual route via Munich and Stuttgart. The Reichsbahn's dispatchers were deliberately misrouting it or refusing the locomotive coal and water, and at stations the police made all the passengers get off and conducted night-long passport controls, and even when they were finally allowed to proceed, the station's exit was often obstructed by an abandoned cattle or timber wagon which no one in the whole of Germany had authority to shunt into a siding without the formal consent of its legal owner, and obtaining this through official channels could be extremely time-consuming.

It had grown cold and dark once they entered Tyrol, where menacingly converging walls of rock towered skyward on either side of the track. When the girl would have had to lie on her back to see the stars in the night sky, she retired to the compartment and lay down to sleep in the cosy fug exuded by her family. Early next morning, however, when the train eventually crossed the Arlberg and picked up speed on the downward run, she returned to her step with the woollen blanket. She watched the valleys widen and the mountain peaks recede, giving way, as the sun rose, first to villages and streams, then to towns and rivers, and finally to lakes.

Her parents have long been accustomed to their daughter's headstrong ways. She used to sit outside on the step even as a little girl. It must have been between Tikrit and Mosul, during their second or third Baghdad tour, that she had first made her way along the corridor for a better view of the cranes on the banks of the Tigris. On the return journey she had sat on the step again, refusing to be parted from the sight of mosquito-infested paddy fields or steppes and mountains blushing in the sunset. She has always sat on her step ever since, whether travelling up the Nile delta from Alexandria to Cairo, or on board a narrow-gauge train in the Lebanese mountains, or in transit from Constantinople to Tehran. She always sits on the step, watching the world go by and singing. She occasionally allows one of her siblings to sit beside her, but only for a while; then she insists on being alone again.

At Kilchberg the scent of chocolate fills her nose as the massive, majestic Lindt & Sprüngli factory glides past behind her. A few sailing boats are cruising on the lake and a paddle steamer is lying alongside a landing stage. The morning mist has dispersed, the sky is pale blue. The countryside has yet to experience a frost, so the fields on the opposite shore are too green for the time of year. The city looms up out of the haze at the apex of the lake. The track traces a long curve and merges with four, eight, twenty other tracks that converge from all directions, draw parallel, and ultimately debouch into Zurich's central station.

It is quite possible that, as she entered the city in November 1924, the girl caught the eye of a young man who often used to sit on the loading platform of a grey, weather-worn goods shed, watching the trains pull in and out and ruminating on the future course of his life. In my mind's eye he kneads his cap in his hands as the Orient Express passes him and catches sight of the girl in the doorway of the rearmost carriage, who eyes him with casual interest.

The youth doesn't really fit with the loading platform and the goods shed. He certainly isn't a shunter or a porter. He's wearing knickerbockers and a tweed jacket, and his shoes gleam in the late autumn sunlight. His regular features testify, if not to a carefree childhood, at least to one devoid of disasters. His complexion is clear, and his eyes, nose, mouth and chin are arranged at right angles like the doors and windows of a house. His brown hair is neatly parted. A bit too neatly, perhaps.

She sees that his eyes are following her, and that he's looking at her the way a man looks at a woman. It is only recently that men have begun to look at her like that. Most of them quickly grasp how young she is and avert their gaze in embarrassment. This youth doesn't seem to notice. She finds him appealing. He looks strong but not aggressive. No fool, either.

He raises a hand in greeting and she reciprocates. She doesn't wave it in a girlish way, nor does she coquettishly waggle all five fingers – just casually raises her hand, like him. He smiles and she smiles back.

Then they lose sight of each other. They will never see each other again, the girl realises that. Being an experienced traveller, she knows that people normally encounter one another only once, because any sensible journey leads in as straight a line as possible from starting point to destination, and the laws of geometry prescribe that two straight lines cannot intersect twice. Repeated encounters occur only among villagers, valley dwellers and islanders, who spend a lifetime treading the same beaten tracks and thus keep crossing one another's path.

The young man on the loading platform is not a villager or islander, but was born and brought up in Zurich and is thoroughly familiar with the city's beaten tracks. He would like to see that anonymous girl in the open doorway again. He will if she gets out in Zurich, he feels sure. If not, he won't.

Nineteen years old, he matriculated four months ago. He now has to decide on a course of study – urgently. Term has already begun and the deadline for enrolment expires at 11 am tomorrow.

His father would like him to study mechanical or civil engineering. Zurich's Federal Institute of Technology, or ETH, has an excellent reputation, and some of the world's foremost industrial firms are located on the city's outskirts. In Baden, Brown Boveri & Cie make the best turbines in the world, Sulzer of Winterthur manufactures the best mechanical looms and diesel engines, and the Oerlikon engineering works produce the finest locomotives. Study mechanical engineering, says his father. As a technician you'll be set up for life.

His father is a grain merchant, not a technician. You can forget about trading in grain with Eastern Europe, says his father, it's a thing of the past. The frontiers are tight as a drum, customs duties are high and the Bolsheviks are crazy – you can't do business with them. Grain was fine for your grandfather, it made him a wealthy man. Wheat from the Ukraine, potatoes from Russia, and a little Hungarian red wine and some Bosnian dried figs for the morale. Those were the good times. The railways had already been built, nationalism had yet to take hold, and a Jew could get by quite well under the crumbling empires. Your grandfather still believed in the grain trade, that's why he sent me off to Zurich. I duly came here and became a Swiss citizen, but I had no faith in it even then. Now I'm here, I'll carry on for as long as I can. The business will see me and your mother out.

But the Ukrainian grain trade won't keep *you* in groceries, my son, which is why I advise you to study mechanical engineering. Everything is machine-made these days. Grain is sowed by machines, harvested by machines and milled by machines. Loaves are baked by machines, cattle slaughtered by machines, buildings built by machines. Music comes from machines manufactured by machines, pictures are produced by cameras, not painters. We'll soon need machines for making love, and have clean, silent machines for dying, and machines will discreetly handle the unobtrusive removal of corpses. We won't worship God any more, but a machine or the name of its manufacturer, and the Messiah who brings world peace and rebuilds the Temple in Jerusalem will be a machine or its maker, not a son of the house of Judah. The world has become one enormous machine, my son, that's why I'm advising you to go the ETH and study mechanical engineering.

His son listens and nods, being a good son who accords his father due respect. Secretly, however, he thinks: No, I won't do mechanical engineering. I know machines, and I'd sooner do nothing at all in life than dance attendance on them. If I do anything, it'll be something totally useless and impractical, something a machine can't harness.

The young man has spent half his childhood and adolescence studying the havoc wrought by machines at long range. He was less than nine years old when his father handed the *Neue Zürcher Zeitung* across the breakfast table, with its Sarajevo headline, and from then on he read the latest reports from the Meuse, the Marne and the Somme every day. He looked up the location of Ypres, Verdun and the Chemin des Dames in his atlas, hung a map of Europe above the bed in his nursery and stuck coloured pins in it, and kept statistics in squared exercise books in which he recorded the dead first in thousands, then in hundreds of thousands, and eventually millions. But he never succeeded in finding any purpose in all that killing. Or any logic. Or a plausible excuse for it. Or a proper reason, even.

To console himself, he spent hours playing the piano in his parents' living room. He wasn't a particularly talented pupil, but when his fingers began to obey him he developed a profound affection for Bach's Goldberg Variations, whose serene, reliable and computable mechanics reminded him of the galactic ballet of the planets, suns and moons.

He was, as he recorded in his handwritten memoirs decades later, a solitary child. At primary school the other children teased him because he spoke Swiss German with a Bohemian accent, and his teacher never failed to remind the class that Felix belonged to an evil, alien race.

His protectress and closest ally was his sister Clara, who was three years his senior. When she died in the second year of the war, having punctured her right foot on a nail, he lapsed for years into a state of hopeless depression. Although developments in early 20th-century science enabled the doctors to explain precisely what went on in Clara's body – bacterial infection, septicaemia, ultimate collapse – they did not know of any therapy that could have saved her from a painful, senseless, banal death. Felix's performance at secondary school deteriorated badly in the months that followed. Why should he make an effort in biology and chemistry if science proved useless in a crisis? Why should he learn anything at all if his knowledge was good for nothing?

The only subject that gave him any pleasure was mathematics, with its dependable, impractical mental gymnastics. Equations with several unknowns, trigonometry, curve discussions – the youngster found it a revelation that something as lucid and beautiful as the relationship between numerals existed. During the autumn vacation of 1917 he spent a whole week calculating the length of an October day with the aid of the earth's rotatory velocity, its axis's angle of inclination to the sun, and Zurich's geographical latitude. The next day he used his pocket watch to measure the lapse of time between sunrise and sunset and was indescribably happy when it accorded with his calculations. The discovery that an idea of his – a trigonometrical calculation – actually had some connection with the real world, and was even in tune with it, filled him with a sense of the harmony between mind and matter that remained with him for the rest of his days.

What most disconcerted him during the war years was the fact that his newspaper-derived knowledge of the world contrasted so sharply with his everyday, empirical observations. When he looked down at Seehofstrasse from his bedroom window he saw no riflemen sprinting along trenches or bloated equine corpses lying in shell-holes, just well-nourished maidservants returning home laden with overflowing shopping bags and apple-cheeked children playing marbles on the pavement. He saw groups of cigarette-smoking taxi drivers waiting for fares from the opera house, and cabbies dozing behind dozing horses, and the knife-grinder going from door to door. The peace that reigned in Seehofstrasse was so complete that one never even saw a policeman. This tranquil street lay in the heart of an inconceivably peaceful city in the heart of an inconceivably peaceful country whose farmers plodded along the furrows of their ancestral acres toward a horizon beyond which Europeans were slaughtering each other on a grand scale. Only on very quiet nights was it possible to hear, from across the Rhine and the Black Forest, the distant thunder of the Franco-German front line.

That thunder pursued him into his dreams, where it swelled to an ear-splitting roar. He waded across stretches of ravaged countryside, knee-deep in rivers of blood, and awoke in time to read the *Morgenblatt* at breakfast, filled with impotent horror by reports of how the war machine was ploughing up the continent and devouring every last thing that could be of use to it. It swallowed monks and spat them out as army chaplains, turned sheepdogs into trench tykes and aerial pioneers into military pilots, gamekeepers into snipers and concert pianists into bandsmen, paediatricians into front-line sawbones, philosophers into warmongers and lyric poets into bloodthirsty jingoists. Church bells were melted down into cannons and the lenses of opera glasses installed in telescopes, cruise liners became troopships, psalms turned into national anthems, the looms from Winterthur wove serge for uniforms instead of silk, the turbines from Baden no longer produced current for Christmas lights but for the electric locomotives from Oerlikon, which no longer conveyed tourists to the Engadine but hauled coal and steel to the furnaces and foundries of the arms manufacturers.

After 1,500 days, or shortly before Felix Bloch's 13th birthday, the war machine faltered for want of fuel and reluctantly ground to a halt. Since then it has remained comparatively inactive, true, but now it is humming once more; before long it will judder and rattle again, and sooner or later its flywheels will start to rotate and its teeth will once more chew up the landscape and devour the flesh and souls of humankind.

It is possible that the machine cannot be stopped, the young man tells himself, but it won't get me. I won't join in, I won't study mechanical engineering. I shall do something thoroughly impractical – something nice and useless which the machine cannot incorporate. Something like the Goldberg Variations. I'll find something all right. I won't go to the ETH, anyway. I won't do mechanical engineering whatever Father says. I'd sooner become a brewer's drayman.

Defiantly, resolutely, he thrusts himself away from the goods shed and jumps off the loading platform. Even before he lands on the gravel below, however, his courage fails and his determination evaporates, and by the time he takes his first few steps along the paved walkway that leads between the tracks to the station concourse, something like a bitter champagne bubble slowly but irresistibly rises from his innards, via his heart, to his head: it's the realisation that he certainly will go to the ETH and study mechanical engineering. This is firstly because he couldn't bear to fall out with his father, secondly because his marks in maths, physics and chemistry are uniformly excellent, and thirdly because he can't for the life of him think what his particular abilities fit him for, other than studying mechanical engineering at the ETH.

A signal between the tracks goes green, denoting that the Geneva Express is free to leave the station. Seated in a first-class compartment on this early November day in 1924 – whether it is really at the same hour on the same day cannot be stated with absolute certainty – is the painter Émile Gilliéron. He has been travelling on business from Greece, via Trieste and Innsbruck, to Geislingen near Ulm, where he had to place an order with the Württembergische Metallwarenfabrik. On the return journey he proposes to make a detour to Lake Geneva in order to bury the ashes of his father, who dropped dead in an Athenian restaurant just before his 73rd birthday, in his native soil.

His father, likewise named Émile Gilliéron, had also been a painter in Greece and a famous man. The artist who had accompanied Heinrich Schliemann on his celebrated excavations of Troy and Mycenae, he had designed a series of postage stamps for the Greek post office, been art master to the Greek royal family, built himself an imposing Athenian residence with a splendid view of the Acropolis, and brought up his son to be an efficient business partner. It had therefore come as a great surprise to the family to discover, when his will was opened, that he had left nothing but debts. Although the Gilliérons lived in great style, it transpired that they had always lived from hand to mouth.

The dead man's dependants were further embarrassed by his testamentary wish to be buried in his old home beside Lake Geneva, because repatriating his remains across three or four national frontiers would have entailed a financial and administrative burden such as only the Pope, the King of England or an American railroad tycoon could have afforded to assume. The only relatively practicable expedient was to cremate him in secret and transport his ashes to Switzerland. Although cremation was strictly prohibited in Orthodox Greece, there were undertakers in the embassy quarter of Athens who specialised in foreign clients. On the day of the funeral they would, for an additional fee, bring the priest an empty coffin weighted down with sandbags and take the corpse to be unofficially and secretly cremated.

Émile Gilliéron had firmly declined to be apprised of the precise details of this service. He had no wish to know which baker or potter had made his oven or kiln available during the night before baking loaves or firing pitchers in it the next morning. It wasn't until he was steaming from Piraeus to Trieste in the Lloyd Triestino mailboat that it occurred to him he would never know if his father had really been cremated or fed to the sharks, and if the cigar box in his suitcase contained a stranger's ashes or the pulverised bones of a mongrel.

Émile Gilliéron junior is a handsome man in the prime of life. His face is still youthfully chiselled and tanned golden brown by years spent with his father at the archaeological sites of Knossos, and his eyes glow like those of his Italian mother Josephine, who plied him and his father with solicitude and jealousy throughout her life. His hair and luxuriant moustache are a trifle too black to be entirely natural, his nose is reddened by a daily bottle of Armagnac, and a trace of bitterness and frustrated ambition lurks at the corners of his mouth. Awaiting him back in Athens are his Italian wife Ernesta, who devotes her spare time to painting pleasant pictures – never of anything but the same view of the Acropolis – on the terrace on their house, and his first-born son, who answers to the name Alfred and is four years old.

2

It would be quite fortuitous if Émile Gilliéron had noticed the girl and the boy as he emerged from Zurich's central station, and I want it to be so. I want him to have sat for too long in the station buffet and have had to run to catch the train. I want him to have removed his hat and coat and put his suitcase up on the luggage rack, panting and perspiring, as the train slowly gathers speed on its way out of the station.

I want Émile Gilliéron to flop down on the seat, gasping for breath, and look out of the window on his right. A dark blue train is travelling in the opposite direction some distance away. Visible through its windows are passengers thronging the corridors in readiness to alight. All the doors are still closed except in the last carriage, where a fair-haired, teenage girl is sitting on the step, yawning, her mouth wide open. A strange sight at this time of year, thinks Émile Gilliéron – the silly thing will catch her death out there. She probably had a row with her parents and is now refusing to go back into the nice, warm compartment. Thinks of her parents as toads or baboons, whereas she herself is the acme of Creation. She ought at least to hold on to the grab handle with one hand, or her youthful arrogance could be abruptly snuffed out, and it would look nicer if she put the other hand over her mouth when she yawns.

The blue train disappears from view on the right. Meanwhile, the left-hand window reveals some goods sheds and a youth shuffling along between the tracks. Another of that type, thinks Gilliéron. The boy looks like someone preparing to throw himself in front of a train because he's too good for this world. Or too bad. Strange that healthy, nice-looking young people should throw themselves under trains. He won't manage to do it under mine, thank God, he's too far away. It always takes hours for everything to be cleaned up so the train can finally proceed on its way.

The conductor comes to check the tickets. Émile Gilliéron lights one of his Egyptian cigarettes with a gold monogram printed on it, then sits back and gazes out of the window at the land of his fathers, whose doll's-house-like neatness fascinates him anew on every visit. The train passes a cute little brewery, a pretty little mill and the shiny steel spheres of a miniature gasworks, then follows the course of an agreeably meandering little river to the outlying wooded, gently undulating range of hills. It makes intermediate stops at neat little doll's-house-like stations belonging to gloomy but equally neat little towns enclosed by medieval walls behind which live people who, although industrious and polite, are not very good-humoured. Or very well-dressed.

Between two small towns the train passes the limestone uprights of a medieval gallows as snow-white and visible from afar as if the last unfortunate miscreant had been hanging there only yesterday. They must be the only nation, thinks Gilliéron, to have banned the death penalty but left the gallows standing. What sort of people not only fail to raze the execution sites of defunct feudalism but clean and maintain them for centuries? Little people in a little country with little ideas, who build little towns and railway stations and incredibly punctual trains. Even the gallows is small. I'd graze my knees if they strung me up from it.

At the eighth small town Gilliéron has to change trains. Thereafter his route takes him past one small lake to the next small lake, then across a range of hills clothed in bare, wintry potato fields and through some ludicrously small vineyards still gilded by the sunset's afterglow. Towering in the south, massive and immovable, is Mont Blanc, Europe's highest mountain. Something big in this country at last, thinks Gilliéron, although he knows that Mont Blanc is in France, strictly speaking, whereas the Swiss content themselves with the view of it. Economically, that's a shrewd decision. The mountain looks beautiful from a distance and the touristic marketing of its idyllic, postcard beauty brings in good money. Seen close up, by contrast, it's just a dangerous and expensive mass of rock and scree.

In Lausanne Gilliéron changes to a local train. Half an hour later he reaches the eastern end of Lake Geneva, his father's birthplace and the goal of his journey.

Villeneuve station is in darkness. There's no one on the platform and no light burning in the station building. The ticket office is shut, the waiting-room doorway littered with dead leaves. There are no cabs, either motorised or horse-drawn, let alone porters. In the station forecourt, which is flanked by some leafless plane trees, pigeons are pecking at the tyre-flattened horse dung on the wet cobblestones. Visible beyond the station are the dark outlines of the Vaud Pre-Alps, and on a slight rise in front of them is the Hôtel Byron, which has spent a hundred years waiting vainly for well-to-do English visitors and has bankrupted all its owners.

Émile Gilliéron puts his suitcase down and sniffs the air. It really is redolent of decay – of the sweet, spicy, marshy smell of the Rhône delta, which his father could inveigh against as tirelessly as if it still lingered in his nose after decades of Greek exile. According to him, prolonged inhalation of Villeneuve's bad air led to consumption and imbecility, rickets and caries, alcoholism, shingles, epilepsy, and all forms of feminine hysteria. He attributed this multiple toxicity to the fact that the marshy smell was simply the stench of rotting, dying organisms that had had a lifetime to collect all manner of pathogens. Interestingly enough, people who fell into the marshes did not decay because, instead of remaining on the oxygen-rich surface, they quite quickly sank to a depth of three or four metres, where the specific weight of their bodies corresponded to that of the surrounding ooze, and where, if they weren't already dead, they suffocated and remained in a stable, airtight state of suspension. Gently tanned by the marsh acids for thousands of years, they preserved a physical freshness of which the Pharoahs' embalmers, for all their skill, could only have dreamed. It could thus be safely assumed that Villeneuve's marshes harboured the well-preserved corpses of hundreds if not thousands of individuals who, though lying peacefully side by side, could never have encountered each other in the light of day: Celtic fishermen beside Burgundian crusaders, Roman legionaries beside German pilgrims bound for Rome, Moorish explorers beside Venetian spice merchants and Alemannic shepherdesses. Some might have owed their drowning to unrequited love, others to the thrill of the chase, and others to drink or stupidity or tight-fistedness, because they were unwilling to pay the Comte de Chillon's road toll; and lying somewhere as if asleep had also to be Villeneuve's 127 Jews, whom the local citizens had massacred and thrown into the swamp for poisoning the wells during the plague epidemic in 1348.

Ah, the citizens of Villeneuve.

Gilliéron's father had spent his entire childhood and adolescence among them, and although he had lived in exile for half a century thereafter, he had remained one of them. Perhaps he had fled Villeneuve as a young man only in order to remain one of them instead of being cast out for good.

The citizens of Villeneuve were fishermen, farmers and carters, industrious Protestants and docile underlings aware of their proper place in a well-ordered world. Every fisherman's son knew that he would ply the lake all his life, and every farmer's son knew that he would farm his inherited acres until the end of his days; this was so much taken for granted that they never thought twice about it. They married in their mid twenties and died at fifty. First-born sons were named after their fathers. Lights out was at half past nine, sex with the wife on Wednesdays, fish for supper on Fridays. On Sundays the men attended Mass wearing black jackets. Not grey jackets, for instance, still less blue ones.

Of course, even in Villeneuve there were always a few youths who sported blue jackets to please the girls, and there had always been a pack of young pups roaming the streets who dreamed of leaving Villeneuve and running off to Italy across the Great St Bernard Pass. The townsfolk sympathised with this because they'd been young once themselves, but they were just as clear that the fun had to stop sooner or later. A young man's pup licence expired at latest after his twentieth birthday. Anyone continuing to wear a blue jacket after that might have done better to disappear across the Great St Bernard.

Ah, the citizens of Villeneuve. Though Papa Gilliéron could

vehemently denounce Villeneuve's marshes, he mildly stroked his white goatee whenever the subject of its citizens cropped up. The son soon realised that his father had to detest the marshes of Villeneuve with such passion only because he wanted to go on loving its inhabitants.

Émile Gilliéron picks up his suitcase again, crosses the station forecourt and plunges into the nocturnal gloom of the Grande Rue, which is flanked by medieval half-timbered buildings. All the windows are dark although it isn't even ten. On the right a chemist's, on the left a bakery, on the right a butcher's shop, on the left the Hôtel de l'Aigle. The food there is said to be really good, but the place is already in darkness. A fishing net is hanging up to dry in one side street, a dung heap in the next smells of cattle.

Splashing in front of the church is a big, isolated fountain. That must be the trough his father had talked about. For many hundreds of years the women of Villeneuve used to wash their laundry in the trough, heedless of the fact that one corner of it was supported by a strange round column bearing the inscription 'XXVI'. The cantonal archaeologist from Lausanne, who passed by one day, informed the inhabitants of Villeneuve that their washing trough reposed on a 2,000-year-old milestone from the ancient Roman military road, and that the numeral 26 recorded the distance in Roman miles from the garrison town of Martigny. The townsfolk nodded thoughtfully, cocked their heads and gave their Roman milestone a look of approval, and many of them muttered '*Tiens donc*' and '*Sacré Romains*' or '*Ça, par exemple*'. But when the cantonal archaeologist asked them to preserve this testimony to the past from the elements and soapy water and set it up inside the church for the benefit of posterity, they defiantly buried their hands in their pockets and thrust out their lower lips because the work would have entailed summoning the stonemason from Vevey and paying him at least 25 batzen. They did not comply until the archaeologist himself deposited 25 batzen on the trough and added another 15.

This had occurred in the middle of the 19th century, while Émile Gilliéron senior was growing up in Villeneuve, the only son of the village schoolmaster and a perfectly ordinary village boy of no particular note. He was averagely tall, averagely robust and averagely brown-haired, and he displayed no outstanding characteristics or discernible talents bar one: he could draw incredibly well – incredibly neatly and expressively and with incredible, almost photographic precision. He had received no special lessons and had not been encouraged or made to practice by anyone. He wasn't even particularly fond of drawing; it was simply something he could do. And since Villeneuve offered few forms of entertainment for young people, he drew the whole time. Even as a seven-year-old he had drawn some amazingly good lightning portraits in charcoal of his schoolmates on the playground flagstones, and on Sundays he went down to the harbour with his box of watercolours and painted the boats and the lakeside willow trees and the snow-covered mountains on the horizon with a facility that convinced those who saw his paintings that they could feel the afternoon breeze blowing inland from the lake.

The townsfolk of Villeneuve had registered his talent without giving it much thought. That's life, they said with a shrug. Many folk can do things other folk can't, no need to lose any sleep over it. Some people can sense the location of underground streams or hear ghostly voices, others can speak in tongues or cure warts. Young Gilliéron can draw well, so what? It doesn't matter or harm anyone. As long as he plays with his crayons, he can't get into mischief.

Gilliéron credited his gift with equally little importance. To him, drawing was merely a pastime that didn't give him all that much pleasure. He wasn't particularly proud of his drawings, either, nor did he hawk them around town or keep them. No sooner were they finished than he deposited them as kindling on the woodpile next the stove.

This did not change until 1866, when he turned 15, donned a blue jacket and started to dream of decamping to Italy forever instead of becoming a Villeneuvian farmer, fisherman or village schoolmaster like the other young pups in his age group. When his father proposed to send him to the college of education in Lausanne, he snorted contemptuously and announced that he would sooner be drawn and quartered than spend the rest of his days shuttling between a schoolmaster's lectern and a blackboard.

Instead, he set up his first studio in an abandoned barn beside the marshes, let his hair grow, and smoked lengths of old man's beard torn from trees and laid out to dry on the floor of the barn. On market days he loitered in front of taverns and looked after the horses of farmers from out of town in return for a glass of Féchy. When he needed money he helped out in the vineyards or cleaned the fishermen's nets. When the weather was fine he spent the evenings with his friends beneath an old weeping willow beside the lake. During the winter his studio served as a rendezvous.

A year went by in this way, then another and another. But when Émile Gilliéron and his friends attained their majority and still showed no signs of exchanging their blue jackets for black jackets, or at least grey ones, the townsfolk of Villeneuve decided that enough was enough. One mild night in spring, for unexplained reasons, his studio was totally destroyed by fire, and two weeks later the postman brought him a letter in which, to his surprise, he was informed by Basel's College of Arts and Crafts that he had qualified for admission to the course for budding art teachers and was to present himself for enrolment between eight and ten o'clock the following Monday morning.

Émile realised that the real author of this letter was not Basel's College of Arts and Crafts but the citizenry of Villeneuve, who must have purloined some of his drawings and sent them off to Basel, and that the letter should be construed as banishment rather than an invitation. And so, snorting contemptuously, he bundled up his things, went off to Basel, and, still snorting contemptuously, discovered after his first term there that he could already do everything the teachers tried to teach him. True, he learned how to sketch, scrape, engrave, etch, model clay and use a palette knife, techniques of which he had never even heard in Villeneuve, and the permanent exhibition in the Swiss capital's Museum of Art opened his eyes to worlds of which he had never dreamt in the marshes of the Rhône delta; back in the classroom, however, he copied, modified and caricatured ad lib any Old Master he had seen, any style and any school. He painted chubby angelic putti like Rubens and arrow-riddled martyrs like Caravaggio, and he made his fellow students laugh by painting angelic putti riddled with arrows and martyrs dancing with drumsticks protruding from their mouths; he threw vases and modelled statuettes of gods and drew Greek temples and statuary as if he had spent his entire life in the Peloponnese, and all this with a casual indifference and disdain for his own talent that fascinated and slightly offended his teachers.

After class he roamed the taverns of Kleinbasel and became notorious as an unrivalled drinker of white wine. His unaffected warmth and bucolic wit made him friends wherever he went, but his fellow students resented the fact that he, who could always do at a stroke what they had laboriously to learn, eschewed any erudite, round-table discussions about art and artistic inspiration because he was more interested in the waitresses' legs and décolletés.

For all his laziness and nonchalance, Émile Gilliéron was indisputably the best student in his year. He won all the competitions even though the college administration invariably had to urge him to enter them and he always completed his entries the night before they had to be handed in, and when the Christoph Merian Foundation advertised a two-year scholarship to the École des Beaux-Arts in Paris, he applied for it only in order to postpone his inevitable return to Villeneuve.

He spent most of the following two years in the bistros of the Marais and Montmartre. Between times, just for form's sake, he put in a little study under the most popular teachers and artists of his day. His monthly scholarship payments covered his financial needs only until the middle of the month, after which he copied works by Millet, Troyon and Courbet and sold them to innkeepers and tourists. His most lucrative source of income, however, was Greco-Roman architectural daubs in the bombastically historicist style so popular with the smug bourgeoisie under Napoleon III.

Although wearing blue jackets was positively de rigueur among the bohemians of Paris, Émile quickly succeeded, even in this comparatively libertarian environment, in making himself unpopular with all the college dignitaries. He permanently damaged his chances in the Parisian art scene right at the start of the annual Salon by turning up with an open bottle of white wine in his hand and grinning broadly throughout the speech delivered by the president of the École des Beaux-Arts. Later on, when he urinated behind a statue of Joan of Arc in the garden and knocked a tray of petits fours out of a footman's hand, two uniformed stewards threw him out into the street.

Time passed quickly, and the day was fast approaching when Émile would be compelled to return to Villeneuve and wear a black jacket for evermore. It so happened that the German millionaire Heinrich Schliemann, who owned a handsome house on the Place Saint Michel and had, in his middle years, taken it into his head to abandon his Russian business interests and become the most famous archaeologist in the world, enquired of the director of the École des Beaux-Arts if his students included a good draughtsman who could be of service to him at his diggings in Mycenae. The director thereupon sent for the unruly but talented Émile Gilliéron, because he thought he needed an outlet and would never, in any case, find his feet in the strictly ritualised Parisian art world. When asked if he would like to go to Greece as a scientific draughtsman, Émile jumped at the opportunity.

The director drew his attention to the fact that Schliemann was a Mecklenburg pastor's son with a domineering, volatile temperament. He had never had a friend in his life, was a restless globe-trotter, and insisted on learning the language of whichever country he was visiting within a few days.

At least that meant he spoke to people, said Gilliéron.

Schliemann didn't speak, he gave orders, said the director. Love and friendship were alien to him. As Schliemann saw it, humanity consisted of superiors and subordinates. He had divorced his Russian wife because he wished to pursue his archaeological venture with a Greek woman at his side. He had written to the Archbishop of Athens asking him to suggest a selection of beautiful young Greek women, and had chosen a 17-year-old on the basis of photographs. More than 30 years older than the poor girl, the bridegroom spent their four-month honeymoon dragging her around the antiquities of Italy and plying her so relentlessly with German lessons that she suffered a nervous breakdown shortly after reaching Paris.

Well, said Gilliéron, he wasn't proposing to marry Schliemann.

He should also bear in mind, said the director, that no one took Schliemann's archaeological pretensions seriously. Professional archaeologists scorned this naive Prussian who had crossed the Hellespont with a spade in one hand and a popular edition of the *Iliad* in the other, promptly convinced that he had found the actual palace of Priam, complete with buried treasure, or the actual battlefield outside the gates of Troy on which Aphrodite had saved her favourite, Paris, from the battleaxe of Menelaus.

For all that, said Gilliéron, the man *had* unearthed quite a lot of nice-looking things.

But not Menelaus's battleaxe, said the director. One might as well go digging for Don Quixote's lance in Andalusia or Hansel and Gretel's bread oven in the Black Forest.

A battleaxe is a battleaxe, said Gilliéron.

The director conceded this, but said it was remarkable how often Schliemann unearthed his shiny gold gewgaws on the last day of the excavations, just when no one was looking, whereas all that came to light in the presence of witnesses were potsherds such as other archaeologists found.

If glamorous gewgaws came to light, said Gilliéron, they

needed accurately depicting. He felt capable of doing that. An artist wasn't responsible for producing certificates of authenticity.

The director said he supposed that was true.

Greece was said to be very beautiful, said Gilliéron. The pay was good and his scholarship was due to run out in the very near future.

❧

When he actually got there, however, Greece presented a great disappointment. He had been so incessantly seasick he'd wanted to die during the three-day voyage from Trieste via Brindisi, Corfu and Patras, and the morning of 23 March 1877 found him standing on the upper deck in pouring rain, desperate to go ashore. Outside the entrance to Piraeus harbour, the elegant, dazzling white steamer belonging to Austrian Lloyd's Egyptian service became embroiled with a pack of smelly, weather-beaten, seagull-infested fishing boats, some of which were putting out to sea and others trying to enter port, the result being that they got in one another's way, jostling and colliding until their timbers creaked and groaned. The captain of the Egyptian service steamer hove to at a safe distance, stationed himself on the bridge in full dress uniform, and waited. When it seemed that none of the fishermen would climb down and give way within a reasonable length of time, the captain sounded his steam siren for two full minutes and then, at half speed ahead, made for the harbour mouth through the middle of the milling throng.

The fishing boats reluctantly scattered, opening up a channel just wide enough for the steamer to negotiate. Émile looked down from the sun deck at the squabbling fishermen, who were shaking their swarthy, hirsute fists and trying to thrust each other aside with rusty boathooks. They were short, thick-set men in baggy trousers, their fat cheeks and black moustaches robbing them of any resemblance to the aquiline-nosed marble statues in the classical antiquities section of the Louvre, on which Émile had honed his mental image of Greece.

Once the steamer had passed the Mole Lighthouse, a view unfolded of the harbour beside which Aristotle, Pericles, Plato and Alexander the Great had once stood: a drab semicircle of grey, one- or two-storeyed brick buildings backed by a range of hills stripped bare of trees for millennia and overlooked by a leaden sky with dark rain clouds scudding inland across them. Some ragged, barefoot figures among the puddles on the quayside were waving excitedly up at the first-class passengers, turning cartwheels and performing handstands or little dances. The passengers tossed coppers to these ragamuffins and watched with amusement as they tussled over them.

Émile Gilliéron's seasickness vanished as soon as his feet touched dry land, but the short ride to Athens in an open carriage and pair left him soaked to the skin. Seated on either side of the muddy road were hundreds of hollow-cheeked children, their big, dark eyes gazing up at the passers-by. When Émile asked the coachman what they were doing there, he was informed that the orphanage stationed them there every morning in the hope that some compassionate traveller would adopt one.

Émile's mood improved somewhat when the white columns of the Acropolis came into view in the rain-shrouded distance; and when he reached the Hôtel d'Angleterre and was installed in the bright, spacious suite Schliemann had booked for him, and the chambermaid took his coat and silently handed him a refreshing glass of ouzo, he was almost reconciled to the place and felt that he would certainly be able to stick it for a few weeks or months. And if Schliemann really paid him as well as he had promised, he would stay a full year and go home to Villeneuve next spring with his pockets full of money. He would buy a small house beside the lake, spend the evenings with friends from the days when he and they were young pups together, and earn a living during the day by painting kitschy little watercolours for English tourists. And of course, whether the citizens of Villeneuve liked it or not, he would wear a blue jacket to the end of his days. Maybe even a yellow one.

Or so Émile Gilliéron thought, but things naturally turned out otherwise. Next morning, when he had drunk his break-fast coffee and was about to go for an introductory walk through the city and up to the Acropolis, he was intercepted at the hotel entrance by Heinrich Schliemann's coachman, who, with silent efficiency, at once conveyed him in an elegant carriage and four to his master's house, where the study was richly adorned with marble statues, brightly painted vases and reproductions of Hellenic frescos.

Seated at his desk, Schliemann craned his tortoiselike neck and inspected Gilliéron with a pair of cold blue eyes framed by circular, steel-rimmed spectacles. Having greeted him curtly in fluent but oddly accented French, he pointed imperiously to the desk in front of him, on which lay a wooden tray bearing three palm-sized fragments of a fresco. One piece of plaster depicted a fist, another a lily ornament, and the third a foot complete with calf.

Schliemann announced that they had arrived from Mycenae the night before and asked what Émile made of them.

Émile shrugged his shoulders. He could see a hand, a foot and a fragment of a lily pattern, he replied.

Don't be impertinent, said Schliemann. He wanted Émile to tell him what the whole fresco could have depicted.

Impossible to say, said Émile.

In that case, said Schliemann, Émile was the wrong man for him.

No one in the world could tell for sure, said Émile.

But one could figure something out, Schliemann retorted.

Yes, said Émile, one could always do that. With a shrug, he bent over the tray and shuffled the fragments to and fro. Then he took a sketch pad lying ready to hand, and, at lightning speed, drew a charioteer with a spear in his fist and his right foot resting on the lily-adorned edge of his chariot.

Splendid, said Schliemann. Can't think why I didn't see that myself, it's so obvious.

Émile thereupon arranged the fragments differently and, on another sheet, drew a temple guard with a flaming torch in his fist and a headdress adorned with lilies.

Well I'm damned, said Schliemann. You're quite something! The charioteer was rubbish, I see that now.

Émile tore off that sheet too, then drew Laocoon fighting off some serpents with his hands and feet.

But … said Schliemann. Are you pulling my leg?

After that Émile drew Theseus in combat with Andromache, then an Attic farmer harvesting olives and a victorious athlete with an olive wreath, and each drawing embodied a fist, a foot and some lily ornamentation. With bated breath, Schliemann delightedly followed the progress of Émile's pencil as he drew bullfighters and shepherds and sailors, then an Amazon pursuing a naked couple with a drawn sword.

But I know those two nudes, said Schliemann. Where have I seen them before?

In the Sistine Chapel, Émile replied. Michelangelo's Adam and Eve being expelled from Paradise.

You're quite something, Schliemann said again.

Émile took another sheet and drew a youth with a ram.

And that? asked Schliemann.

John the Baptist by Caravaggio.

Émile quickly drew a little Botticelli and a Degas, then Schliemann snatched the pencil from his hand.

Enough of these biblical jokes, he said, it's time for lunch. You'll stay, I won't take no for an answer. We eat *en famille* and *sans façon*. My wife has ordered moussaka. After lunch we'll draw up a contract. You'll stay for a year at least.

Six months, said Émile.

A year, said Schliemann.

Six months at most, said Émile. Beside Lake Geneva the grape harvest begins in October. I must be home in time for that.

Why so? asked Schliemann.

My father owns a vineyard, Émile lied.

You'll stay for a year, said Schliemann, I won't take no for an answer. We'll go to Troy, Mycenae and Tiryns together. After that I'll need you here in Athens. And now, *à table*!

Well, well, thought Émile as he followed his employer into the dining room. *En famille* and *sans façon*. So the man won't take no for an answer. We shall see.

৯৯

Half a century has elapsed between young Émile Gilliéron's departure for Greece and the return of his ashes to Lake

Geneva. Émile's son carries his suitcase down to the harbour, his footsteps ringing on the cobblestones. Holidaymakers' winterproofed sailing dinghies are lying at anchor with seagulls perched asleep on their spars. He looks at his watch. There is still an hour till the next train leaves for Brig, where he will take the night train to Trieste. Tomorrow afternoon the mail-boat leaves there for Athens, where his wife will welcome him home and show off her latest oil painting of the Acropolis.

Émile Gilliéron junior walks to the end of the quay, sits down on a bollard and removes the cigar box from his suit-case. It contains a small quantity of dove-grey ash, maybe three or four handfuls. Whether they are really his father's ashes or those of some other creature has ceased to matter. He has complied with the will, that's all that counts.

He looks down at the dark water lapping softly against the harbour wall, lets the ashes trickle slowly into it, and tosses the cigar box after them. This was really a sailor's burial, but where in Villeneuve could he have found a quiet patch of ground in which to lay his father to rest unobserved? Small towns like Villeneuve are silent at night, but they do not sleep; every street houses some grief-stricken widow or toothache-tormented spinster who will hurry to the window in the dark if a stranger's heels ring on the cobblestones. Émile realises that he has taken hardly one step unobserved since he got out of the train. He couldn't have gone to the vineyards because of the watchdogs on guard there; nor to the marshes because he and his suitcase would have been visible from afar, thereby attracting the suspicions of the citizens of Villeneuve.

He is also under observation down at the harbour, that is equally clear to him, but here the citizens will regard him as a harmless tourist who has inadvertently got off the train one station too soon and is having to kill time for an hour until the next train comes along. That he is not pacing up and down the platform but has gone for a walk down by the harbour is noteworthy, to be sure, but not entirely out of order. And if he perches on a bollard and fiddles around with his luggage, that, too, is nothing to get worked up about. All that matters is that he gets up and returns to the station in good time. Then the lonely widows and spinsters can go back to bed.

His father's ashes are immersed in the dark water and no longer visible. The bigger fragments of bone will have sunk vertically to the bottom of the lake; the ashes will become widely dispersed and merge with the sludge on the bottom. Sludge is simply soil, Émile reflects. Even the remains of a burial at sea are ultimately reunited with Mother Earth. The cigar box is bobbing beside the harbour wall. Just a common or garden cigar box, it will drift away during the night, get washed ashore somewhere in the next few days and peacefully rot away in a mound of jetsam.

3

Felix Bloch never again set eyes on the girl in the Orient Express because she didn't get out in Zurich. That November afternoon, Laura d'Oriano travelled on via Basel to Belfort, where, while Felix Bloch was calling at the ETH's enrolment office and Émile Gilliéron waiting for his steamer in Trieste, she boarded the express to Marseille with her parents, who proposed to settle down there and take over a distant cousin's music shop. It was time the family's odyssey came to an end. The d'Orianos had been on the move for half a century. As a young cabaret artiste, Laura's mother had spent 20 years touring the luxury hotels of the Near East. Now she was tired and fast approaching the day when her garter and her cleavage would cease to be of help to her on-stage. Her husband was tired too and suffering from liver trouble, and it was time for the five children to settle down.

Thanks to all their travels and the luxury they had been able to sample in grand hotels as artistes' children, Laura and her siblings had become wilful and spoilt. They had table manners like the children of an English milord and could dance like Cossacks, and they conversed together in a mixture of English, French, Greek, Russian and Italian. They smoked like Turks and took an interest in prices on the London Stock Exchange, they knew the fares on the Bosphorus ferries and how to eat an orange with a knife and fork. But they had never played cops and robbers with the children next door because they had never lived next door to any children. They had always spent Christmas in the company of hotel guests, and their only friends had been chambermaids and porters who recognised the d'Orianos from previous visits and greeted them by their first names.

Like all nomads, they settled into the routine of travelling. Laura, the eldest, felt at home in the ever-changing rehearsal rooms and artistes' dressing rooms to which her mother had taken her along, even as an infant, in order to breast-feed her during intermissions. In the afternoons she listened to the musicians practising, in the evenings she watched her mother putting on and removing her make-up, and all day long she shared in the everlasting, unchanging agonies of artistic self-doubt, cosmic despair and lack of understanding that unfolded behind the scenes. Not a day, not an hour could go by without some minor psychodrama or other. There would be vows of fidelity, fainting fits and paroxysms of weeping, champagne glasses were forever being smashed and doors slammed, and standing in the midst of it all was little Laura, clasping her doll to her childish tummy and growing up in the certainty that this was real life in the real world.

When Laura was old enough to traverse long corridors on her own, climb backstairs and be sure to knock on doors bearing the right numbers, grown-ups would send her off with little notes or imprecations learnt by heart. Laura carried out these missions conscientiously, transmitting the direst curses with a radiant, innocent smile, and afterwards she carefully memorised who was linked with whom in amity or enmity because of a stolen kiss, a professional insult or an unpaid

gambling debt. Before long, because she found this all so exciting, she no longer contented herself with an errand girl's role
but played that of a blonde, curly-haired little imp who, on her
own initiative, sowed death and destruction in an artless lisp.

Laura thoroughly enjoyed this puppet show. She deposited ladies' garters in places where they shouldn't have been,
insulted leading actors by lowering the curtain in the middle
of a scene, or crept into the auditorium and giggled at inappropriate moments. She mendaciously claimed that A wore a
toupee, that B's teeth were false and that C's sexual indiscre-
tions had occasioned a visit to the urologist. There were times
when a knowing look in her childish blue eyes was enough to
bring grown men out in a cold sweat.

It sometimes happened that Laura's machinations were discovered before the d'Orianos had set off on the next stage in
their odyssey. On such occasions she would weep, plead childish irresponsibility and hide in her mother's dressing room
until the dust had settled. Because there was nothing to do in
there, she softly joined in when her mother was practising her
coloraturas, and it wasn't long before she felt she hit the notes
as well as her. Or even a bit better. Which was true. Then,
during one long train journey, came the day when she sat out
on the step for the first time.

When Laura's brothers Umberto and Vittorio Emmanuele
were born, her mother couldn't take them to rehearsals as well,
so she left them in the care of their father, whose nightly tin-
kling on the piano constituted the limit of his artistic ambitions
and had long ceased to require any practice. Consequently, the
boys spent their childhood in their father's orbit at racecourses,
on seaside promenades and in the smoking rooms of grand
hotels, where they developed into shrewd poker players who

played each other for very high stakes in dead earnest. Sometimes one was indebted to the other for life and de facto his slave; a few days later it was the other way round.

By contrast, the two youngest children, Marina and Maria Teresa, grew up in the care of a nursemaid, a simple soul who spent a great deal of time instructing the girls in the application of mascara and nail polish. Before they went to sleep at night she enlightened them on the interrelationships of the European royal families and told them of dream-like weddings and tragic deaths. The girls listened, let it all sink into their absorbent childish heads, and were soon convinced that every girl's supreme ambition in life should be to marry a Russian prince; this idea became so deeply embedded in their skulls that it refused to dissipate later on, when their skulls had grown harder. As a result, Marina and Maria Teresa merely cast their eyes up to heaven when their parents tried to get them to do their sums and explained that girls, too, had to do something in life because the world had always contained many more girls than Russian princes, and the few Russian princes there were had recently all been shot or become taxi drivers in Paris. When told these things, they merely smiled in disbelief and gazed wistfully out of the window.

It really was high time the d'Orianos settled down. Their protracted wanderings had turned them into experienced, well-travelled cosmopolitans whose horizons spanned the whole world, but they were rootless and devoid of ties and, in their heart of hearts, a little stunted. This process was now into its third generation.

The family's odyssey had been initiated half a century earlier in the Neapolitan fishing village of Pozzuoli by the children's grandfather, Vincenzo d'Oriano. A smouldering-eyed young fisherman, Vincenzo had been singing a song atop a pyramid of herring barrels when a wealthy Englishman sailed into the harbour on his yacht and impulsively engaged him on the spot as his personal balladeer. During the crossing to Palermo the Englishman could not hear enough of the picturesque young fisherman belting out Neapolitan songs from his place in the bow. But then the yacht sailed on to Corfu and Piraeus, Heraklion and Naxos, and by the time it reached the Turkish coast of the Aegean, Vincenzo must have bawled his repertoire at the Levantine skies a hundred times, so the bored Englishman was relieved to be able to dismiss him at the port of Smyrna with a generous gratuity and best wishes for the future.

How young Vincenzo d'Oriano kept his head above water during those first few years so far from home is shrouded in the mists of time and cannot be ascertained. It is, however, on record that in Smyrna Cathedral on 29 January 1877 – 14 Muharram 1294 by the Islamic calendar – he married a certain Teresa Capponi, who, in the ensuing 24 years, bore him eight children, all of whom were christened in Smyrna Cathedral, the third-youngest being a boy named Policarpo. In May 1910 – yet again in Smyrna Cathedral – 24-year-old Policarpo married the beautiful and still optimistic 20-year-old chanteuse Aida Agnese Caruana, toured the Near East with her in the capacity of protector and accompanist, and fathered headstrong Laura and her four siblings.

That was over now – that world no longer existed. The Ottoman Empire had disintegrated during the Great War into a vast number of traumatised, hysterical little nation states that fought each other to the death, invented hitherto unknown ethnic incompatibilities, and developed their newly drawn frontiers into insurmountable barriers. Trade and traffic came to a halt, ships lay idle in harbour. The grand hotels of Beirut and Alexandria had no guests, the nightclubs closed, the musicians were sent home.

Bereft of employment and income, the d'Orianos moved into the late Vincenzo's house in Smyrna. They spent two inactive years in the beautiful old seaport, which many called the Paris of the Orient and others the capital of tolerance because people of all races and religions had lived peacefully together there since Homer's day. For many centuries they had peacefully cohabited under the Greek colonists, under the emperors of Rome and Byzantium, and under the aegis of the caliphs; they had peacefully cohabited until 15 May 1919, when Greek nationalist troops invaded the city and massacred the Muslim population in a Hellenistic frenzy; whereupon, three-and-a-half years later, Atatürk's troops likewise invaded the city, massacred the non-Muslim population in a Kemalistic frenzy, and burnt Smyrna to the ground.

It must be surmised that the conflagration deprived the d'Orianos of their worldly possessions, which would by then have been very meagre. We do not know whether they managed to escape in the nick of time by ferry or inland across the coastal range on foot. The only certainty is that two years later they caught the Orient Express in Constantinople and, travelling by way of Budapest, Vienna and Zurich, headed for Marseille to begin a new life.

I can imagine that, on arrival at the Gare Saint-Charles that morning in November 1924, the d'Orianos engaged a porter who trundled their suitcases down the Canebière to the Vieux-Port on a handcart. It is very probable that the sun in the friendly skies of the Côte d'Azur was bathing the broad streets and lighting up the palatial new houses of the commercial aristocracy.

Marseille had recently been largely rebuilt as the gateway to France's colonial empire in Africa and the Far East. There was a whiff of the Orient in the air. In the streets you could see black beards and caftans, baggy Turkish trousers and turbans, but also stand-up collars *à l'anglaise*, white military uniforms and French berets, and all their wearers travelled harmoniously by tram, did business with each other in cafés, or kept watch for ships entering and leaving port.

The harbour boasted big new docks, quays with modern cranes, and freight trains for the transportation of exotic produce. Most of the vessels lying in the harbour basin, on the other hand, were not new steamships but old-fashioned, wooden-hulled sailing ships. Huge 19th-century Hanseatic five-masters lay alongside elegant American clippers, Norwegian fore-and-aft schooners alongside Arab dhows, and even Chinese junks put in occasionally. Modern, steel-hulled steamships, by contrast, were seldom to be seen because most of the world's modern shipping had been sent to the bottom of the ocean between 1914 and 1918. After the war, therefore, shipowners had recommissioned all the semi-seaworthy wooden vessels they possessed, and since a large proportion of the world's seamen had drowned, they had also combed retirement homes and exerted gentle pressure on any white-bearded, toothless old salts who could still stand semi-erect and still had some command of their five senses.

The d'Orianos' new home was a half-timbered 18th-century building in the Vieux-Port. The music shop was on the ground floor; the living quarters, which occupied the two floors above, comprised four small bedrooms and a sitting room that overlooked the harbour basin. The walls were whitewashed and the staircase smelt of floor polish. Laura inspected the building in the knowledge that she would have to stick it out there for three years. She would go to school and give no cause for complaint, and at home she would do the shopping and the washing-up and help out in the shop in the afternoons. After six months' good behaviour she would ask her mother's permission to take singing lessons at the Conservatoire de Marseille and attend an occasional concert. But on her 16th birthday, of that she felt quite sure, she would pack her bag and go off to Paris.

Alone, what was more.

Felix Bloch was one of those rare people who experience a sudden, revelatory awakening in life, and he would remember it to the end of his days. It occurred shortly after half past five on the last day of the four-week practical that concluded his first year at college, when he was standing for the last time at his drawing board in the office of the Fritz Christen foundry in Küsnacht. The foundry itself was already silent, the workers having gone home for the weekend. The secretary had clamped her coat and handbag under her arm and taken her leave, the boss was still sitting over his books beside the window. A ship hooted out on the lake, the light was gradually fading. Soon it would be time to turn on the electric lights.

Felix Bloch put the finishing touch to his ink drawing of a manhole cover the foundry was planning to put into production the following winter. He had spent nine hours a day for four weeks on this project, so he knew it like the back of his hand: a circular cast-iron manhole cover 60 centimetres in diameter, including the rim, and 5 centimetres thick, with an inset handle and the firm's name in the centre, 24 concentrically arranged drainage holes for dispersing surface water, and anti-slip grooves running at right angles to each other.

On his first day the boss had handed him a sheaf of pencil sketches and technical specifications and instructed him to convert them into usable technical drawings for the workshops and the sales department. Manhole covers were a good, reliable source of business. Road and sewer construction was booming now that more and more people owned cars. Manhole covers were indispensable and demand for them had been steadily increasing for years. Public authorities were by far the firm's most important customers; they paid promptly and ordered in bulk, not individually or by the dozen.

By the end of his practical, Felix Bloch knew his manhole cover better than anything else in the world – better than his mother's eyes, better than his pocketknife, better than the switch of his bedside light, better than his own hands. He had drawn the cover perpendicularly from above and perpendicularly from below, each time on a scale of 1 to 4, 1 to 8 and 1 to 12, and he had also produced a – not very useful – lateral view. His drawings from a 45-degree angle had been particularly time-consuming, and for each drawing he had also produced a technical supplement specifying dimensions and weights, the carbon content of the steel and its shock- and pressure-resistance per square centimetre.

To his surprise, he had enjoyed his four weeks working on the manhole cover. After a first day's astonishment at the object's unsurpassable simplicity, he had derived pleasure from immersing himself in his task with monastic contemplation. It did not occur to him to question the point of his activity. For one thing, the industrial practical was an obligatory part of the course at the end of every academic year. For another, manhole covers were undeniably good and sensible things because they kept streets free from mud, thereby benefiting the economy, facilitating people's freedom of movement and serving the cause of hygiene and public health. Thirdly, they were of no discernible military use. Fourthly, Felix Bloch discovered how satisfying it could be to possess sound technical knowledge in a clearly defined field. From the middle of his second week onwards, he could justifiably claim to be an expert on cast-iron manhole covers 60 centimetres in diameter.

Every day for four weeks he had cycled from Zurich to Küsnacht and drawn manhole covers with pleasure and enthusiasm. He was first in the office every morning and the last to leave at night, and the boss had peered over his shoulder while he was standing at the drawing board and growled approvingly. Lunch hours he spent in the workers' locker room, sitting with them on the benches that ran round the walls, propping his elbows on his knees like them and, like them, eating bread and cheese out of the tin he'd brought with him. He listened to their conversations, wisely kept his trap shut and was grateful to them for not making him feel they despised him too much even though he was a student.

At the end of the second week the boss had slipped him five francs and growled that, if Felix was in search of a job when he completed his studies, he should apply to him first. At the end of the third week he slipped him another five francs and growled that he wasn't too enamoured of testimonials and diplomas, and so, as far as he was concerned, Felix could ditch his course and simply stay on. The foundry was expanding fast and he needed a bright lad whom he might later transform into a partner.

Felix Bloch had naturally been gratified by the boss's praise and paternal goodwill, and during the last week of his practical he had pictured what it would be like to actually drop out of his course and embark on a new life as an adult with his own home and a regular profession as an expert on cast-iron manhole covers. He would pay taxes and get married and design a new factory for cast-iron manhole covers down beside the lake, and he would make business trips to Cologne and go for skiing holidays in the Engadine and visit Italy with his wife. Later he would build a house in a green field and take over the foundry altogether, and at some stage he would retire, hand over the production of cast-iron manhole covers to his sons, and devote himself to his grandchildren and his cactus collection.

But during the final minute of his final day at the foundry, when he laid down his pen and screwed the top on the bottle of ink for the last time, then took his coat from the hook and said goodbye to the boss, who accompanied him to the exit in a spuriously casual manner and gruffly muttered that his door would always be open – at that moment, when Felix Bloch emerged from the building and mounted his bicycle, he was transfixed like an electric shock by the realisation that he would never return, because a cast-iron manhole cover was never more than a cast-iron manhole cover and he would never in his life muster the humility to devote his creative energies to the manufacture of cast-iron manhole covers. Or the production of crankshafts. Or piston rods. Or gas turbines.

At that moment he realised that he would not study mechanical engineering for another single day because he had been right the previous autumn on the loading platform of that goods shed, when, for the space of a few seconds, he had resolved to spend his life doing something beautiful, useless and utterly impractical. He pedalled away with a will. He would go straight home and tell his father that he could not do otherwise than embark on a new life at once.

At that time, Zurich's College of Technology did in fact house a few men whose profession it was, day in, day out, to entertain beautiful, incomprehensible thoughts that had no discernible practical use and bore a certain resemblance to the Goldberg Variations. They peered through new-fangled telescopes into the depths of the universe, postulating that the cosmos must be curved and that human beings, if only they could see far enough, would see the backs of their heads in the darkness of space. They heated salts and metals, fed the light they emitted through glass prisms, and, from the resultant colours, made assumptions about the behaviour of atoms and electrons, which bore a surprising resemblance to the ballet of the planets, suns and moons.

Albert Einstein had written his general theory of relativity in one of the ETH's offices. In that same summer of 1925, Erwin Schrödinger was puzzling over the question of why electrons behaved like waves and, at the same time, like particles. It was there, too, that Hermann Weyl had produced the mathematical proof of Einstein's theory of relativity and Peter Debye had experimentally proved that the smallest particles of matter really did behave as erratically as Max Planck had predicted.

Felix Bloch had studied mechanical engineering for a year at the same place: Mechanical Technology I with refresher lessons, Chemistry I with refresher lessons and exercises, descriptive and projective geometry, metallurgical study of technologically important alloys, economics, slide rule exercises, and lectures on mechanical elements for two hours a week.

He had also, purely for fun, attended a few lectures on

quantum mechanics. He hadn't understood much of them, but the poetry of ideas, the metaphysical beauty of their language and the antimechanistic and anticausal character of their logic had enchanted him. An additional factor was that atomic physics was predominantly a young man's field. There were world-famous professors little older than Felix Bloch himself, and all of them were younger than his father. Heisenberg was 24, Paul Scherrer 36, Schrödinger 37, and Weyl and Debye were under 40.

His homeward journey took half an hour, but this time his courage didn't fail. While pedalling along the lakeshore, he worked out what he was going to say to his father. He would tell him about curved space-time, to the extent that he had understood it, and about Heisenberg's uncertainty principle and Paul Scherrer's X-ray camera, about the wondrous stability of matter and the mysterious simplicity of natural laws. He might even speak of his suspicion that lying deep beneath the surface of atomic phenomena was a bedrock of remarkable intrinsic beauty.

If his father asked him whether he thought mechanical engineering possessed no intrinsic beauty, he would tell him that a manhole cover was just a manhole cover and he wouldn't be able to endure this lack of mystery in the long run. If his father then accused him of arrogance, he would agree but say he couldn't do otherwise. If his father pointed out that not everyone was an Einstein, he would concede the point but add that scientific research needed journeymen as well as geniuses, and that bricklayers were never out of a job when kings built palaces. If his father then asked about his potential earnings, he would say he was going to acquire a teaching diploma on the side, and if the worst came to the worst he could teach physics at secondary school. And if his father asked whether he wanted to wind up like his own physics teacher, a confirmed bachelor who, after 40 years' service, lived in a little attic apartment with no electricity or a separate WC and spent the long, lonely winter nights swathed in a rug in front of the stove – if his father asked him that, he would answer: Yes, if I have to, I'll wind up just like Herr Seiler.

He eventually extracted his father's blessing on this change of course by arguing that the faculty of mathematics and physics was crediting his first two semesters in full, so he wouldn't be wasting any time. His father expressed surprise at this, and Felix himself found it remarkable that his expert knowledge in the field of cast-iron manhole cover production should be equated with a basic study of atomic physics. However, it soon turned out that physics students at Zurich's College of Technology enjoyed a measure of freedom that verged on neglect.

There were no compulsory introductory lectures, fixed curricula or intermediate examinations, nor was there a mandatory number of years' study culminating in a final exam. The 24 students who had enrolled in the faculty of mathematics and physics that winter semester of 1925/26 were left largely to themselves; they devised their own course as they pleased with the aid of the college calendar, their own inclinations being the only guidelines they were obliged to follow. All that was expected of them was to fall in love with one special area in the course of their studies and, at some indeterminate point in time, when the professor encouraged them to do so, to write a dissertation on one narrowly defined and partial aspect of their special field.

What accounted for this old-fashioned, Humboldtian freedom was the fact that the exact sciences were more unpopular after the Great War than they had been for a century. Wide sections of the European public – newspaper readers, political educationists, primary school teachers – had lost faith in a rational world order after the catastrophe and were now seeking salvation in an irrational world order. Professional astrologers outnumbered astronomers ten to one in Zurich alone, and great popularity was enjoyed by spiritualism, anthroposophy, psychoanalysis, religious recipes for salvation, opium cures, sexual libertinism and vegetarian diets. The exact sciences, by contrast, had to shoulder prime responsibility for the mechanised slaughter on the battlefields. Although they had not deliberately brought it about, they had done their best to carry it to extremes that would not have been possible without their contribution.

In addition, the world of industrialists had largely lost interest in physics since their steam engines, locomotives and turbines all functioned perfectly well. They wanted no truck with new lines of research that promised to be of no practical use and threatened to cast doubt on Newton's simple, serviceable mechanics with all their to-do about relativity. As for the unworldly oddballs at universities, industrialists had absolutely no use for them.

Although Felix Bloch didn't mind the fact that no one was interested in him or issued him with instructions, he would have welcomed a certain amount of guidance at the outset of his studies. There being no one in the faculty whom he could have consulted, he put together his programme of lectures according to whether he liked the sound of their titles. For instance, he attended Debye's 'Quantum Theory of Serial Spectra', Scherrer's 'Röntgen Rays' and Weyl's 'Philosophy of Mathematics'. Employing the same method, he chose as his first specialised lecture 'Atomic Structure and Spectral Lines' by Professor Arnold Sommerfeld of Munich.

To Felix's relief, the professor wrote that he wanted 'to allow the non-academic reader to enter into the new physics of the atom', so 'inordinately abstract mathematical developments had to be avoided' in order briefly and without any incomprehensible formulae to develop the 'introductory physical and chemical facts' on which the new atomic physics was based. Even on the first page Felix stumbled across terms assumed to be known but utterly unfamiliar to him, and after the first chapter he had to concede that he had failed to grasp even the 'introductory facts' because he lacked the requisite prior knowledge. And when he tried to acquire this prior knowledge it turned out that he lacked the prior knowledge for that too.

Even on page one, for example, there was talk of an 'electromagnetic field'. In order to find out what this was, he went to the library and borrowed *Theory of Electricity* by Max Abraham. Abraham also asserted in his foreword that his supreme maxim in writing the book had been general comprehensibility, yet even in his first chapter he employed mysterious terms such as 'corpuscular rays' and 'cycle theory' whose explanation Felix had to seek in other borrowed works.

He did his best to acquire a basic knowledge of his subject, but discovered that the human intellect resembles a muscle that tends to develop symptoms of paralysis if subjected to unwonted exertion and becomes only relatively more efficient even with regular training.

When he read the second chapter, in which Professor Sommerfeld dealt with the 'Central and Peripheral Properties of the Atom', Felix came close to giving up, and when the fourth chapter proved to be an 'Introduction to the Theory of

Quanta', the narcissistic injury to his weak brain muscle was so painful, he seriously considered returning the book to the library and his rueful self to the world of mechanical engineering and manhole covers.

He may have stuck with atomic physics mainly because he was unwilling to look foolish in front of his father. Besides, after a few weeks and months he was gratified to discover that even the hardest ideas become readily comprehensible once one has grasped them. Moreover, the gaps in his knowledge gradually diminished – or he gained at least an inkling of their extent. Although he still felt like a polar bear marooned on a little ice floe of knowledge in an ocean of ignorance, other ice floes appeared in the course of time, enabling him to jump from one to the next. They became more numerous and the distances between them shorter until, towards the end of his second semester, several ice floes combined to form an island of pack ice on which he had already secured a very firm footing.

He also got to know his fellow students, who were in the same position. Each was balancing on his personal, rather random ice floe in the hope of some day discovering virgin academic territory. Some attached electric cables to salt crystals and endeavoured to understand what was going on inside them, others crossed the Rhine in order to buy radioactive Doramad toothpaste from German pharmacists and spread it on ultra-thin sheets of metal foil, and still others looked out into the cosmos and pictured vast explosions in the heart of stars.

When spring came, Felix Bloch struck up a friendship with two German doctoral candidates named Fritz London and Walter Heitler, who had come to Zurich as Schrödinger's assistants. Five years older than Felix, they were trying to trace the bonding forces in molecules by heating hydrogen and irradiating it. At weekends he went walking on the Höngerberg with them or took them hiking in the Glarner Alps. Fritz London and Walter Heitler profoundly impressed Felix Bloch by their ability to compose differential and integral equations and solve them in their heads while chatting in the midst of an alpine meadow. He spent most of the time trailing after them and trying to understand what they were talking about.

On the last weekend before the summer vacation, when they set off on a walk across the Urnerboden, they were joined by a Danish doctoral candidate. While they were frying some sausages over a campfire, the Dane poked fun at the outdated atomic model of his teacher, Niels Bohr, and casually mentioned that he himself had done some rather complex molecular calculations that could, if necessary, be checked by means of ultraviolet spectroscopy.

Felix still had no clear idea of what atomic models were, nor did he know what molecular calculations and ultraviolet spectroscopy really signified, but he did suspect that a nice ice floe was drifting past him and that it might pay to jump aboard. So he asked the Dane what sort of calculations these were and how they could be experimentally checked. The Dane thereupon took an outline of his work from his rucksack and handed it to Felix, who laid aside his sausage and read it. It comprised five quarto sheets. Although he was far from being able to comprehend it fully, he did at least grasp its drift and felt that it would be just the job for him: limited in extent but not unimportant.

On the way back to Zurich in the mail bus, he plucked up his courage and asked the Dane if he might copy his outline and try to produce the experimental proof himself. The Dane gave him a derisive sidelong glance and asked if he had a spectrograph handy. Afraid not, said Felix. He'd guessed as much, said the Dane. To the best of his knowledge, no such gadget existed anywhere between Rome and Copenhagen.

The following Monday, Felix took the outline to Paul Scherrer, his professor for experimental physics. Scherrer read it with care, stroked his chin approvingly and handed it back with the comment that proving it experimentally would require a spectrograph. He was aware of that, said Felix – that was the whole problem. The professor thereupon took several quartz prisms from a drawer in his desk, went over to the window and held them up in the sunlight, bathing the floor in all the colours of the rainbow. The two men stood there in silence, gazing at the spectacle, until Scherrer put the prisms away and the rainbow was extinguished.

You could build your own spectrograph if you wanted, he said. How persevering are you?

Felix Bloch spent the next ten months in a windowless basement two floors below ground level in the ETH's main building. He left his parental home early in the morning and returned late in the evening, and in the intervening hours he only briefly left the basement to attend a lecture or stroll on the terrace so as not to render his eyes entirely unaccustomed to daylight. He shaved only once a week and lived on black bread and dried figs. Other than that, he devoted himself completely to his DIY.

He screwed his prisms into brass mounts and fashioned little shades for his metal-vapour lamp out of sheet copper. He went to a department store and bought dozens of make-up mirrors, scraped tiny holes of different diameters in their silvering, and placed the lenses between the lamp and the prisms to focus the light. He grew salt crystals, placed these in the beam and observed how it fanned out into a rainbow. If the rainbow was missing a certain colour he made a note of it and raised the temperature of the salt crystal by ten degrees Celsius. If another colour was missing he made a note of that too and heated the crystal another ten degrees.

Felix spent week after week and month after month in the gloomy basement. The more data he collected the more obvious it became that his results really did tally with the Dane's predictions. And the more clearly he saw that here, once again, an abstract idea had its equivalent in the world of things, just as it had when he had calculated the length of an autumn day in Zurich, the more convinced he became that the rainbow colours on his basement wall really were a visible reflection of atoms.

When spring came round again Felix resumed his long walks with Fritz London and Walter Heitler, but with a difference: this time it was he that talked away during a climb while the other two panted in his wake. He spoke of frequencies and absorptions and impulses, diffusions and amplitudes, and when they questioned him he answered them with the self-assurance of an expert who was possibly more conversant with his specialism than anyone else in the world.

4

Needless to say, Émile Gilliéron senior's sojourn in Greece lasted very much longer than a few months, even though he felt homesick after a week or two, when the oriental charm of his new home palled and he began to be irked by the Greeks' bucolic uncouthness, their torpid religious credulity and the frowstily provincial atmosphere of their capital city, which reminded him in many ways of his native Villeneuve. On lonely evenings he would sit with a bottle of red wine on the terrace of the Hôtel d'Angleterre, contemplating the Acropolis in the fading light and dreaming of the cottage beside Lake Geneva which he would soon be building in a secluded cove a few hundred metres from the harbour. When the bottle was empty he would sometimes open another, and when that was also empty he usually resolved to write a letter to Villeneuve the very next day and request the childless old fisherman who owned the real estate around the cove to sell him a plot of building land.

But next morning, when he was sitting thick-headed over his breakfast coffee, he never wrote the letter after all. In the first place, the fisherman wouldn't sell him the land because no inhabitant of Villeneuve would ever have sold any land unless God, the Shah of Persia or Lausanne's official debt collector was holding a knife to his throat. Secondly, the citizens of Villeneuve would never grant him permission to build his cottage

– they had already burnt his studio down. And thirdly, they would never welcome him as one of their own while he still had a blue jacket in his luggage. Unless, of course, there was money in the pockets – a great deal of money. And this money, Émile realised, could only come from Schliemann.

In order to earn some money, Émile accompanied his employer to Troy and Mycenae. His drawings were much clearer and more comprehensible than the misty photographs produced by Schliemann's personal photographer with his wooden box and his glass plates. Furthermore, unlike the photographer Émile was able to depict things that weren't there at all. If Schliemann so desired, he filled in blank spaces on murals, supplied damaged statues of gods with missing limbs, or developed potsherds into splendid vases.

Émile had the wealthy Prussian eating out of his hand from day one. Schliemann refused to dispense with his services because he was a quick, painstaking and reliable graphic artist capable of depicting any statuette, coin or vase in great detail and with great precision. But that wasn't all. What distinguished Émile from the hordes of other art students who had, with pan-Hellenistic fervour, converged on Athens from all over Europe in the hope of making a living out of classical antiquity, was his unerring feel for Schliemann's wishes, which he fathomed more clearly than his own. He detected his weakness for glamorous golden gewgaws and his aversion to the profane, and he realised that unsolved mysteries were abhorrent to Schliemann's dictatorial personality. Accordingly, he conjured the face of Poseidon out of every anonymous scrap of beard, and a clay pot filled with ashes did not remain simply an urn but became the last resting place of Agamemnon. Or Penelope. Or even Theseus.

Émile resurrected all the glories of antiquity in as perfectly mint condition as Schliemann would have envisioned them, had he possessed the requisite imagination. So the pair jointly developed into a well-practised team. Whatever Schliemann unearthed with relentless perseverance, Émile's playful powers of imagination brought to life. And if it so happened that Schliemann had previously buried the shiny treasures he unearthed, Émile knew nothing about it.

Schliemann appreciated the fact that Émile didn't bother him with any undesirable philosophical debates about the borderlines between originals and copies, reproductions and forgeries, nor did he sound off about artistic scruples or scientific misgivings. He simply did as he was bidden; nothing else concerned him. If Schliemann wanted a head on a headless statue of Hermes, he gave Hermes a head; and if a ship on a vase lacked a prow, he gave it a prow. He was relatively indifferent to antiquity and archaeology, although he respected the unearthed artefacts for what they were: remarkable examples of craftsmanship by competent fellow artists who had laid down their brushes and mallets forever a millennia or two ago.

What interested him far more were the 300 French francs he earned at the end of every month, his bottle of red wine after work and the giggles of the Anatolian village girls who fluttered around his drawing table.

He had little contact with his employer except at the archaeological sites. When it became too hot in summer and when autumn storms sent rain clouds scudding across the Aegean, the two of them returned to Athens. In the winter Schliemann and his young wife made lengthy trips to Rome, Paris and London while Émile saved money by remaining behind in his overheated but unpleasantly draughty hotel room, bored stiff until springtime because Athens had yet to became a real European metropolis and resembled a sleepy, provincial, Ottoman dump.

For all that, Émile found a peace of mind abroad he might never have attained at home in Villeneuve. He was happy that indigenous Athenians would regard him as a foreigner until the end of time and never accept him as one of their own. That meant he wouldn't have to submit to their initiation rites, whose sole and acknowledged purpose in all societies throughout the world was to bind and gag young men. Since this danger had now been averted, he felt absolved of the obligation to outrage respectable citizens by wearing blue or yellow jackets. Nor, in Athens, did he have to antagonise local dignitaries, but could treat them with the same discreet courtesy they extended to him as a certified foreigner and recognised artist.

Every few months he extorted a raise from Schliemann by threatening to depart and never return. And, like every émigré, he reluctantly put down roots as time went by. The process began when he moved out of the Hôtel d'Angleterre, it being too expensive in the long run, and rented a handsome apartment with moulded plaster ceilings and a pleasant, shady terrace. He also engaged a housekeeper who served him faithfully and forwarded his mail when he was away at diggings with Schliemann. He learnt Greek and made friends among the bohemians of Athens, and gradually acquired a certain reputation in the Greek capital's diplomatic circles as Schliemann's right-hand man.

Then there were the women who cast languishing glances at him. He was a handsome, unattached, courteous man in his early thirties, and he had money in his pockets. In the seventh year of his exile he became acquainted with Josephine, the daughter of an Italian businessman, who kissed him with unbridled ardour, swore eternal love and pursued him with passionate jealousy from the very first. For Émile Gilliéron, this was an entirely new experience. True, he'd had two or three pragmatic love affairs back home in circumspect, Calvinist Villeneuve, and had, as an art student in Paris, sampled the sweet poison of capricious female fellow students who could talk incessantly of love, passion and soulmates, but, in their heart of hearts, remained the coldly calculating French *bourgeoises* they really were. But Josephine gave herself to him with utter abandon, leaving him in no doubt that he was her idol, and that she would remain his own true love to the end of her days. In Émile, all this Mediterranean passion aroused an enthusiasm he had never known before, so they married in May 1884. Eleven months later, on 14 July 1885, their only son, Émile junior, was born.

It is apparent from the aliens' register of Marseille that Laura d'Oriano returned from Paris on 12 July 1930 and resumed living at her parental home on the Quai du Port. She was 19 years old, 22 months having passed since she'd carried her suitcase to the Gare Saint-Charles. It now contained quite different things, for 22 months is a long time. She read different books and smoked a different brand of cigarettes. Her hairbrush was different, as were her face powder, eye shadow and perfume. And her clothes, of course, were anyway quite different from the ones her mother had bought her.

Only her suitcase was the same. It was a small but expensive pigskin suitcase adorned with brass fittings and labels from grand hotels in Cairo, Baghdad and Beirut. Its leather was stained and scuffed from overuse but darkly, nobly patinated by many years of loving care; the hinges were well lubricated and the silk lining had been replaced more than once. Laura's mother had always insisted that the family should have first-class luggage, because nothing could be more irksome when travelling than burst suitcase lids, torn-off handles or broken hinges. One could and should dispense with many things en route, but not with decent luggage. People as peripatetic as the d'Orianos had to be able to rely on their luggage. After all, the nomads of Arabia would never venture into the desert on second-rate camels, just as the Cheyenne Indians had always let the fastest and hardiest ponies live and converted all the others into jerky.

Laura had carried this suitcase around since her earliest childhood, and the handle had moulded itself to her hand perfectly after so many years. The exterior smelt discreetly of leather, the interior of eau de cologne, and she had long been accustomed to the fraudulent effect it created. It had happened yet again before her departure for Paris that the porter had carried the noble object to a first-class carriage in expectation of a tip Laura could not afford. And when the suitcase was finally installed in the rack above her seat in a third-class compartment, she'd had to endure meaningful glances from her fellow passengers, who drew discreditable conclusions from the discrepancy between the patrician piece of luggage and the modest appearance of its owner.

On arrival in Marseille she hefted her suitcase off the rack and waved all the porters aside. Having made her way to the station on her own 22 months ago, she would also return to the Vieux-Port by herself. That was why she had not informed her parents of the day and hour of her arrival.

We may assume that Laura moved back into her old room on the second floor, which afforded a fine view of the harbour basin, and that she once more washed dishes and went shopping for her parents and helped out in the shop. But not everything had remained the same during her absence. Laura's siblings had flown the coop. The two boys, who were working as office juniors in Cannes, squandered their earnings in Monte Carlo on Sundays, while her sisters attended a boarding school for young ladies in Nice and kept watch for Russian princes on the promenade. Now that their adolescent clamour had fallen silent, so had the daily cacophony of parental admonitions, threats and vituperations. In the hush that pervaded the building, its three remaining residents quietly and considerately avoided each other.

Laura's father was troubled by his liver complaint and the unwonted monotony of a settled existence enforced on him by chronic impecuniosity. He could not get used to waking up in the same bed every morning or to listening to the same regular customers exchanging the same small talk outside the same cafés in the Vieux-Port. Laura's mother, for her part, was glad that their wanderings had ceased. But on quiet nights, when the wall clock was ticking and her husband had fallen asleep with a half-empty glass of cognac in his hand, she did, for all that, yearn for the footlights' glare and the yells of appreciation when she displayed her garter.

What was more, the couple were bored by their daily work in the music shop. They had never dreamt that commercial life could be so monotonous, so they were grateful when their daughter took over responsibility for the shop on her return. Laura ran errands and cleaned the shop window, swept the pavement every morning and wax-polished the floor after closing time, and after breakfast on the fourth Monday she appropriated the shop key, telling her parents to take it easy and go and read the paper in the café, which they did. They went to the café the next morning and the morning after that, and before long they only showed their faces in the shop late in the afternoon and left the business entirely to their daughter.

This was all right with Laura. She preferred to be on her own because it gave her a free hand, and the shop didn't make much work in any case. During the quiet morning hours she stationed herself behind the counter and sang scales. In the afternoon she took a chair and seated herself outside the door on the sunlit pavement, smoking cigarettes and watching the goings-on in the harbour. If customers entered the shop she followed them into the gloomy interior and looked out the requisite sheet music. Most of them were emigrants eager to buy a last-minute piece of musical nostalgia before embarking on their long voyage – Mozart, Schubert, Vivaldi, Chopin, Bach, Beethoven, Mahler – and many of them took along a harmonica as well.

Laura could fulfil almost every one of their requests because she carried a wide range of items, and the stock the d'Orianos had taken over from their predecessors was so inexhaustible, it would be a while before she needed to worry about replenishing it. Since there were no purchases, rent or wages to pay, she could put down all her takings as profit. This made the bookkeeping considerably easier.

The turnover tripled under Laura's management. She was a good saleswoman who treated all her customers in the same businesslike but friendly way and could converse with most of them in their mother tongue. She also knew her way around the shop and could unerringly pick out whatever they asked for. When they left the shop, satisfied, she watched them until they disappeared into the tide of humanity passing by. She pictured them crossing the ocean with their sheet music and settling down in some jungle, savannah or trading post on the other side of the world – pictured them doing some kind of work by day, and then, in the evening, streaming with sweat as they practised their Mozart, Schubert or Chopin by the smoky light of a paraffin lamp with chimpanzees screeching in the background. They would do this for many hundreds of hours until one day, very sick, very rich or very disillusioned, they returned to their old homeland.

It was noticeable that most of the shop's customers displayed extremely good manners. This was attributable not to their love of music – fools and boors have always been particularly well represented among musicians of every era – but to their travel plans. Laura's customers were courteous because they were emigrating. They had an end in view and had no wish to endanger it by causing needless aggravation, so they strove to be inconspicuous and inoffensive.

Before leaving home they might have been perfectly ordinary, averagely uncouth village louts who had felt tough and invulnerable in the snug warmth of their father's pigsty and thus not obliged to be particularly polite to their fellow mortals. But then, for whatever reason, they had left home and spent a lot of money on a ship ticket, so until they embarked they wanted as far as possible to refrain from doing anything that might inhibit them from going aboard.

They did not take siestas on park benches or drown their homesickness in pastis, nor did they cut up rough if a tobacconist short-changed them; they simply accepted it. When they came into Laura's shop they spoke softly and said please and thank you. They never tried to haggle and always paid cash, and it would never have occurred to any of them to risk their berth on an emigrant ship at the last minute by shoplifting.

Apart from the emigrants, there were some regular customers from the *quartier*: a few secondary school pupils, a piano teacher, and two or three elderly ladies. Occasionally, however, the shop was visited by a seaman who purported to be interested in music. Then Laura knew she was in for an unpleasant quarter of an hour, because ships' crews still consisted of those limping, grizzled, toothless individuals who had been recruited from retirement homes to replace young seamen drowned during the war.

The old salts never paid Laura compliments or invited her to a gin fizz on the esplanade, as the young ones would have done, but cracked obscene jokes and got her to fish out scores of song sheets without ever buying one. They harried her from shelf to shelf and up her little ladder, the better to appraise her legs and possibly even to tweak her skirt with gnarled fingers. And if that didn't work, they spat tobacco juice on the floor and cracked a last off-colour witticism, which might have been comprehensible in the previous century, before stomping to the door.

Laura had soon learnt that it was the old seamen she needed to beware of, not the young ones. Young seamen were harmless – you always knew what they were after. They simply wanted to pub-crawl in packs, drink as much as possible for as long as possible, and finally, if they could manage it and their money hadn't run out, get laid somehow, somewhere and with someone.

The dangerous ones were the crafty old salts who had, in a lifetime at sea, acquired personal experience of all the dirty tricks and vile behaviour in the world. The majority remained on board their rotten hulks and went to bed early, to dream of the good old days they might never have known, but some of them bestirred themselves after nightfall, dragged their weary bones down the gangway and plunged into the Vieux-Port's murky alleyways. Those were the driven, the distracted, the unreconciled – the truly dangerous ones.

These old seamen never hunted in packs, always alone. They could say a friendly good evening to some old woman with a dog on a lead and slit the animal's throat in passing. The simple amusements of youth had ceased to be enough for them. If they bought themselves a whore, it was only for the pleasure of infecting her with the disease that had given them years of torment when passing water, and when they roamed the water-front taverns they did so not in order to sing and laugh like the young ones; they were only waiting for an excuse to slice off another ear or gouge out another eye.

Laura knew all this. It would be a few more years before newly constructed steamships brought some healthy young seamen to Marseille; till then she would beware of the old ones. At dusk she used to fetch her chair and sit down in the light of the nearest street lamp, where she was clearly visible from a long way around, and if she went out again at night to buy cigarettes or fetch some laudanum for her mother, she avoided the narrow alleyways and kept to the big, gaslit boulevards.

In Paris, on the other hand, it had been young men, not old, of whom Laura had had to beware. If you saw an old man on the streets of Paris, you could assume that he wasn't a new arrival and had survived for several decades in the City of Lights. If a man had managed to keep his head above water for that length of time, it meant that he had found his place in the world. He had a pension and an apartment and, with a bit of luck, a wife to fry his escalope and scratch his back when need be; and if he didn't have all those things he would have a place to sleep under some bridge and his own method of procuring his daily bread and ham and red wine. Besides, the old men of Paris were continually, daily surprised to be still alive at all after the wars, crises and upheavals of recent decades, so they did no one any harm and were happy to be left in peace.

But the young men of Paris were as dangerous as their elders were innocuous – tens of thousands of homeless, motherless, hopeless youngsters who had crawled out of Europe's trenches after the war and drifted through the city pursued by their ghosts. Even after ten years, many still had eyes dilated with terror, many others still stammered and trembled and could not sleep at night, and all were hungry and thirsty and greedy and desperate and unsparing of themselves and everyone else.

Laura recognised those youngsters from afar when she encountered them in the street. She learnt to avoid their eye and ignore their whispered invitations, and she also learnt not to be taken in by the one-man dramas they staged on the pavement – the fainting fits, the declarations of love, the spurious threats to throw themselves off bridges – and not once in the 22 months she spent in Paris had she made the mistake of getting into conversation with one of them.

After passing the Conservatoire's entrance examination and paying the terminal fee, she had moved into an attic room in the Rue du Bac. Unbearably hot in summer and bitterly cold in winter, it had stained wallpaper and a window that overlooked the inner courtyard. Her room was one of a row of eight, and across the passage were another eight attic rooms whose rent was a little higher because they overlooked the

Rue du Bac itself. These 16 rooms were occupied by 16 relatively young women, all of whom had enrolled at the Conservatoire, could sing tolerably well, and cherished the same ambition: to become, at some stage in their lives, great singers. Many already entertained a vivid picture of themselves standing bathed in the footlights of the Théâtre des Capucins, the Mathurins, the Olympia, or even the Opéra; others simply had this big, expansive feeling in their chest and hoped to express it someday.

Laura had originally welcomed the proximity of 15 likeminded neighbours and had hoped to make friends with one or another of them. However, she was soon compelled to accept that these future goddesses of song, if she bumped into them in the passage, would at best murmur a perfunctory greeting and brush past with fluttering eyelashes as if terribly pressed for time before dining at the Ritz, having shaken off several admirers on the pavement, signed countless autographs and paid a quick visit to their agent, their dressmaker and their financial adviser.

The truth was, none of them knew a soul in the big city apart from the teachers at the Conservatoire and the woman who ran the greengrocer's stall on the corner, from whom they bought a kilo of apples every day. They had no money for cinema or theatre tickets and none for smart restaurants; nobody knew their names and they hadn't the slightest prospect of paid employment unless they were accosted in the Métro by some bourgeois from Passy and agreed to become his mistress for 20 francs a week. This meant that their only pastime was a daily stroll in the Jardin du Luxembourg or the Jardin des Plantes, where they watched the changing seasons reflected in the colour of the plane trees and dreamt that their dreams would be fulfilled in the not too distant future. And because the parks' haughty iron gates were locked at night with great big keys, they spent their evenings alone in their attic rooms.

The 16 residents of the Rue du Bac formed a monastic community. By day they conscientiously attended their singing lessons, by night they obediently practised their scales. They made sure they got enough sleep and observed the arcane regimens confided to them by their teachers or older fellow students. Many of them swore by fennel tisane and dark chocolate because they made the vocal cords flexible, others swallowed raw eggs and practised octaves standing on their heads. Still others massaged their diaphragms with almond oil or slept with lavender under their pillows.

Laura complied with her teachers' instructions to give up smoking, which she didn't find particularly difficult. She missed cigarettes only as a way of passing the time between practice sessions in her room, when she was listening through the thin walls to the voices of her 15 competitors and their own vocal exercises, which were eternally the same and eternally faltered in the same places. Many had thin, hoarse, girlish voices; others had rounded, well-bred, womanly voices. Then there were four or five voices – one on Laura's left, one across the passage, and two or three at the far end – that drowned all the rest, thrusting them aside and overpowering them with strident, relentless, uninhibited fervour.

Those voices were imbued with such passion because inordinate sorrow had robbed their owners of all shame. You did not have to know their life stories to grasp that these woman were weeping for their brothers, fathers or sons, or their childhood, or their sisters' virginity, or the ruin of their native village. Laura listened to this singing – this keening, sobbing and weeping from the depths of the soul – and squirmed with embarrassment for the women who gave vent to it, wondering how much sorrow a singer's voice could endure before it became ridiculous.

To her disappointment, however, Laura failed to find any voice, anywhere along the passage, that she wanted to emulate. The hoarse, girlish voices interested her least of all because she herself had one such. The well-bred, womanly voices she despised because they were guilty of failing to fulfil their potential. What appealed to her most were the uninhibited voices of the afflicted, even though they never hit the note first time and would never know any score other than that of their own spiritual torment.

But genius – that little, unlearnable, additional something, the only thing that really mattered – was denied to all of them.

After a month Laura felt almost certain that none of the residents of the Rue du Bac, herself included, possessed the makings of greatness. They were all tender, sensitive souls, to be sure, but none of them would ever become a great singer, a true artist who touched the innermost recesses of her audiences' hearts because she had a unique message of her very own, one that was so important and true that humanity would still remember it a hundred years hence.

Some might become cabaret chanteuses, and the prettiest of them – with a bit of luck, and if they showed off their garter and cleavage nicely – might be privileged to warble a song at the Folies Bergères or the Moulin Rouge; others would try their luck as street singers for the space of a summer; and the most courageous would possibly tour the nightspots of Barcelona, Madrid and Rome as 'danseuses orientales'. If they were wise, however, all of them would sooner or later go back to their home towns and get married to some dentist or solicitor or publican whom they had known since childhood – and who would not insist on knowing precisely what they had got up to in Paris.

And what of that great, expansive feeling to which Laura had hoped to give expression someday? Oh, that was nothing special; all her fellow students nursed the very same sensation in their bosoms. Laura could tell this from the way they ran their fingertips absently over the grimy wallpaper and sometimes, for no apparent reason, sat down at the top of the stairs and gazed into the far, invisible distance, lost in thought, as if they could see the most glorious scenery through the wall. She came to realise that the wallpaper was grimy only because countless generations of students had run their fingertips over it, and when she had come to terms with that idea, she discovered that butchers' boys, too, developed this abstracted, faraway look at quiet moments, and even policemen toyed dreamily with their holsters when they thought no one was looking. The fact was, this feeling in which she had invested all her hopes for so long was merely the sound of the workings of the soul – something that all mortals perceive when they take a brief respite from the world's hurly-burly and pay a little attention to themselves.

But there was something else. For a while now, when she was lying in bed with her eyes closed in the silence of her room, Laura had heard a kind of hum that seemed to come not from her breast but from far outside herself, perhaps from the depths of the cosmos. It resembled the distant echo of a sound that disclosed to her, plainly and comprehensibly, in simple harmonies, what constituted the world in her innermost self. When Laura heard that sound she felt happy and at one with the universe. But the next morning, when she hesitantly raised her voice in some secluded corner of the Jardin des Plantes and tried to reproduce that sound, what emerged was no all-embracing cosmic formula, just commonplace, soulless squawks no different from those of her neighbours.

Laura found it terribly disappointing that she failed to give expression to her feelings. True, her voice had grown purer and fuller at the Conservatoire, and she now hit notes with greater assurance, but that wasn't what mattered. Laura didn't delude herself. Because she was too much of an artist to shut her eyes to the fact that she wasn't one, it came as no surprise to her when, at the end of the third semester, her singing teacher, with thoroughly Parisian cruelty, informed her that although she possessed quite a decent voice, it was incapable of further development, so there was no point in keeping her at the Conservatoire for a fourth semester.

That night she wept in her attic room in the Rue du Bac, as did those in the neighbouring rooms who had received the same news the same day. Unlike them, however, she did not console herself for her defeat by blaming a hostile environment, the malignity of the times or the obtuseness of her teachers. Instead, she faced facts: her voice was incapable of further development. That verdict was sad but not unjust. At ballet schools too, 99 out of 100 careers were cut short by overly broad haunches and overly short legs; that was genetically predetermined and nobody's fault. Not every would-be dentist could become one, after all, and many a youth who aspired to become a celebrated football star had been compelled to take over his father's greengrocer's shop.

For her few remaining weeks at the Conservatoire, Laura valiantly attended her lessons and assiduously practised her scales at night. But she no longer refrained from smoking ciga-rettes. At least she still had that feeling inside her. And that cosmic hum. And quite a decent voice.

That, at least.

5

Then came the day when Felix Bloch concluded his experiments, returned to the light of day and discovered that he had become something of a celebrity in the little world of atomic physics. Word had got round, at first in Zurich, then at other Swiss colleges and universities, and finally at those European institutes that went in for atomic physics, that someone was doing unusual things in the ETH's basement. Though only 22 and still a long way from committing his dissertation to paper, Felix was invited to congresses in Göttingen, Hamburg and Copenhagen. There he lectured to small groups of predominantly young men on the behaviour of electrons at different temperatures, after which he had to submit to questioning by grumpy old professors who were at odds with younger physicists' talk of uncertainty and fuss about imprecision.

Felix withstood all these inquisitions unscathed because he never indulged in speculation about wider issues but kept both feet planted on the relatively firm foundation of his personal ice floe, simply reporting on the spectrograph's chromatic changes as he had observed them and as anyone with a suitable apparatus could verify.

He now felt thoroughly at home in atomic physics. His professors and fellow students had become a second family to him and he often sat with them over bread, cheese and red wine in the Institute's kitchen until late at night, discussing the latest results of research and the state of the world with like-minded individuals.

It transpired that most of the students shared his pacifism and his hopes for a better future, transcending crude mechanics. Many of them were so inimical to anything industrial and mechanical that, as scientists, they fundamentally rejected the basic principle of the machine – the law of cause and effect – as a fiction of the human mind. As against this neo-romantic existentialism, their elders argued that, from an empirical point of view, machines clearly worked when they worked, which was sufficient proof that, in physics at least, certain things had a cause and many had an effect. To which the younger ones retorted that machines worked only as expressions of a human idea and invariably led to death and destruction because their causality principle was (a) man-made and (b) the negation of everything living and organic, which always grew out of and into itself without any cause and effect. To which their elders, in turn, rejoined that the moon could hardly be said to be guided by human ideas when it kept to its precisely predictable orbit; to which the younger ones objected that it would be naive to regard atomic physics as a kind of astronomy in miniature.

Such were the subjects discussed in the Institute's kitchen. At some stage late at night, when a few bottles had been emptied and the older students had gone home, conversation among the young ones inevitably turned to Einstein's *Manifesto to the Europeans* and to the disgraceful assiduity with which many of his colleagues had made themselves into willing accomplices of war.

They spoke, for example, of Fritz Haber, the professor of

chemistry from Berlin who had overseen the first large-scale poison gas attack in history outside the small Belgian town of Ypres on 22 April 1915, which killed 18,000 French soldiers within a few minutes. They also spoke of his beautiful and brilliant wife, herself a qualified chemist, who was so ashamed of her husband's achievements that she shot herself with his military pistol in the garden of their Berlin home. Personally rewarded by the Kaiser with promotion to the rank of captain, Fritz Haber left that very day for Galicia to prepare for the next gas attack, so her funeral had to take place without him. Yet another topic of conversation was the nuclear chemist Otto Hahn, who, with patriotic fervour, had joined Fritz Haber in turning on the chlorine gas bottles, only to run across no-man's-land, conscience-stricken, and soothe some Siberian soldiers' burning lungs with oxygen. There was also the daft idea Hahn and Haber came up with in the middle of the war, when they suggested that a million German army rifles should have their sights smeared with radioactively luminescent radium so that soldiers could shoot at night as well as by day. The Minister of War had eagerly adopted this idea and commandeered every available pinch of radium in the Reich – until firing tests at Bruck an der Leitha demonstrated that it was preferable to illuminate the target rather than the sights. A year after the war Fritz Haber was awarded the Nobel Prize for chemistry. He had spent years thereafter sailing the Atlantic Ocean in a vain attempt to pay Germany's reparations debts by extracting gold from sea water, and he was now, as Reich Commissioner for pest control, developing a poison gas for combating rodents and other vermin. The physics students could not have known in the spring of 1927 that Haber's gas would go down in history under the name 'Zyklon B'.

Felix Bloch took the fate of Hahn and Haber as a warning, but it did not shake his decision to devote his working life to physical research. Those men had served the machine because they had been children of their age and their empire, but he himself belonged to another age and was Swiss, not German.

He had spent almost the whole of his life hitherto in Zurich, having left it only to go skiing in the Engadine with his parents and, later on, to go for long hikes in the Glarner Alps. He now spoke the Zurich dialect almost without an accent and had acquired the Zwinglian, rather wry Zurich sense of humour, which finds its own hilarity a trifle embarrassing. On Saturdays he went to football matches at the Letzigrund stadium, and on Wednesdays he ate fried sausages on the Limmatquai. He felt valued and secure at the ETH, and his research work had a purpose in which he found it easy to believe.

And then, from one day to the next, he became homeless when his family of physicists scattered in all directions overnight. At the end of the summer semester of 1927 he had to take leave of Fritz London and Walter Heitler, his friends and fellow hikers, because the former was returning to Munich and the latter going to Berlin with Professor Schrödinger. At the same time, Peter Debye, the director of the ETH, accepted an appointment in Leipzig. The Institute's kitchen fell silent and Felix now spent the evenings with his parents in Seehofstrasse. It dawned on him that, once the summer vacation was over, Professor Scherrer would be the only person in the whole of Zurich with whom he could discuss electrons.

One afternoon he called on Scherrer at his office and deposited the quartz prisms on his desk. Surprised, the professor raised his eyebrows and asked if Felix had completed his work.

Far from it, Felix replied. The truth was, he still had no idea if his electrons performed the high jump, the long jump or some other neat trick.

Scherrer laughed. Well?

For the time being, said Felix, he had no further use for the spectrograph. If he needed prisms in the future he would get hold of some replacements.

Nonsense, said the professor. Pushing them back across his desk, he asked what Felix's plans were.

Actually, Felix said with a shrug, he still wanted to discover why electric currents passed through metals so unaccountably fast. Other than that, he was going to enrol in a teacher-training course that autumn and prepare to enter the teaching profession. There would be a vacancy at Seefeld High School next year.

Is that what you want? asked the professor.

Felix nodded.

To become a schoolmaster? To torment bored youths with the fundamentals of mechanics and thermodynamics?

Felix nodded.

For a lifetime? Over and over again for the rest of your days?

It's a respectable job, said Felix.

But not yours, said the professor. Your job is to watch electrons performing the high jump or the long jump or some other neat trick. You must leave education to others.

Felix said nothing.

I understand, said the professor. Listen to me, Bloch: you must go out into the world, you'll find Zurich a pretty lonely place in the near future. Go to Göttingen or Copenhagen. Or Leipzig – Debye is redeveloping the Institute for Theoretical Physics there with Heisenberg.

I can't afford it, said Felix.

I'll call Heisenberg if you'd like me to. I've heard he's looking for a second assistant.

Felix said nothing.

I understand, the professor said again. Your father?

Felix nodded. My father isn't very susceptible to the charm of electrons.

Be a man, said the professor. Inform him of your decision and he won't withhold his blessing.

§∂

If truth be told, Laura d'Oriano wasn't altogether unhappy about her rejection by the Conservatoire and her enforced departure from Paris. Her failure to make it as an artist had certainly been a stinging defeat, but leaving behind the northern greyness of the City of Lights that had so mercilessly cold-shouldered her for 22 long months had also come as a relief to her Mediterranean cast of mind.

She felt at home in Marseille. The harbour's quasi-oriental bustle reminded her of carefree childhood days in Smyrna and Damascus, and she heard more laughter there in a day than she had in a year in Paris. Mind you, life here was a struggle. The morgue's horse and cart toured the quarter every morning to pick up any poor wretches who had reached the end of their road during the night, having died alone and unaided in some backyard, on some cellar stairs, or behind some stack of timber. Nevertheless, as long as the poor wretches were still more or less mobile and robust enough to obtain their own daily crust and a dry place to sleep, the old port tolerated them like long-established residents.

Laura now knew all the denizens of the quarter and

exchanged *bonjours* in all directions when she went to fetch her breakfast croissants. At night, when the walls still gave off the warmth of the departed sun, she often sat outside the shop in the light of the streetlamp until long after midnight, smoking cigarettes and enjoying the company of any friends from the district who joined her. Waiters from the neighbouring bistros spent their cigarette breaks with her and the oyster seller would present her with half a dozen *belons* as he passed by. Sometimes schoolboys sauntered up and boldly requested a light for their stolen cigarettes, and in the evening prostitutes rested their aching feet and warned Laura against the dangers of this world as if she were an innocent country girl.

Word had soon spread that she possessed a nice voice, and friends sometimes pressed her to round off the evening with an oriental love song. Happy to oblige, she would then mount her chair and fill the night air with her wistful singing. But if the waiters suggested getting her a guest appearance at some dance café or music hall, she declined. Why? Because she realised that she would have to enlist the aid of her garter and cleavage while singing there, just as her mother had done, and that she had vowed from her earliest childhood never to do.

However, childish vows expire at the end of childhood and Laura was now 20 years old, so she gave the matter some more thought. She was bored by her salesgirl's existence and continued to hanker after the stage, and if a young woman wanted to go on the stage, showing her garter was the price of admission; that had been so in every age and in every branch of show business.

And so, in March 1933, Laura finally accepted an engagement at the Chat Noir and appeared there on five successive nights. The proprietor's stage props included a Cossack costume trimmed with fake ermine. It fitted Laura like a glove, so she sang Russian love songs and danced the kozachok. Her audiences went wild, she herself enjoyed the footlights and the applause, and the 15 francs she received at the end of the night came in very handy. After each performance she was awaited outside the rear entrance by a waiter friend who protected her from the attentions of overenthusiastic members of the audience and chivalrously escorted her home.

Laura was naturally aware that her performance was modest from the artistic point of view, and that her voice had grown a trifle rusty since her time in Paris. All the same, she undoubtedly gave her audiences pleasure, and wasn't pleasing an audience the supreme goal of any artiste? Furthermore, if you could enhance your public's pleasure by showing a smidgen of leg or cleavage, why shouldn't you do so?

She did not get all that many engagements. Marseille was the second-largest city in France but a provincial city nonetheless, so there were only a limited number of music cafés. Once she had performed in one, she had to wait at least a year before she could consider appearing there again. Later on, when her name had become better known, perhaps she would embark on a little tour of the Côte d'Azur, taking in Cannes, Nice and Monaco.

Laura was putting down deeper roots in Marseille than she had ever done anywhere before. Her parents had aged perceptibly and the music shop's stock remained inexhaustible. Then, one afternoon, the door was opened with a flourish by a young man wearing a white linen suit, white spats and a white fedora on his pomaded head. He planted his legs apart, hips swaying, and cast short, sharp glances at every corner of the shop as if he were the kind of man who led a dangerous life and needed to be permanently on his guard against powerful adversaries. At length, eyeing Laura keenly, he tipped his fedora back with a forefinger and said:

Bonjour, mademoiselle.

Bonjour, young man, Laura replied. She saw him wince at the implied diminutive, and then, to give him a treat, lowered her eyes in a spuriously bashful way.

I need some sheet music, he said, rocking up and down on his toes so that the leather of his spats creaked. I was told you carry an extensive stock.

That's true, monsieur. Do you require anything specific?

I have a number of requirements, very specific requirements, he replied, producing a thrice-folded sheet of paper from his breast pocket. Do you have Mozart's clarinet concerto?

Certainly.

Laura opened a cupboard and smiled. This foppish young man who played the macho adventurer to camouflage his innocuousness made a welcome change from the endless succession of obsequious migrants and malign old seamen. He looked good in his white suit, and there was a defiant curl to his upper lip which she wouldn't have minded kissing away. He was light on his feet – a good dancer, probably – and he spoke French with a smooth and melodious, almost girlishly lilting accent that Laura couldn't place.

I'd also like Beethoven's Moonlight Sonata, the young man said.

So you don't want the clarinet concerto?

I want both. The clarinet concerto *and* the Moonlight Sonata.

He drew in his breath sharply.

As you wish, said Laura, opening another cupboard.

I need five copies.

Five copies of the Moonlight Sonata?

And three of Chopin's Preludes.

Laura glanced at the young man in surprise, but she opened another cupboard.

I also need the B minor orchestral suite by Johann Sebastian Bach. One copy of that.

The whole score?

No, just the flute part. Plus two copies of Brahms's Hungarian Dances and three of Mussorgski's Pictures at an Exhibition. That's it. Oh, no, I'd also like Beethoven's 'Für Elise'. Twelve copies.

Twelve copies of 'Für Elise'?

Twelve, I'm afraid.

Forgive me for asking, but is this a practical joke?

I have money, mademoiselle, I'll pay cash.

They went over to the till, and he introduced himself while she was making out the bill.

The young man's name was Emil Fraunholz. He was a 25-year-old Swiss who had been born and brought up in Bottighofen, a farming village beside Lake Constance. He had fled to Marseille two or three years earlier to avoid having to do national service in the Swiss army. Since then he had scraped a living by means of various odd jobs and artful schemes whose primary purpose was keep him as far away as possible from military service and agricultural drudgery.

His most profitable scheme consisted in getting middlemen in the colonies to collect letters from members of the Foreign Legion and smuggle them past the military censors and across the Mediterranean to Marseille, whence – for a fee – he would forward them to their addressees by ordinary mail. As a further service to the legionnaires, he supplied them – payment in advance – with desiderata that were unobtainable in Sidi bel Abbès, Saigon or Nouméa: a photograph of some actress, a tin of *crème de marrons*, a kilo of dried cod, ten grams of opium, or the Moonlight Sonata.

Sometimes his pockets overflowed with money and sometimes he was flat broke. His commercial dealings were subject to strong fluctuations. Business was best when the barracks were occupied by battle-hardened veterans who knew the ropes and wouldn't shrink from bribing an amenable sentry with a bottle of spirits or putting an incorruptible one out of action with a well-gauged blow to the back of the head; business was worst when the barracks were occupied by recruits to whom regulations were still sacred.

Emil Fraunholz also came unstuck whenever one of his middlemen got caught, which happened every few months. He would then have to brace himself for a visit from military policemen who wore stiff white kepis, asked unpleasant questions and could get pretty stroppy if you lied to them. On such occasions Emil deemed it advisable to give business a rest and visit a non-existent aunt in Nice or Cannes.

But in May 1931, when he first set foot in Laura d'Oriano's music shop, business was good. And because his pockets were full of money that afternoon and the girl behind the counter enchanted him more than any he'd ever met before, he laid aside his macho mask and asked her, quite shyly, if she would care to join him for coffee and cakes on the terrace of the Hotel Excelsior next Sunday.

From then on, Laura and Emil spent all their Sundays together, and sometimes their weekdays as well. Laura had never before met a man like Emil Fraunholz. His veneer of machismo had completely disappeared the moment he first asked her for a date, revealing an amiable and reserved but shrewd and alert young man who listened to her attentively and liked to make her laugh. What particularly appealed to her was the unaffectedly gentle manner that was probably a legacy from his peaceful homeland, which had been spared destruction and disaster for many generations.

Emil did not talk of war or grind his teeth, feign attempted suicide or slit puppies' throats, nor did he knit his brow for no good reason; he told Laura, in his almost girlishly high-pitched voice, about the beautiful eyes of Bottighofen's cows and the sweet taste of fresh apple juice pressed from windfalls gathered free of charge from the wet grass of other people's orchards.

But Emil also told her that his parental farm afforded a fine view of Lake Constance, on which the yachts of the wealthy cruised so majestically, and that he had vowed, even as a young child, to exchange hard graft and cow dung for quaffing champagne on board white yachts in the company of beautiful women. When Laura smilingly asked if he had fulfilled his ambition, he brought a bottle of Veuve Clicquot to their next date and, at the Quai des Belges, ushered her aboard a white sailing boat that doubtless belonged to some friend or business associate who owed him a favour.

And when Laura trailed a hand in the water during their boat trip and admired the hilly beauty of the Provençal coast, he turned up for their next date in a Bentley or a Peugeot and invited her to come for a spin. And when she got in he drove her up into the hills, and when she felt hungry he spread out a rug in some pretty little spot and unpacked a picnic basket filled with delicacies he hoped she would like. And when she ran out of cigarettes there was a packet of her favourite brand in the glove compartment, and when dusk fell he drove her home without ever having put a hand on her knee all day.

The relationship between Emil and Laura went well because it evolved simply, devoid of guile or ulterior motive. When they drank champagne, they drank champagne, and when they lay on the sand together, they lay on the sand. He described his business deals and cunning schemes and was pleased when Laura laughed at them, and she told him about the big, expansive feeling in her chest and the cosmic hum, although those things seemed quite unimportant now. And it pleased her when he listened intently and made no comment.

And when they slept together they slept together.

When Laura had an engagement at a music café she felt embarrassed and concealed it from him. And when he got wind of it all the same, he sat wide-eyed at her feet the whole evening, kissed her hands afterwards and swore that he'd never heard anything lovelier in his life. And when she called him a flatterer he protested and volunteered to drop dead if he wasn't telling the absolute truth. Then she believed him and felt happy.

In the late summer of 1931, however, the couple could no longer shut their eyes to the fact that Laura was pregnant. This made everything more difficult. Laura wept because it had probably put paid to her singing career, but Emil took her in his arms and said that all would be well because he was giving up his shady deals and would ask her parents for her hand in marriage.

Her father and mother were not overly enthusiastic about the unexpected advent of their daughter's suitor because they scented the country bumpkin under his white linen suit and doubted if he had the mental strength and agility to sustain a long-term relationship with their headstrong daughter. However, human nature having created an indisputable fact whose elimination they, being sensitive souls, could not bring themselves to suggest to Laura, they gave the couple their blessing.

They were married on 18 August 1931 in the little church of Sainte Marie-de-la-Charité, after which the wedding party drove in two hired cars to a country inn outside the city. It was only a small party – apart from the newly-weds, only Laura's parents and her four siblings were present – but they nonetheless managed to stage a complete music hall programme after the meal. Laura sang an Egyptian ballad and Emil performed his party piece, which consisted in juggling with five wine glasses at once. Laura's brothers did card tricks, made coins disappear and retrieved them from the bridegroom's auditory canal. Everyone cracked jokes about the fact that marriage had transformed Laura into a Swiss citizen. In conclusion, mother and daughter sang a duet – something they had never done in public before – and the bride's father accompanied them on the taproom piano, which was appallingly out of tune and missing several keys.

When they had all wiped away their tears they ordered *cafés cognac*, and when they were all tipsy they drove back to town.

§

On an overcast autumn day early in October, Felix Bloch alighted from the train beneath the massive dome of Leipzig's central station, collected his bicycle from the mail van and rode it to the Institute for Theoretical Physics, which was situated on the outskirts of the city between a cemetery and a psychiatric clinic. Having dumped his suitcase in an assistant's attic room, he paid a preliminary call on Heisenberg.

Feeling immediately at home in his new surroundings, Felix set up his electrical apparatuses in a windowless basement room. The spectrograph remained in its packing case for the time being. In the mornings he functioned as Heisenberg's lecture assistant and held exercises for the first-year students; in the afternoons he corrected their work and engaged in his own experiments.

The student body of the newly founded institute was small, and Felix knew all its members by name after a week. Word had yet to spread that young Werner Heisenberg, the man who had shaken the world of physics with his uncertainty principle and ran his institute like a troop of Boy Scouts, was teaching there. The lecture rooms were far too big. The students sat in a circle on their desks, brewed tea on Bunsen burners and munched the pastries Professor Heisenberg brought with him from the bakery around the corner.

They were a boisterous bunch of youngsters. Heisenberg had installed a ping pong room in the basement of the institute, and everyone had free access to it. Felix looked after the equipment and a Hungarian student named Edward Teller, who had fallen under a tram in Munich and lost a foot, always made tea for everyone. Professor Heisenberg was the undisputed ping pong champion and regarded as invincible, at least since his lecture tour of the Far East. The only person who beat him regularly was a Japanese named Yoshio Nishina. A bad loser, Heisenberg is said to have gone to earth for three days after one such defeat.

At weekends the students and lecturers jointly explored the city, which had grown rich over the centuries thanks to its worsted and wool-combing mills, its printers and publishers and its trade in furs and grain from Eastern Europe. They rode the carousels and roller coasters in the Alter Messplatz and patronised the Rote Mühle cabaret in Windmühlenstrasse, whose outward appearance resembled that of the Moulin Rouge, its Parisian prototype. At night they visited the political cabarets that had sprung up like mushrooms after the war, among them the Retorte, the Bauch and the Litfasssäule. In summer they went to the open-air pool in Schönefeld or the lido in the grounds of the trade fair, in winter to the toboggan run in Schönefelder Park. Over Easter, Heisenberg would invite his closest friends to stay at his ski chalet in the Bavarian Alps.

Felix Bloch spent the late evenings alone in his room, reading technical journals or writing to his parents. Before turning out the light he would fall to musing, staring at the bulb in his reading lamp and wondering if the electrons inside the glowing filament were really doing what he imagined. When he lay in bed in the dark, the walls were so thin that he could hear Heisenberg at the other end of the passage, playing the brown mahogany grand he had ordered from Julius Blüthner's Leipzig piano factory. That autumn of 1928 it was the allegro vivace from Schumann's piano concerto in A minor at which Heisenberg toiled night after night for hours on end. Listening until he fell asleep, Felix was surprised that Heisenberg should have chosen to tackle such a melancholy, romantic piece, which was one long fantasy about Schumann's courtship of Clara and the bliss he felt at their union.

The two young men developed a restrained but genuine friendship. At Christmas 1927, Heisenberg took Felix aside and asked how he was progressing with his electrons.

Not badly, Felix replied; the results of his measurements were fully consistent with his initial theory.

So wasn't it time he wrote everything down as a dissertation? asked Heisenberg. With a bashful smile, he added that he hadn't yet supervised a doctoral candidate in the course of his brief professorship, and that he would consider it an honour if Felix became his first.

Felix devoted the following six months to his dissertation, which he submitted on 2 July 1928 under the title 'On the quantum mechanics of electrons in metal lattices'. In this, he examined the hitherto unsolved mystery of why an electric current flows extremely fast even through very long metal wires. He explained the remarkably small resistance it encounters by positing that the metal ions are arranged in the form of a crystal lattice, which renders a collision with the electrons passing them extremely unlikely; furthermore, the lower the temperature the more stable the lattice and the less likely a collision. His experiments in the basement had, in fact, demonstrated that the conductivity of metals increases as their temperature drops. Heisenberg, his doctoral supervisor, would a little later adopt the lattice idea and suggest that the entire cosmos is organised into a single lattice, like a gigantic honeycomb.

Felix's dissertation aroused interest all over Europe when it was published in Berlin's *Zeitschrift für Physik*, and everyone wanted to make the young man's acquaintance. During the winter semester of 1928/9 Wolfgang Pauli invited him to the ETH in Zurich. Thereafter he visited Niels Bohr in Copenhagen, Max Planck and Otto Hahn in Berlin, Paul Ehrenfest in Leyden and Max Born in Göttingen, where he got to know an American doctoral candidate named Robert Oppenheimer, who could talk the hind leg off a donkey about Sanskrit, Dante or the Buddhistic concept of time and was to play a momentous role in Felix's subsequent life.

One would like to have been present at Easter 1932, when the young 'quantum mechanics' from Leipzig went to Copenhagen for the spring conference at Niels Bohr's institute. Werner Heisenberg and Felix Bloch undertook the hours-long train journey accompanied by Carl Friedrich von Weizsäcker and Edward Teller, their doctoral candidates, and Otto Hahn's assistant, Max Delbrück, joined them in Berlin. On the way, the young scientists discussed the year's most exciting topic in the field of atomic physics: the discovery by James Chadwick of Cambridge that, in addition to the positively charged atomic nucleus and the negatively charged electrons, there were also neutrons, or uncharged particles. This raised the prospect that atomic nuclei were far from being an indivisible whole, as had been assumed hitherto, but composed of several parts and capable of being split.

Since the centenary of Goethe's death was looming, one of the travellers had a copy of *Faust* in his luggage, so Heisenberg, Bloch, Teller, von Weizsäcker and Delbrück hit on the idea of enlivening the conference with a quantum physical skit on Goethe's drama.

The idea was promptly put into effect, the nub of the parody being the question of what holds the innermost structure of the world together. It was performed in the institute's big lecture room on Easter Sunday 1932 and watched by many of those attending the conference.

Professor Paul Ehrenfest of Leyden took the part of Faust and Léon Rosenberg from Belgium that of Mephistopheles. Felix Bloch, who played Almighty God himself, presided over the experiment table seated on a high stool, wearing a top hat and a home-made mask whose features bore an unmistakable resemblance to those of Niels Bohr. The Chorus

Mysticus consisted of Heisenberg, Oppenheimer and four other volunteers.

Faust aroused much laughter when he took the stage and declaimed:

I have, alas, learned Valence Chemistry,
Theory of Groups, of the Electric Field,
and Transformation Theory as revealed
by Sophie Lie in eighteen-ninety-three.
Yet here I stand, for all my lore,
no wiser than I was before.
M. A. I'm called, and Doctor. Up and down,
round about, the pupils have been guided
by this poor erring Faust and witless clown;
they break their heads on Physics, just as I did.
But still I'm better than the cranks,
the Big Shots, monkeys, mountebanks.
All doubts assail me; so does every scruple;
and Pauli as the Devil himself I fear.
[…]

A moving moment was provided by the Danish student Ellen Tvede, who played Gretchen. Dressed up as a neutron with a big plus-minus sign over her face, she sang the following words to the tune of Schubert's 'Gretchen at the Spinning Wheel':

My Mass is zero,
my Charge is the same.
You are my hero,
Neutrino's my name.
I am your fate,

and I'm your key.
Closed is the gate
for lack of me.
Beta-rays throng
with me to pair.
The N-spin's wrong
if I'm not there.
My Mass is zero,
my Charge is the same.
You are my hero,
Neutrino's my name.
My psyche turns
to you, my own.
My poor heart yearns
for you alone.
My lovesick soul
is yours to win.
I cannot control
my trembling spin.
My Mass is zero,
My Charge is the same.
You are my hero,
Neutrino's my name.

6

On his return from Copenhagen, Felix Bloch made some pre-liminary notes for a work on the stopping power of atoms with several electrons. Meanwhile, in Marseille, Laura d'Oriano made some preliminary efforts to accustom herself to her new role as a wife and mother-to-be. It would doubtless have been possible, from a purely practical point of view, for Emil Fraunholz to have moved in with the d'Orianos above the music shop. It would also have seemed sensible, in view of the Depression and mass unemployment, for the young couple to have minimised their living expenses by pooling their income with Laura's parents. However, since they were all intelligent people and knew that nothing good could come of such an arrangement in the long run, Emil set about fulfilling a plan he had hatched on the off chance some time ago. A legion-naire who had originally been a pharmacist in Grasse, and had been compelled for unknown reasons to abandon his former livelihood in a hurry, had offered to sell him – for a song – his business and the flat that went with it.

While Emil was busy forging plans, Laura cautiously objected that Grasse was a provincial dump at the back of beyond, and that Emil, unless she was much mistaken, did not know the first thing about pharmaceuticals. Emil coun-tered this by arguing that the air of the Alpes Maritimes would be incomparably better for their baby than that of Marseille harbour, and that Grasse, being the world capital of perfume manufacture, was a destination popular with rich American tourists. Finally, as far as the pharmacist's profession was concerned, it really wasn't witchcraft; you sold Sirolin syrup for coughs and Anaxa opiated plasters for corns and referred any more serious cases to the local GP.

So the young married couple packed their belongings and got Papa d'Oriano to drive them to Grasse in a rented Fiat, collected the key from the legionnaire's mother and moved into their new home. There, Laura and Emil made the surprising discovery that everything in the pharmacy and the flat above it was so consistent with their needs, tastes and dimensions that they might have been their own predecessors. The slippers inside the door to the flat fitted Emil's feet perfectly and the dressing gown in the wardrobe was his exact size. On the dressing table in the bedroom Laura found a new eyebrow pencil of her usual make and a bottle of her favourite perfume, and standing beside their bed, complete with pillow and eiderdown, was a cradle that seemed only to have been awaiting their baby's arrival.

Emil, said Laura, what is all this?

It's incredible, he said.

Is this one of your practical jokes?

I'm utterly mystified, he said. Hand on heart, I'm as surprised as you are.

This isn't funny, Emil. I want to know if you've been here before.

Never, I swear.

Then Laura believed him, because she knew that although he was a smart alec, he wasn't a liar. He had never been in

Grasse before and knew the legionnaire only from letters. It really was pure chance that the premises suited them to a tee. Laura and Emil were not surprised, later on, to discover in the shop two pharmacists' white gowns that fitted them perfectly, or to find the shelves dust-free and well stocked and two copies of the latest inventory lying on the counter.

All Emil had to do at eight the following Monday morning was put on his white gown and unlock the shop door. Laura would look after the household and the baby, when it arrived, and possibly help out in the shop when it was asleep. If the business prospered they would buy a used car and drive to Cannes or Nice for the weekend, and on high days and holidays they would sometimes visit Laura's parents and siblings in Marseille.

Emil was firmly convinced that the pharmacy would feed him and his family for the duration of the economic crisis because people were always falling ill and needing medicines they could have faith in. This, alas, was a misapprehension. On the day of the reopening he had only one customer, on the second day none, on the third day two. It transpired that the Depression had killed off the tourist industry. The Americans stayed away and the perfume trade collapsed. The citizens of Grasse had ceased to earn good money, and because they couldn't afford to become ill they simply stayed healthy. Those that became genuinely ill refrained from showing it because they preferred to spend the little money they did have at the butcher's, not the chemist's. They could live without corn plasters and tincture of opium, at a pinch, but not without their *escalope de bœuf.*

Emil stood behind the counter for days on end, all on his own, but the bell over the shop door remained silent. When he closed in the evening, the till was as empty as it had been that morning. His savings and Laura's dowry were running out, and it wasn't long before Laura could no longer obtain credit from any of the little town's bakers or greengrocers. She had already paid two visits to Marseille to ask her parents for money and she had no wish to go a third time. In April she gave birth to the baby, a girl whom she christened Renée. The shopkeepers now took pity on Laura and extended their line of credit, but when she became pregnant again a few months later and queued up for bread or sausage with a bulging belly, they stared straight through her until she got the message and went home empty-handed.

In March 1933 a second baby girl was born. Emil and Laura christened her Anna. They were now in dire straits and short of everything. When Laura had somewhat recovered from the birth, she called all three music cafés in Cannes, asked them for an engagement and demeaned herself to the extent of vocally auditioning over the phone. When she actually did land a Friday-night engagement and drove off in the omnibus in evening dress, Emil fell prey to such an unprecedented fit of jealousy that he abandoned his two sleeping daughters in the flat, purloined a neighbour's bicycle and pedalled the full twenty kilometres to Cannes, where he watched Laura's performance in the darkened auditorium and made the most terrible scene afterwards because she'd exposed her garter and cleavage to the footlights.

Then came the summer, and life became a little easier because at that time of year the South of France was a horn of plenty. Come October, though, money was again needed to buy coal for the stove. One night after the couple had gone to bed, Emil cautiously asked his wife if she could contemplate leaving Provence for the time being and riding out the Depression at his parents' farmhouse in Switzerland.

But you'd have to do your military service, she said sleepily.

They won't want me any more, he replied. I'm a married man with two children, you know.

Laura sat up and turned on the bedside light again.

Emil, look at me and pin your ears back.

I'm listening.

I came to Grasse with you even though I'd sooner have stayed in Marseille.

True.

I'll be your faithful companion for better or worse, the way we promised the priest.

I know.

But you're asking too much of me. It'd be more than I could stand, you hear? I'd sooner be divorced or shot like a dog than bury myself in that village of yours.

What are you talking about? he said. It's not *my* village. We'd have a roof over our heads and the children would have enough to eat. Any amount of potatoes and apples and fresh milk.

What's the name of the place again? Bottikov?

Bottighofen. After all, it doesn't have to be forever. A year or two, just till the crisis is over.

Bottikov ... Where is it, in Russia? And what's there, cows? Apple trees?

Lake Constance is beautiful, you'll see. Tourists come from far and wide.

I'm staying here.

In the South of France? For evermore?

What have you got against the South of France?

Nothing, said Emil.

You've got something against the South of France.

The South of France is lovely, said Emil.

But?

It does have its darker sides – everywhere does.

For instance?

Forget it.

For instance?

Well, for instance, in the South of France waiters teach young foreigners to eat little birds with a knife and fork.

And that's why you're homesick for Bottikov?

If you like, yes. We don't eat little birds, but we've plenty of potatoes and fresh milk.

Laura wouldn't hear another word. As far as she was concerned, moving to Bottighofen was out of the question. She turned out the light and went to sleep, and at breakfast the next morning she again insisted that Emil abandon all thought of it once and for all. She would certainly have stuck to her guns, had not the bailiff turned up three days later and sealed the door of the pharmacy, and had not the bank five days thereafter given them notice to vacate the premises by the end of the month because they were six months in arrears with their mortgage payments.

Felix Bloch handed in his thesis after returning from Copenhagen, then delivered some lectures on the general theory of relativity, the quantum theory of magnetism and the absorption of high-energy particles by matter. The year 1932 was a happy one for the sciences, the discovery of the neutron having opened up new horizons in many fields. In Germany, however, the annus mirabilis, as physicists called it, began to wane long before the autumn.

This was brought home to Felix by the ever-increasing numbers of flags hanging in the old quarter of Leipzig. Demonstrations and torchlight processions were forever being held, and brawls and shootings resulted in bloodshed every few days. The university steps and entrances were picketed by members of the National Socialist German Students League (NSDSTB), who beat up the pamphleteers of other political parties. Uniformed students seated in the lecture rooms kicked up a din if they suspected a lecturer of being Jewish. A professor of radiophysics named Erich Marx was shouted down by Brownshirt students and compelled to resign. The NSDSTB demanded that quantum physics be deleted from the curriculum on the grounds that it disseminated Jewish ideas. It was not long before the theory of relativity ceased to be taught at German universities and Einstein's name was no longer uttered. At Berlin's Lehrter Station on 10 December, Albert and Elsa Einstein and their six suitcases boarded a train for Antwerp, whence they eventually sailed to New York.

Felix, too, was booed. Shortly before Christmas he was compelled to abandon a lecture for the first time. It started – seemingly innocuously – when one uniformed student dropped a coin on the floor. Even before it had stopped jingling, a second coin hit the floor, followed in quick succession by 10 or 20 more. Another student compounded this cacophony by slapping his desk with the flat of his hand, whereupon a hundred more hands slapped the desks in unison with a sound like boots on the march. Imperturbably, Felix Bloch continued to write his formulas on the blackboard, but when the first coins came flying in his direction he laid the chalk aside and left the room.

On that day, Felix was forced to acknowledge that his pacifism offered no protection from the hatred of misguided people. He was powerless against the malign stupidity and unbridled violence that was spreading, not only in the university's lecture rooms, but in the streets of Leipzig as well. When he cycled through the inner city he was recognised by students who yelled abuse and sometimes threw stones at him, so he soon took to travelling by tram and hiding behind a newspaper.

Winter was slow to come that year, and the weather remained unnaturally mild until well into the new year. Many home-owners had already convinced themselves that they would get by on only half the usual amount of coal when, in the middle of January 1933, the big freeze set in. Pigeons dropped dead and fell off roofs, streams, sewers and water mains froze. Tram windows were thick with frost flowers, outside and in. Felix several times missed his stop because the conductor had failed to call it out.

On Sundays, to escape the incessant chorus of hatred, he often went ice-skating. The toboggan run was still closed for want of snow. In the evenings, because it was so cold in his attic room, he went to the cinema. Tom Tyler was starring in *The Return of Tarzan* at the Alberthalle and Marlene Dietrich in *Blonde Venus* at the Capitol.

On the last day of the cold snap 20,000 socialist workers demonstrated in Messplatz. Next morning, Leipzig was engulfed in a violent winter storm. Thirty centimetres of snow fell to the accompaniment of thunder and lightning, then it grew warmer. When the National Socialist Students League held its daily demonstration in the university courtyard, the snow beneath its uniformed members' boots turned to grey slush.

Felix must by then have realised that his time in Leipzig had run out. After the Reichstag elections of 5 March 1933 the university acquired a new rector who, in the presence of the assembled staff, marked his assumption of office by personally hoisting the swastika flag on the roof of his institution. New subjects such as 'Blood and Soil' and 'Nation without Space' were incorporated in the curriculum. On 21 March a torchlit procession of 300,000 people marched from Messplatz to Augustusplatz. Schoolchildren, students, soldiers, workers, townsfolk, farmers – all joined in.

The sound of marching boots and of many thousands of voices raised in song came wafting through the streets and out to the Institute for Theoretical Physics, where Felix Bloch and Werner Heisenberg doubtless heard it but did not comment. The signs of the times were so obvious and the impending disaster seemed so inevitable that there was nothing to be said, so they shunned the subject early in the morning, when they drank coffee together and discussed the day's agenda. It remained equally taboo in the evening, when they played ping pong in the basement.

The same reticence applied when Heisenberg and his friends went skiing in the Bavarian Alps at Easter 1933. It was already four in the afternoon when Heisenberg set off from Oberaudorf station, not far from the Austrian frontier, accompanied by Niels Bohr, his son Christian, Carl Friedrich von Weizsäcker and Felix Bloch. The climb to the ski hut, which stood on the southern slopes of the Grosser Thraithen, was a tiring one. In summer it could easily be done in two or three hours, but because a metre of snow had fallen the previous day it would now take twice or three times as long.

The route led steeply upwards through woods deep in snow,

and their rucksacks were heavy. During their first stop to rest, Heisenberg jokingly remarked that what would now be nice would be some 'inverse mountaineering' of the kind he'd done in the Grand Canyon. Travelling by sleeping car, you got to the edge of a big desert plateau and could comfortably descend to the Colorado River, which was almost at sea level. The only trouble was, you were then faced with a 2000-metre climb back to your sleeper.

Darkness had fallen by the time they reached the most strenuous part of the climb, at an altitude where the snow had lost its stability and was alarmingly powdery. Heisenberg trudged on ahead in silence followed by Niels and Christian Bohr and von Weizsäcker, who was lighting their route with a lantern. Felix Bloch brought up the rear because he had the most stamina and was the most experienced mountaineer.

The men were panting now, and no one uttered a word. They made slow progress because Bohr, who was the oldest by 20 years, was starting to tire. Shortly after ten o'clock, Heisenberg, as he later wrote in *Physics and Beyond*, suddenly had the strange sensation that he was swimming in nocturnal darkness, engulfed in snow and bereft of control over his limbs. He couldn't breathe for a while, although his head remained clear of the masses of snow. Then everything came to rest. He extricated himself and turned to look for his friends but could see nothing in the darkness. 'Niels!' he called, but there was no answer. This shocked him, because he could only suppose that his friends had been carried away by the avalanche. Having dug his skis out of the snow with the greatest difficulty, he peered into the darkness once more and spotted a light – von Weizsäcker's lantern – on the slope far above him. That was when he grasped that the avalanche had swept him away but not his friends, who had remained standing on the path. He quickly clipped on his skis and climbed back up to the others. After breathlessly assuring each other that all was well, they continued on their way in silence.

They reached the ski hut next morning, after wading through dazzling white masses of snow beneath a dark blue sky. They didn't feel like skiing yet, not after the alarms and exertions of the night, so they shovelled the snow off the roof of the hut and lay in the sun. And when they had found their tongues again they didn't talk, for instance, about Leipzig's police commissioner, who had banned the social democratic *Leipziger Volkszeitung* by decree, nor about the Brownshirt hordes who had closed down Held, the Jewish department store in Merseburger Strasse, nor about the fact that the city of Leipzig had granted honorary citizenship to Hitler and Hindenburg a few days previously, nor about the eight university professors who had been summarily suspended.

They talked about none of these things because they felt ashamed of their powerlessness, and because no words would have been adequate to describe the extent of the disaster. Instead, with the splendid alpine panorama as a backdrop, they discussed the question of whether positively charged antiparticles could exist as well as neutrons and negatively charged electrons, as their colleagues Dirac and Anderson had recently asserted. The latest issue of the *Physical Review*, which Niels Bohr produced from his rucksack, contained a cloud chamber photograph that seemed to prove this. It showed the vapour trail of a particle that had penetrated a lead plate inside the cloud chamber and flown past a powerful magnet. The remarkable feature of the photograph was that the vapour trail did not curve towards the magnet, as it should have done if the particle had been a negatively charged electron, but, on the contrary, curved away from the magnet, which indicated that it was positively charged.

The five men discussed this phenomenon for hours. They kept passing the journal around and puzzling over the photograph, in which nothing could be seen in addition to the vapour trail but a lateral view of four screw heads and the lead plate. Their search for some explanation for the strangely curving trajectory continued until the sun went down behind the snow-capped mountain peaks.

Then they went inside. Heisenberg lit a fire in the stove. They drank grog, played poker for toy money in the light of the paraffin lamp and played some rubbishy hit records on an old gramophone. Before long, because the mountain air seeping through the cracks in the walls became bitterly cold after dark, conversation lapsed and they lay down to sleep on their palliasses.

Next morning, because the snow had firmed up in the sun, the men went skiing. They again spent the afternoon on the roof of the hut, discussing physics and philosophy; no reference was made to anything else. Heisenberg made no mention of his now having to preface each of his lectures with the Hitler salute. Carl Friedrich von Weizsäcker refrained from mentioning that, although he condemned the crudity of the Nazis' hatred of the Jews, he was fascinated by the revival of the German nation's hopes for the future, or that he would two weeks hence be taking part in Leipzig's May Day celebrations, at which the Führer was scheduled to deliver a speech. For his part, Felix Bloch did not mention that the new civil service law of 7 April had compelled him to declare his Jewish grandparents, or that from 1 October onwards he would be receiving a Rockefeller bursary of 150 dollars a month, which would render him financially independent and free to pursue his research wherever he chose.

And so the days went by. On Easter Monday, 16 April 1933, the vacation came to an end. The five men put on their skis, shouldered their rucksacks and descended the shorter, western route to the valley between Bayrischzell and Landl. It was a warm, sunny day. The snow had become a bit karstic but provided a good, firm foundation. Liverwort was flowering between the trees down in the valley, where the snow had disappeared, and the alpine meadows were sprinkled with cowslips.

On reaching the Zipfelwirt inn, the atomic physicists got two horses hitched to an open farm cart and drove through the vernal Bavarian countryside to the nearest Oberlandbahn station. And because they had never, in all this time, uttered a word about the dark shadow that had fallen over Germany and Leipzig, the university and every last one of them, they also restricted their conversation during the train journey to splitting atomic nuclei and made no reference to the unavoidable fact that their ways would part at Munich's central station. Niels and Christian Bohr, being Danish citizens, went home to Denmark. Heisenberg and von Weizsäcker, who were loath to abandon their institute, boarded a train for Leipzig in the hope of preserving their oasis of civilisation from the age of barbarism. But Felix Bloch took a train to Zurich by himself. He would never again set foot on German soil.

At the end of October 1933, Emil and Laura and the two girls set off for the station and travelled north by way of Cannes,

Aix and Lyon. Everything might have turned out differently had they arrived in Switzerland on one of those fine, crystalline autumn days on which a warm katabatic wind from the snowy mountains wafts a last hint of late summer into the valleys, the air is filled once more with teeming insects and women wear light dresses for the last time. For Emil Fraunholz, the train journey from Geneva to Lake Constance would then have been a triumphal progress. He would have been able to show Laura the vineyards in their spectacular, flame-coloured autumn robes and the majestic white sweep of the Alps, which would have been visible through the right-hand window throughout the journey. They might have made an intermediate stop in Zurich, walked down Bahnhofstrasse to the lake and inspected the opera house. They might even have crossed the path of Felix Bloch, who was at that time living with his parents in Seehofstrasse and preparing to emigrate to America – not, of course, that Felix and Laura would have recognised each other. Laura would have walked up to the theatre with her husband and children, then past the art museum, through Niederdorf and back to the station. They would then have got to Kreuzlingen late that night, when the last bus to Bottighofen had already left, and spent the night at a hotel. Next morning, because the weather was still fine, they would have made a circuit of Lake Constance in a trim white paddle steamer before taking the bus to Bottighofen and paying their respects to Emil's parents.

But it wasn't like that. It poured with rain throughout the train journey and the sky was so overcast it became dark by midday. What was more, an icy wind lashed the windows with such bucketfuls of rain that Emil and Laura wasted no thought on touristic diversions but concentrated exclusively on keeping their luggage and their children dry. The bus ride from Kreuzlingen station to Bottighofen post office took 20 minutes, the walk up to Emil's parents' farm a quarter of an hour.

Then they were standing outside the farmhouse in the dark. They had dumped their suitcases at the Zum Bären inn and were carrying the sleeping children in their arms. It had stopped raining. Emil called his father first, then his mother. The door opened and his parents came out into the muddy yard in their clogs, his mother lighting the way with a paraffin lamp. Awkward salutations and embraces ensued, and the new arrivals were ushered into the house.

The children were admired and put to bed. Bread, sausage and cheese were laid out on the table in the parlour, together with a bottle of wine and a jug of milk. Emil's father bade Laura welcome in a smattering of French picked up during his military service. His wife smiled at Laura encouragingly, patted her forearm and gestured to her to help herself to the food and drink.

Laura smiled too and asked Emil to convey how sorry she was that she couldn't yet speak a word of Swiss German. Then she sat back and listened to her parents-in-law talking with their son, whom they hadn't seen for five years. Looking at their flushed faces and gnarled hands, she told herself that she had come to rest among decent, placid, hard-working people with whom she shouldn't find it too hard to live in peace for a while.

After the meal Emil and his father walked down to the inn to collect the luggage while Laura got her mother-in-law to show her where the lavatory and wash-house were. Before going to bed she hung her clothes in the wardrobe, firmly resolved to settle down and refrain from thinking at once of moving on.

In the last week of October it was a long-standing custom in Bottighofen for the farmers to install secondary windows and place sausage-shaped draught excluders on the window sills. Laura inferred that the winter would be hard and long, and that windows, once secured, would not be opened again until springtime.

It was the dreariest time of the year. The nights were long and the days so short that dawn and twilight seemed to merge without a break. From time to time a little snow fell. Bedraggled cows stood beneath the leafless apple trees, hanging their heads. Emil made himself useful by replacing the shingles on a barn with his father. Meanwhile, Laura helped her mother-in-law in the kitchen and ensured that the children got some fresh air by going for walks in the hills overlooking the village.

In the second week, however, the old woman conveyed to Laura by means of friendly gestures that it was cold outside, and that she was welcome to leave the children in the kitchen with her if she wanted some fresh air. And when Laura got back from a long, carefree walk – her first chance in a long time to concentrate simply on setting one foot before the other – she returned to the kitchen to find the two little girls and their grandmother positively radiant with happiness. No one in the house even noticed when she again set off on her own the next day, so from then on she always went for walks by herself and stayed out for as long as she pleased.

There was a bench outside the Liebburg, a ruined castle overlooking Bottighofen, from which Laura had a fine view of Lake Constance, whose leaden grey waters faded into the distance and fused with the mist that clothed the German shore. She sat there every afternoon, smoking cigarettes and practising the Swiss German words her mother-in-law, half bashful, half proud of her stubbornly rustic idiom, had taught her. Laura memorised them with ease, and she imitated the soft, limpid Thurgau dialect that suited women so well and lent men's voices, too, a feminine quality, with the assiduity of a musician who already has the right note in her head and is ambitious enough to hit it precisely.

Laura was firmly determined to speak perfect Swiss German in the shortest possible time. Her in-laws were friendly, good-natured, generous people, and she wanted to remain with them. She was better off here than anywhere else.

When she made her way down the muddy farm track and her heart grew heavy at the sight of the squat farmhouses and the crows hopping around between the furrows, pecking up seed, she consoled herself with the thought that the days would lengthen after Christmas. It wouldn't be long before the thousands of apple trees on Bottighofen's hillsides, so black and seemingly dead, burst into pink and white blossom once more.

But then came one sunny morning when she emerged from the wash-house, a small shed beside the farmhouse, with a basket of washing. Melted snow was dripping from the roofs. Emil Fraunholz was standing on the path to the front yard with his left hand held to his cheek like someone who has some unpleasant though not particularly important news to impart. Laura came to a halt and looked at him.

Everything all right? he asked.

Laura nodded.

Going to hang up that washing?

As you can see.

Listen, Laura. Emil scratched his neck and gave her a sheep-ish, sidelong look. I was wondering …

What?

I was wondering if, in the future, you could kindly hang up your washing behind the house, not in the front yard. Beside the goat pen, in other words.

There's no washing line there.

My mother has just put one up.

It's shady and sheltered from the wind behind the house, said Laura. The washing will never dry there.

You're right, the thick things won't, said Emil. But the thin ones will.

You want me to hang the thick things in front of the house and the thin ones behind it?

Just the underclothes, said Emil. Just your underclothes.

Just *my* underclothes?

It's my mother who's asking.

Your mother has put up a line just for me? For *my* underclothes?

Emil nodded.

What has she got against my underclothes?

Nothing. Please don't get me wrong.

No?

It's just that people can see your underclothes when they're hanging up in the front yard.

I wear quite normal underclothes. They aren't in the least –

It isn't that, said Emil.

So what is it?

People can see your underclothes there, that's all. Please give me the basket, I'll carry it for you.

Laura laughed and turned away to prevent him from taking it.

What about your mother's underclothes? Are they invisible, or something?

No, but one can't tell at a distance who they belong to.

And with mine one can?

They advertise the fact far and wide, said Emil.

This is absurd, said Laura. My underclothes are almost as respectable as your mother's. I make sure of that, God knows.

It isn't that. Now give me that basket, please.

So what *is* it about?

With your underclothes, people can tell at a glance that they aren't from round here. It's as if your name is written on them, understand? My mother's underclothes are perfectly ordinary, locally purchased underclothes, that's why no one can tell they belong to her. They look just like my sister's. Or the woman next door's.

That's true enough, said Laura. Or your father's, for that matter.

My mother thinks your underclothes are very pretty, incidentally. But people can tell they're yours.

I'm sorry if my underclothes embarrass you.

We aren't in Marseille, Laura, you've got to understand that. People will look at our washing line and know exactly whose underclothes are which. Then they'll turn round in church on Sundays and grin because they know what you're wearing under your skirt.

Is that so?

I'm sorry.

Emil and Laura looked at each other across the washing basket. No further words were necessary; they had both said and understood everything. Emil spread his arms with the palms upturned like someone seeking acknowledgement of an obvious fact. Laura nodded thoughtfully.

I'll go behind the house, then.

That afternoon she removed her dry underclothes from the line, took them up to the bedroom and packed them in her handsome old suitcase together with her skirts, toilet articles and passport. Then she surreptitiously carried the suitcase outside and concealed it behind a woodpile.

After supper she put the children to bed, made up the stove with coal for the night and went outside to take her usual stroll in the apple orchard and smoke her last cigarette of the day. As she passed the woodpile, she picked up her suitcase in one sweeping movement, strolled unhurriedly to the end of the orchard, climbed over the fence and walked along the stream to the mill before heading uphill. When she got to the ruins of the Liebburg she sat down on her bench, gazed down in farewell at Bottighofen wrapped in darkness and wept for her daughters and Emil Fraunholz. She took a handkerchief and dried her tears, then rose to her feet and resolutely strode on southwards to the nearest railway station.

7

The longer Émile Gilliéron remained in Greece, the more his pockets filled with money – not only Greek drachmas but French gold francs, pounds sterling, gold marks and US dollars. After ten years in Schliemann's employ he was quite well-off enough to have built his house beside Lake Geneva. He could also have furnished it nicely and devoted himself for quite a while to *dolce far niente*, but he kept postponing his return home from one year to the next. Every few months he received a letter from his mother enquiring whether he was getting proper meals in Greece and was warmly enough dressed, and whether he didn't feel homesick. He invariably replied that his dearest wish was to come home at once, but being a married man he could no longer take the important decisions in life on his own.

This was probably true. His wife had more than once made it very clear to him that, as a native Athenian, she would find it hard to reconcile herself to the thought of spending the rest of her life in a snowbound alpine valley haunted by wolves and bears. Furthermore, they would have to take her widowed mother and unmarried sister with them, not to mention their son Émile junior, who was happily growing up into an Athenian street urchin.

Émile Gilliéron really was inhibited from returning to

Villeneuve by all these things, but the principal inhibition, which he guiltily forbore to mention to his mother, was money. He was doing too well to give up. For all his love of *la vie bohème*, he had in his heart of hearts remained a rural schoolmaster's son who couldn't resist picking apples when they were ripe. And because his apples were genuinely ripe and no end to the crop was in sight, he postponed his homecoming year after year and became settled and prosperous against his will.

Money was pouring into Athens during this period. Heinrich Schliemann's Trojan discoveries had sparked an unprecedented craze for all things Greek throughout the West; when he announced to the world that he had unearthed Priam's treasure, everyone wanted to see it. However, since Priam's treasure could not be simultaneously exhibited in every museum in Berlin, Paris, London and Boston, unsuccessful applicants insisted on at least acquiring faithful copies – at any price.

Émile Gilliéron supplied them with these copies. He was just the man for the job. For one thing, he had been present at the excavation sites when the precious pieces were brought to light after thousands of years; for another, he was artistically equipped to assess their value; and thirdly, he was the first person to clean and reassemble these finds when they were broken – which almost all of them were, since tons of earth had been lying on top of them for millennia.

Émile derived great pleasure from fitting these jigsaws together. He was brilliant at juggling with possibilities, using the facility he had so impressively demonstrated to Schliemann the first time they met. If an important piece of a jigsaw was missing, for instance the left arm of a gold statuette, he would climb down into the trench himself and look for it. If the arm was nowhere to be found, he produced a sketch of the way logic dictated that it must have looked and commissioned the finished article from an Athenian goldsmith whom he trusted. And if a vase was so badly smashed that it was past saving, he had a new vase thrown and painted it himself with motifs he had found on the original fragments. If he liked the result he would have three or four copies made – sometimes as many as ten – and before sending them out into the world he produced watercolours and ink drawings of them and sold these for good money to scientific journals, encyclopedias and women's magazines.

And so the years went by. His son Émile junior was joined by three more children named Gaston, Gemma and Lucie. The apartment was becoming cramped, particularly as his mother-in-law was getting old and had to be taken in together with her maidservant and the spinster sister-in-law. So Émile built a large villa for his Greek family on a hill on the northern outskirts of the city, where sheep still grazed and real estate was cheap. He had to spend all his savings on the house, but it had a fine view of the Acropolis and was a good investment because Athens was rapidly expanding and would soon have swallowed up the vacant land. On the other hand, his exchequer was empty again. Until recently a well-to-do young man with dazzling prospects, he suddenly found himself a paterfamilias burdened with a great deal of responsibility and manifold financial commitments. There was no doubt that he would remain in Schliemann's employ for a long time to come.

When his first-born turned five, it miraculously became clear that the boy had inherited his father's talent. As soon as Émile junior got hold of a pencil and paper he drew everything around him – his parents and his little brother and sisters, the fruit bowl on the dining table, the old woman who sold firewood on the corner of the street – not only with incredible clarity and attention to detail but with the same indifference to his own talent that had characterised his father in his youth. The latter looked on with mixed feelings as his son produced some very adequate lightning sketches of the Acropolis and sold them to admiring tourists for good money. On the one hand, he rejoiced that the boy had inherited his abilities, and that he was displaying commercial acumen in selling his work; on the other, he felt that it diminished his personal merits if his artistry was no more than an effect of the Mendelian genetic doctrine. Nonetheless, he did recognise the commercial prospects that would open up if father and son cooperated, so he soon took Émile junior to archaeological sites with him and, insofar as he was able, schooled him in all forms of drawing and painting.

Shortly after Christmas 1890, however, Heinrich Schliemann died in terrible pain of a suppurating cholesteatoma, or cyst in the middle ear, on which his German physicians had vainly tried to operate. Although his young widow immediately proclaimed that she intended to carry on her husband's work in the same spirit, she privately advised Émile Gilliéron to look around for a new source of income because she did not propose to squander any more of her assets on Homeric daydreams.

Émile had no difficulty in doing this, having over the years acquired a comfortable status as the best, best-known and best-paid artist in Greece specialising in works from the ancient world. Although money trickled through his fingers like water because his numerous family had become accustomed to a certain standard of living, the French Archaeological Institute regularly employed him as a scientific adviser and artist. It valued his services highly because he could, if so required, put aside any Schliemannesque daydreams and combine crafts-manlike skill with the most scrupulous academic exactitude. He also gave painting lessons to the children of the Greek royal family, becoming such a frequent visitor to the palace that the royal dogs no longer barked when he took a short cut through the garden. In his second year as royal art master the queen gave him permission to leave his slippers in the vestibule, and in 1896, when the first Olympic Games of modern times were held in Athens, Prince Nikolaos commissioned him on behalf of the Olympic Committee to design a set of postage stamps for the Greek post office.

But Émile Gilliéron's main source of income after Schlie-mann's death was making faithful reproductions for the inter-national market. He was hard hit in 1899, therefore, when the Greek parliament passed a law prohibiting the export of ancient artefacts and the manufacture and sale of copies on pain of up to five years' imprisonment. Although he had no dif-ficulty in discreetly maintaining production in inconspicuous backyards, orders underwent a dramatic decline because major institutions like the British Museum and the Louvre could not afford to give house room to exhibits of obscure provenance.

So Émile's income dwindled while his financial require-ments remained substantial. Not a young man any more, he was nearing 50 and his vigorous goatee beard was gradually turning white. He had grown accustomed to certain amenities, and his wife, mother-in-law and sister-in-law had fixed house-hold expenses and requirements of their own. As for Émile junior, now 15 and starting to wear blue jackets, he was attend-ing the French *lycée* and, in his free time, devoting himself to the expensive pleasures of the local *jeunesse dorée*.

It therefore came a great relief to Émile Gilliéron when, early in April 1900, he received a letter from Crete urgently requesting his help with excavations. The sender was an Englishman of private means named Arthur Evans, whom Gilliéron had met at the archaeological sites of Tiryns and Mycenae in the 1880s. He knew that Evans, the son of a successful paper manufacturer, received a generous allowance in sterling that assured him of almost boundless wealth in the impoverished countries of the Mediterranean. Ever since his wife Margaret had died of tuberculosis in Alassio, he always wore black ties, used black-bordered writing paper and had been roaming the Mediterranean area as a lonely widower with an interest in archaeology.

Arthur Evans was extremely short-sighted – almost unable to discern anything beyond his immediate reach – but refused out of vanity to wear glasses. Being unable to see the ground when visiting an excavation site, he felt his way with the aid of a stick. Close up, however, his blue eyes saw things with great clarity, and he often spotted details that escaped other people.

Evans was a shrewd, sensitive and patient man. Ever since Schliemann's excavations he had been driven by a desire to lend his hitherto leisurely existence the grandeur it had lacked until now. After his wife's death in 1893 he had gone to Crete and bit by bit, over a period of six years, used guile and trickery to buy up all the grazing land and olive groves on the malaria-ridden hill of Kephala south of Heraklion, the island's capital, which had long been suspected to be the site of the Bronze-Age settlement of Knossos.

On the morning of Friday, 23 March 1900, when all the excavation permits had finally been secured, Evans had ridden his donkey out of Heraklion to an inn where several hundred men and women of all ages were waiting for him. Having engaged 32 of them as diggers, porters and washerwomen, he provided them with digging and sluicing equipment and led them into the olive groves with the express intention of discovering an advanced but ancient European civilisation that would be able to hold its own against that of the pharaohs and the Sumerians.

And because Evans knew so precisely what he was looking for, he found it.

After a few days' not very productive exploratory digging, he directed his labourers to the very top of the little hill that overlooked the centre of the plain. What came to light there was a bewildering maze of prehistoric walls running parallel and at right angles to each other and covering an area of several hectares. Evans immediately recognised what was confronting him: the labyrinth of King Minos, son of Zeus and Europa, in which Theseus had slain the cannibalistic Minotaur and found his way out with the aid of Princess Ariadne's ball of red wool. When a basin was unearthed at the foot of a wall, Evans identified it as Ariadne's bath, and when one of the chambers was found to contain a stone seat with a high back recessed into the wall, he became convinced that it was King Minos's throne.

This, of course, was nonsense in the purest Schliemann-esque tradition, because the throne was simply a 4000-year-old stone seat and the bath an ancient basin. As for the walls, all that could honestly be said of them was that they consisted of rough-hewn stone and together formed a maze of a thousand small chambers that might, until their destruction by an earthquake 4,000 years earlier, have been used for some unknown purpose by some unknown people.

But the finds Evans's labourers unearthed among the walls

surpassed all expectations: vast numbers of exquisite ceramics lodged in the excavators' sieves, as well as jewellery and finely engraved seals, water basins of stone and copper and delicately carved ivory figurines. There were also hundreds of small clay tablets, inscribed in a hitherto unknown language, which Evans construed as the earliest legal documents to be found on European soil. The most important discovery of all, however, was that the walls of Knossos were covered with colourful frescos in which a rich and voluptuous civilisation – Evans christened it the Minoan – had left evidence of itself.

Remnants of painted plaster were still adhering to the walls, but hundreds and thousands of fragments had flaked off and were lying in the soil, whence the labourers shovelled them into sieves. Many of these fragments bore representations of human arms, legs and ears or geometrically arranged lilies, roses and fern fronds, others depicted bulls' horns, peacocks and pheasants, monkeys' tails, dogs, olive trees and sailing ships. Many were the size of soup plates, others as small as fingernails, and they now lay strewn around exposed to the elements, the labourers' boots and marauding goats. If these fragments were not to be reduced to dust they had to be salvaged, cleaned and reassembled at once. And for that task, Arthur Evans knew, no one was better equipped than Émile Gilliéron.

It appears that Émile dropped everything in Athens as soon as the wealthy Englishman's invitation reached him. In good weather the mailboat took a day and a half to get from Piraeus to Heraklion, and the wooden-saddled mule ride from the harbour to Knossos would have taken a further hour and a half. Arthur Evans noted in his diary on 10 April 1900 that Émile Gilliéron had arrived at the excavation site and begun to sort the fragments without delay.

One would like to have been there. It was the time of the Notus, the warm southerly breeze that blows sand from the Libyan desert across the Mediterranean, absorbing a great deal of moisture and turning the sky over Crete an ominous yellow. One can picture the two men in the olive grove, sweating as they stood at a big table in the shade of a white awning, eager as schoolboys, and shuffled the 4,000-year-old fragments to and fro. One can imagine how they tried azure pieces up against azure and scarlet up against scarlet, and how they triumphantly shook hands when two pieces fitted together perfectly. But such successes were rare. Small joined-up areas were always surrounded by big, gaping lacunae. And because human beings are so constituted that they cannot bear the idea of incompleteness, it was not long before Evans and Émile began to guess at what might once have occupied the gaps between the completed areas, where only the table's bare wood could be seen.

We shall never know, said Émile. He had often conducted conversations of this kind with Schliemann and was seizing the opportunity to discover what made his new employer tick.

Of course not, said Evans. But if we simply content ourselves with these fragments in front of us, the result will be meagre indeed. They convey very little, don't you think?

That's true, alas, said Émile.

But it doesn't take an awful lot of imagination for one to visualise how the mural used to look.

Certainly not.

For instance, where there's a knee, there would doubtless have been a thigh and a calf, wouldn't there? And at the top of the leg there would very probably have been – pardon me – a posterior. And if there are eight palm trees in the background, it wouldn't be so unthinkable to extend the row by a ninth and a tenth if necessary, don't you agree?

I quite understand, said Émile. One could always amplify a bit – the world possesses a logic of its own, after all. I would only point out that, from a purely scientific point of view, nothing non-existent can exist. In science, as you know, only facts count.

Oh, science and its facts, said Evans. Science is also full of holes.

True, said Émile. But it's duty-bound to declare those holes and live with them for as long as they exist.

On the contrary! Evans exclaimed. Scientists are the first people to embellish the gaps in their knowledge with daydreams – they *have* to do so! Archaeologists and historians would have nothing to say if they kept strictly to their empirical facts. All scholarship is narration – it vaults one gap in knowledge after another, leaps from fact to fact. Facts are the smallest, indivisible parts of science, and between them are yawning gaps of cosmic dimensions. Do you know of a single scientist who can interpret his facts without resorting to metaphysics?

No, said Émile.

Do you know what would be left of science if it kept strictly to facts and refrained from amplifying?

Not a great deal.

Nothing whatever. Fact-mongering – just dull, lifeless fact-mongering.

I expect you're right, said Émile.

Look, that's why we have an obligation to fill in the gaps. Human knowledge is always fragmentary, it's part of our fate. It's the only reason why we carry faith, love and hope in our hearts – so that we can correlate our fragments of knowledge and believe that everything this side of the grave has some meaning. Don't you agree?

I agree entirely, said Émile, who had now got the measure of his new employer and only wanted to discover what sort of pictures Arthur Evans had in mind.

So you believe, he said cautiously, that this really is the palace of King Minos?

Allow me to explain, said Evans. It seems clear to me that this is the biggest and finest palace ever built in Crete. You agree?

It would appear so, said Émile.

That poses the question of who built it. Who built the biggest and finest palace in Crete? One can read the answer in Homer, Hesiod and Herodotus – they're unanimous on the subject. Who do *you* think built the biggest and finest palace in Crete?

King Minos, said Émile, concealing his annoyance at being lectured like a schoolboy.

You see? And where in Crete could Minos's palace have stood, if not here? Has anyone found an architectural complex of similar size and splendour on this island? Or, to put it the other way round: Who could have built this enormous palace here, if not King Minos?

Having settled that point, they got down to work. From now on, the big table under the white awning was Émile Gilliéron's workplace. The labourers brought him all the fragments that lodged in their sieves. Arthur Evans increased their number first to 100 and then to 140. For his personal accommodation he erected a military tent on the edge of the site and hoisted a Union Jack in front of it.

Evans and Émile were the first to reach the site before

sunrise and the last to leave it at dusk. The two men, who were within a few months of each other in age, worked together like an ill-assorted married couple. What the short-sighted Evans had discovered in the way of details, Émile built into the overall picture they had previously dreamed up together. The ground was still heavy and damp from the winter rains, and the anopheles mosquitoes proliferated like mad. Émile did not contract malaria, but Evans suffered badly from it. When he could no longer stand he lay down on a camp bed in front of his tent and the labourers had to bring all their finds to him for a preliminary inspection.

Despite suffering from the shakes and diarrhoea, Evans spent the happiest days of his life at Knossos in the spring of 1900. The finds surpassed his wildest dreams. He really had unearthed an ancient and hitherto unknown civilisation whose vivacity and refinement surpassed Schliemann's discoveries. Not only had the Minoans left behind written testimony – something which Schliemann had vainly sought in Troy, Tiryns and Mycenae – but their iconography bore witness to a delight in spontaneity and improvisation and a sense of the fleeting beauty of the moment compared to which the art of the ancient Egyptians, Sumerians and Greeks could not fail to seem stiff and masklike.

An additional factor was that, in many ways, the Minoan island kingdom reminded a Briton like Arthur Evans of his native land. It seemed obvious to him that, like London, Knossos could never have wrested its wealth from the barren soil of its environs. From this he inferred that the Minoans, like the British, must have been a race of seafarers and traders who protected their far-flung colonial empire with a powerful fleet. It seemed equally obvious that King Minos's empire had attained its final and finest efflorescence shortly before the decline which also – not that Evans knew it – lay in store for the Victorian British Empire: it was, in Shakespeare's words, 'a precious stone set in the silver sea which serves it in the office of a wall.'

It gave Evans the greatest pleasure that all his finds fitted almost seamlessly into the picture he had formed of the Palace of Minos from Homer's description of it. The labyrinth, the staircase, the throne – everything was there. All that was missing was the alabaster dance floor built for Princess Ariadne by Daedalus before he and his son Icarus escaped by air on home-made wings.

Consequently, there was great excitement when, on 3 and 4 May 1900, the labourers discovered eight fragments of a fresco in a newly unearthed chamber. When fitted together, these showed a slender figure of blue complexion with strangely contorted arms and legs. One look convinced Evans that he was confronted by the depiction of a dancing girl, so the chamber had to be Ariadne's ballroom – especially as the floor consisted of white alabaster. He recorded this find in his notebook, then asked Émile Gilliéron for his opinion. Although the latter was long accustomed to letting his employer have his own way, he recommended that the fragments be thoroughly washed. Once this had been done, Evans had to agree that the headless figure was far too muscular and narrow-hipped to pass for a girl, and that the youth was picking saffron in a flowery meadow, not dancing at all. So he crossed out the dancing girl in his notebook and recorded his new finding while Émile used a mixture of plaster, mortar and pigments to supply the blue figure with a human face and amplify the background into an uninterrupted field of crocuses.

This picture, which went down in art history as the 'Blue Boy', was regarded as a impressive example of the facility and humanity of Minoan art, and it retained that status even when, many years later, additional pieces of the puzzle revealed that, far from being a boy, the Blue Boy was a crocus-picking monkey whose long, curly tail Émile had failed to recognise as such – he had inserted it in the flowery meadow a long way away from its owner.

So work continued. On 16 May 1900 the diggers unearthed a chamber whose walls had been adorned with representations of bulls and bullfighting. Arthur Evans concluded that he had now reached the heart of the Minoan labyrinth – the actual chamber in which seven Athenian youths and virgins had met a sad end every nine years.

For his part, Émile realised that it would be Evans's dearest wish to be able to present the world with some graphic and impressive bullfighting scenes. The trouble was, the fragments differed widely in structure, coloration and thickness because they belonged to different frescos and had adorned different walls. Despite the fact that most of them were little more than brown flakes that simply conveyed the clods of earth around them, Émile fitted them together and shuffled them around the table until, irrespective of their disparate sources, they combined to form an attractive, integrated bullfighting scene; that is to say, until the pieces of the jigsaw puzzle fitted into the bullfighting scene that Émile had previously envisioned.

The finished result depicted a magnificent bull galloping full tilt with a youth performing a handstand on its back, flanked to left and right by two young women, one of whom gripped the bull by the horns while the other stood behind it with her arms extended as if to help the youth dismount. This flew in the face of common sense, because no one on earth has ever considered gripping a mature, galloping bull by the horns, and it would have been absolutely impossible to perform a handstand on the back of a beast galloping at 20 miles an hour. As for the young woman who had taken up her position near the animal's hind legs, she could only have done this with suicidal intent.

But Arthur Evans was delighted.

Fantastic! he exclaimed. Definitely a ritual human sacrifice to the Minoans' taurine deity, don't you think?

Quite possibly, said Émile. Not for the first time, he wondered why all the archaeologists he had met in his life instinctively reacted to depictions of young people by fantasising about ritual slaughter. On the other hand, he added cautiously, it might also be an athletic contest or some kind of game.

Ritual human sacrifice, Evans insisted. To me, that seems as plain as the nose on your face.

I would only point out, said Émile, that I had very little to work with. I took a lot of liberties.

I quite understand, said Evans, but it's the finished result that matters.

It's risky, said Émile. We're skating on thin ice.

It has paid off, though! Evans exclaimed. A magnificent bullfight! But for your temerity, what would we have? These few brown flakes here?

So Émile continued to work in the same manner.

Immediately north of the throne room the labourers unearthed a chamber whose walls were adorned with numerous female figures. In many cases only their feet and the hems of their skirts had survived, in others only their eyes or a bare shoulder, but because the female form, too, possesses an inherent logic, Émile supplied them with complete figures. By the time he was through, the murals were as vivid and vibrant as if the Minoan ladies had sat for the painter only yesterday. Many had their heads together as if exchanging the latest Minoan gossip, others were toasting each other in goblets of wine, and twelve of them were – remarkably enough – seated on camping stools with thin metal legs. They all had huge, almond-shaped eyes, sensual, bright red lips, and long black hair dressed in ringlets that sometimes dangled coquettishly over their foreheads. Many were wearing flat gym shoes, short skirts and open blouses as if fresh from the tennis court, others sported skimpy boleros and proudly bared their bosoms at the beholder. Still others wore diaphanous shirts, had coloured ribbons woven into their hair and were boldly cocking their chins as if to say: Come with me, young man.

Arthur Evans was delighted once again, and Émile Gilliéron's paintings caused a furore in the world of archaeology when they were published. Europeans weary of technology were gratified to rediscover their cultural roots in a civilisation whose refinement and *joie de vivre* were so dissimilar to the austerity of classical Greece. Moreover, Minoan art's floral ornamentation reminded many observers of Art Nouveau, which was then all the rage.

However, some people were puzzled that the frescos in Knossos made such a modern impression and were so devoid of archaic characteristics. '*Mais, ce sont des Parisiennes!*' Edmond Pottier, a visiting archaeologist and art historian, exclaimed at the sight of Émile's camping-stool belles, and Evelyn Waugh said it was not easy to assess the merits of Minoan art 'since only a few square inches of the vast area exposed to our consideration are earlier than the last 20 years, and it is impossible to disregard the suspicion that their painters have tempered their zeal for accurate reconstruction with a somewhat inappropriate predilection for the covers of Vogue.'

8

After walking for an hour-and-a-half across dark, snow-covered fields, Laura d'Oriano must have reached Weinfelden, whence the last passenger train was scheduled to leave at 10:48 pm. If she managed to catch it, she would have got to Zurich's central station at 23 minutes past midnight and, because the next train to Geneva did not leave until 6:34 am, spent the night on a wooden bench in the second-class waiting room. She could not have encountered Felix Bloch again that night because he had left Zurich at the end of March 1934 and was on the other side of the world, where it was broad daylight.

Felix had not planned his escape to America; it had come over him like the Damascene conversion that had propelled him to atomic physics from the production of cast-iron manhole covers. After his last skiing holiday with Heisenberg he had returned to his parental home in Seehofstrasse, there to spend the summer free of charge and wait until the monthly payments from his Rockefeller bursary commenced in October. He resumed the habits of his youth, went swimming in Lake Zurich and hiking in the Glarner Alps. On Saturdays he attended football matches at the Letzigrund. It is also quite possible that he cycled over to Küsnacht and acquainted himself with the latest developments in cast-iron manhole cover production at the Fritz Christen foundry. On

Mondays he went to the colloquium of the Institute for Theoretical Physics, where the main topic of conversation was the newly discovered neutron. In the evenings he read technical journals, which also had much to say on the neutron.

Everyone was talking about the neutron that summer of 1933. It was the most exciting discovery in physics for a long time and the greatest hope of those engaged in experimental research. There was nothing vague or imprecise about the neutron; above all, it lent itself to use as a projectile because, instead of being diverted by positively or negatively charged particles, it always flew straight ahead. Felix surmised that it would be possible to achieve something with it in the laboratory – more, in any case, than with electrons, of which one never really knew whether they were performing the high jump or the long jump or some other neat manoeuvre.

He therefore decided to devote the duration of his Rockefeller bursary to a trip around Europe visiting other atomic physicists and bringing himself up to date on the latest state of neutron research. First he would go to Rome, where Enrico Fermi had taken it into his head to bombard all the elements in the periodic table with neutrons, one after another, and see what happened. Then he would look in on Niels Bohr in Copenhagen and float his idea that neutrons, even if electrically neutral, might nonetheless carry a magnetic charge. Finally, he would spend a few months in Cambridge with James Chadwick, who was the very first person to prove the existence of neutrons experimentally.

That was his plan, but it never came to pass. The longer the summer of 1933 went on, the clearer it became that the time for innocent educational trips around Europe would soon be over for a long time to come. Zurich was a mass of flags and pennants, and the lobby of the university was patrolled by grey-uniformed storm troopers of the Swiss National Front. Felix's friends and fellow students Fritz London and Walter Heitler had fled to England, as had his teachers Erwin Schrödinger and Hans Bethe. Albert Einstein had announced in America that he would not be returning to Europe in the foreseeable future. Even Fritz Haber, the German patriot and poison gas veteran of the First World War, had resigned his posts in Berlin and accepted a chair at Cambridge.

By summer 1933 it was obvious that the war machine had set its wheels in motion again and would sooner or later spin out of control. The newspapers Felix read every morning told of overcrowded concentration camps and parliamentary punch-ups, of book bonfires at German universities and summary executions of kulaks in the Soviet Union, of huge warships being launched and shortages of coal, of tighter visa restrictions, mass unemployment, all-embracing Nazification, pogroms, rearmament and food riots.

Such was the situation when he received a telegram in which the Dean of Stanford University offered him a professorship of theoretical physics. Felix did not have the faintest idea where on God's earth Stanford was, but because the salary offered was quoted in US dollars he decided to take a chance on America.

The rough ten-day Atlantic crossing in winter was his very first sea voyage. It took a week for his stomach to become inured to the pitching and tossing, and when he finally went ashore in New York harbour he made an interesting discovery: he felt nauseous once more because his stomach's reaction to the sudden immobility of terra firma was a kind of inverse seasickness.

Since he had 20 hours to kill before the next stage of his

journey, he tottered through Manhattan and took a look at everything – the tall buildings, the wide streets, the huge automobiles – but was disappointed to find himself unenthusiastic. True, the buildings were very tall and the streets remarkably wide – probably wider than many alleyways in the old quarter of Zurich were long – and the cars were huge and glittered like Christmas trees as they cruised past sidewalks thronged with a never-ending tide of humanity.

It may have been Felix's weakened state that caused him to find the omnipresent immensity impressive but not particularly interesting. As he saw it, no matter how high into the sky Manhattan's buildings soared, they were merely utilitarian structures with windows and doors through which people went in and out. For all their six or eight lanes, the streets were merely thoroughfares along which cars and lorries drove. Despite their chrome and gleaming paintwork, the cars had only four wheels like cars elsewhere in the world. As for the people, they were simply people. Many might have different-coloured skin, hair or eyes, and all were unknown to him, but that didn't make them unfamiliar. The people were people, nothing to get excited about.

Next morning he went to Grand Central Station, where the train that was to transport him across a continent to the other side of America was already waiting. When he passed beneath the dome of the huge, immaculately white, brightly illuminated concourse, whose vastness was so utterly devoid of any human dimension, sense or utility, he experienced a first pang of nostalgia for dreary old Europe.

The train journey took four days and four nights. Felix travelled through the suburbs of Chicago and across the interminable bridges that spanned the Mississippi and Missouri at a dizzy height. He crossed the Rocky Mountains and followed the Colorado River through orange-coloured canyons streaked with yellowish white. Through the windows of his compartment he saw grazing moose, fleeing deer and circling eagles. The train stopped in Salt Lake City, Reno and Virginia City, and it toiled across the Sierra Nevada and down into the fertile valleys of California, where farmers picked apples three times a year and nuggets of gold lay exposed in the furrows of ploughed fields. At the end of the fourth day the Golden Gate Bridge came into view through the right-hand window and the train finally came to a stop in San Francisco's very modest railroad station.

Felix had spent many hours in the previous four days and nights gazing out of the window, and by the end of the journey he had learnt one thing: in this country he would need a car. It wasn't that he found the American countryside to be on a considerably bigger scale than the European, for from what he'd seen a mountain in America was a mountain and a river a river. A kilometre measured no more than 1,000 metres here too, and the distance between New York and San Francisco was, objectively speaking, less than that between Lisbon and Moscow. What was more, as far as he could tell from the window of the train, most Americans lived away from the big cities in small towns on the European scale, with a few thousand inhabitants, a church and a hostelry or two.

The difference was that these small towns were situated not within sight of each other but separated by endless expanses spacious enough to accommodate the entire Black Forest, half the Swiss Alps or the whole of Tuscany, and that a paterfamilias wishing to pick up some fresh bread for breakfast would have to drive through three canyons and across a prairie grazed by 10,000 buffalo.

Felix would need a car in this country, of that he felt convinced as he carried his suitcase out of San Francisco station, so he flagged down a taxi and asked to be driven to the nearest second-hand car dealer. There, within minutes, he plumped for an almost rust-free 1928 Chevrolet Sportster with wooden spoked wheels, a claret-coloured bonnet and an engine that, to judge by the sound, seemed to run pretty well. Since he had never sat behind a steering wheel before, the dealer had to explain how the vehicle worked and accompany him on a few circuits of the firm's parking lot. Then, jolting and jouncing, he drove out of the city and headed 30 miles south through the eternal springtime of that fortune-favoured part of the world.

It took Felix barely an hour to drive along the brand-new, asphalted, four-lane Bayshore Highway. If he looked out of the right-hand window he saw gently undulating hills that reminded him of the Swiss Jura. Through the left-hand window he saw long-legged birds strutting around in the brackish grey waters of San Francisco Bay. The road was level, firm and free from dust. Looking straight ahead, he could see that the ribbon of black asphalt was flanked on either side by telegraph poles, gigantic hoardings and garages, as well as gas stations and lunch counters in the most fantastic guises; many of them assumed the form of Hindu temples, gigantic lemons, outsize Hansel and Gretel cottages, or wigwams. Driving along ahead of Felix and behind him were gleaming, luxurious automobiles in which lonely people sat in ones or twos, followed by buses the size of cathedrals and, quite often, decrepit old Fords whose hollow-cheeked occupants had tied an assortment of cooking pots, tent poles and suitcases to the roof and running boards.

In Palo Alto he turned off to the right. Beyond the railroad station he came to a long avenue of palm trees that led through a park full of exotic trees to Stanford University. He parked his car, made his way through a Romanesque arch richly adorned with reliefs and found himself in front of a squat church in the neo-Byzantine style. Abutting on this and arranged in a rectangle were some cloisters in rough-hewn red sandstone with terracotta-tiled roofs. They were reminiscent of a Mexican hacienda, a medieval Romanesque monastery, or the translation into stone of some deracinated railroad magnate's historical fantasy.

In later years, when journalists asked Felix Bloch about his arrival in Stanford, he recalled friendly faces, the Dean's firm handshake and the pleasant feeling of being genuinely welcomed with open arms. He recalled a spontaneous party the lecturers had thrown in his honour and his amazement at the sight of the tanned and seemingly happy students of both sexes, all of whom looked as if they were just back from the beach and had to go straight on to a barbecue.

In April 1934, Stanford really did resemble a country club for wealthy young people. Available to them on the campus was a spacious 24-hole golf course reputed to be the finest on the whole of the Pacific coast. There were two artificial lakes on which sailing and rowing regattas took place, a polo field, a stadium that could hold 90,000 spectators and any number of excellently equipped gymnasiums and sports halls in neo-classical white marble, with integrated indoor pools, handball courts and bowling alleys.

Stanford was home to 5,000 male and 1,000 female students at this period. To judge by the names listed in the yearbook for 1934, nearly all were of Anglo-Saxon, Scandinavian or German origin. Most of them played games and had broad shoulders, sturdy legs and healthy complexions. The men wore corduroy trousers and lumberjack shirts, the women straight skirts and tennis shoes; they were unfamiliar with the formal dress code of the Ivy League universities on the east coast. There were no elitist secret societies, either – the kind whose members affected English accents and held silly initiation rituals with skulls and gory masks behind secret doors wreathed in ivy. Stanford students went out into the foothills at weekends to fish for trout and shoot rabbits, or they drove in overladen cars to San Francisco to dance at the Mark Hopkins or the St Francis Hotel, which they nicknamed 'the Frantic'.

In 1934, the fifth year of the Great Depression, more than half of them had cars of their own, and many owned aeroplanes. They all lived in the serene certainty that America was unassailably powerful, and that they themselves, thanks to their inherited wealth, would remain proof against hunger, sickness, poverty and any other form of misfortune to the end of their days.

Felix Bloch realised that he had landed on the sunny side of life and left the world's darkness behind, but Stanford had no institute for theoretical physics. It would be his task to establish one.

The first event he organised at Stanford was a seminar devoted to Enrico Fermi's theory on beta radiation. In the lecture room he found a dozen well-nourished, rosy-cheeked students who eyed him curiously with their sharpened pencils expectantly poised above the first pages of their brand-new notebooks. When he started to speak, however, their pencils did not speed over the blank paper; they remained poised because none of those present understood a word he was saying. Felix realised that he was dealing with youngsters a decade younger than himself – less than 20 years old, in fact – and that they lacked the requisite basic knowledge for an introduction to quantum physics. So he laid his notes aside and improvised a new lecture programme in which he endeavoured not to assume that his students possessed any prior knowledge or were familiar with technical terms. First he would explain why apples fall to the ground whereas the moon remains in the sky; then he would discuss why steam in a kettle whistles and icebergs melt but don't sink; and at the end of the academic year, if there were still time, he would talk about the reasons why lightning always strikes the highest branches of a tree but as far as possible leaves the lower vegetation untouched.

Felix had been aware that atomic physics was an unploughed field in the west of the United States, and he had also known that Stanford was a practically oriented university whose principal interest in theory was its concrete application. He was staggered, nonetheless, to find that he was almost the only person within 2,000 miles who had ever concerned himself with quantum mechanics, and that it would be his task to preach the quantum-mechanical gospel in this part of the world.

As a physicist, Felix felt like a fish out of water at Stanford, and even in his leisure hours he found it hard to participate with due enthusiasm in the social rituals customary on the campus. He felt uncomfortable when obliged to take part in one of the traditional bachelor booze-ups on Friday nights, and fishing for trout the next morning bored him. Shooting rabbits he found banal and repellent, and it would remain a lifelong mystery to him how, Sunday after Sunday, 90,000 people could succumb to quasi-religious fervour in the baseball stadium. It was consequently a source of great happiness to him that another apostle of quantum mechanics had come to live not far away a few years earlier. Robert Oppenheimer, whom he had met at Göttingen in his student days, had taken a professorship at the University of California, Berkeley, and established the chair of theoretical physics there. Since Felix badly needed someone with whom he could discuss his half-completed theory about the magnetism of the neutron, he drove up the Bayshore Highway and took the ferry across to Oakland.

The meeting between two such different men could have been a total failure. Felix was a friendly but reserved young man whose main interest in life was physics and whose favourite recreation was mountain walks; Robert Oppenheimer, 18 months his senior, he had known in Göttingen as a volatile dandy from a wealthy New York family who chain-smoked Chesterfields, accompanied other people's remarks with a rhythmical 'Yes … yes, yes … yes … yes, yes … ', interrupted them at the first opportunity, and finished off their sentences in the belief that he knew what they meant to say better than they did themselves.

The fact was that Oppenheimer really did grasp other people's ideas more fully and quickly than they did themselves, and that he possessed a gift for incorporating new concepts in his own world of ideas. It was also true that Felix and Oppenheimer were equally glad to have discovered a companion in the quantum-mechanical solitude of California. When Felix outlined his theory about the magnetism of the neutron, Oppenheimer listened eagerly, fixing him with his pale blue eyes and saying 'Yes … yes, yes … yes … yes … ' Then he broke in and, off the cuff, pursued the idea in just the direction Felix had hoped he would.

Every Monday from then on, the two men held joint seminars on quantum mechanics for doctoral candidates, alternating between Stanford and Berkeley. Felix usually opened the meetings of this 'Monday Evening Journal Club', as it was christened, by presenting a new paper on quantum physics from the *Physical Review* or the *New Scientist,* whereupon Oppenheimer would break in and question the paper's actual content. They and the students would then explore ways of pursuing research in the relevant field by means of their own experiments and theoretical work.

The students were delighted. Instead of reeling off academic certainties learnt by heart, their youthful professors concentrated on unsolved problems and thereby made them feel they were transcending the boundaries of human knowledge in company with the physics avant-garde. Sparks flew at the 'Monday Evening Journal Club'. Felix and Oppenheimer generously shared their ideas with all who were capable of absorbing them. If anyone needed a research subject for their thesis, a rich selection was on offer every Monday.

Discussions with Oppenheimer were a source of intellectual enrichment for Felix, too, but he soon sensed that the man's brilliance was at once the cause and effect of a peculiar mental failing. Curious about everything, Oppenheimer grasped any new idea right away and retained all that he had grasped in his memory. Because he found everything so easy, he had a predilection for the most difficult things. If he was in the mood for poetry, he would go for French medieval rather than Emerson, Yeats or Rilke. When he discovered Hinduism, he learnt Sanskrit in order to be able to read its sacred texts in the original. And when he looked into the cosmos through a telescope, he didn't confine himself to knowing the names of heavenly bodies but enjoyed indulging in quantum-mechanical speculation about the nuclear reactions inside them.

He had not gone in for theoretical physics because he had

a penchant for it, but because of insufficient care and perseverance in the laboratory when a chemistry student, and he had specialised in quantum mechanics because it was the most abstract and incomprehensible theory ever devised.

But because he so easily and quickly grasped what others had to rack their brains over for years on end, he also found it easy to come up with any number of alternative solutions to the same problem. Being able to spot the weak point in any theory, he could never arrive at a firm belief in some idea but remained permanently mistrustful, even of his own ideas, and never attained the confident perseverance essential to the attainment of grand objectives. Finally, he derived enjoyment from scientific theorising not for the knowledge it yielded, but purely as fuel for his own vanity.

Being incapable of deep feeling, he needed powerful stimuli. His apartment was furnished with Navajo rugs and statuettes of Indian goddesses, and he kept the windows open summer and winter alike. When he cooked for his students, he produced diabolically hot nasi gorengs which, being under close observation, they felt bound to eat. He raced trains behind the wheel of his Chrysler, and when he crashed the car and injured a female passenger, he made amends by presenting her with a small Cézanne from his father's collection.

His students revered him. They called him 'Oppie' and copied him in every way. They chain-smoked Chesterfield cigarettes like him and wore broad-brimmed hats like him, and they couldn't stand Tchaikovsky because Oppie couldn't stand Tchaikovsky either. They said 'Yes … yes, yes … yes … ' when someone other than Oppie was speaking, and, like their master, produced their lighters with a flourish when someone took out a cigarette.

After the seminar Oppenheimer would drive privileged students to 'Frank's' in San Francisco, a smart seafood restaurant down by the harbour. There he showed them how to decant French red wine, shuck oysters and open coconuts, meanwhile reciting Plato in ancient Greek or discoursing in his dulcet voice on Navajo rugs and Hegel's dialectics. And when the bill came he always insisted on paying.

Felix went along to these evening parties at first, but later his appearances became less frequent, because he felt he'd been sufficiently schooled in decanting French red wine. Thereafter he spent his evenings alone. He was homesick for Zurich and Leipzig, Heisenberg and his parents. Never a day went by that he did not peruse the *Neue Zürcher Zeitung* in the reading room of the university library.

At weekends he drove up into the hills, parked the Chevrolet on Windy Hill or in Palo Alto Foothills Park and walked across the deserted highlands on his own, wading through ferns the height of a man and passing beneath sequoias like Gothic skyscrapers until the Pacific came into view. Then he would take his bread and cheese from the old rucksack he had brought with him from Europe, sit down on a rock in the company of sapphire-blue jays, brightly-coloured woodpeckers and inquisitive chipmunks, gaze out across the ocean and immerse himself in the sight of rolling waves and the shadows cast by scudding clouds.

9

Laura d'Oriano arrived in the South of France at almond blossom time. Swallows circled above the roofs of Marseille, café proprietors were putting out tables and chairs on the pavements and a smell of disinfectant and freshly washed curtains was issuing from the tenement buildings. Laura's parents were surprised, though not unduly so, when their daughter turned up at the Vieux-Port with her old suitcase but unaccompanied by her family. They embraced her without asking too many questions and gave her back the room she'd left on her wedding day. She removed her wedding ring and put it in an empty powder box, which she stowed in the left-hand corner of the top drawer of her chest of drawers. And then, for a moment, it was almost as if she had never been away.

But it wasn't really so, of course. As soon as she was alone in her room and had come to rest, she wept bitterly for her two daughters, whom she had put to bed the night before, and for Emil Fraunholz, with whom she had shared a bed every night for the past three years, and whose gentle masculinity had always managed to make her feel at home in the world. She spent the night agonising over the question of whether she'd really had to leave Bottighofen, whether she'd had the right to do so and whether there had genuinely been no alternative.

Finally, at dawn, she decided that there hadn't been any

other possible course of action because she would have taken it anyway, and that it was time to regain control over her life. It was clear that she would now have to earn her own living because her parents were barely getting by on their savings. She would have preferred to take over the music shop again, but her parents had sold the business to a Polish Jew stranded in Marseille because the USA was no longer issuing visas to Polish Jews.

So Laura went to the advertising department of *Liberté* and placed a small advertisement offering her services as a secretary, pointing out that she could speak and write French, Italian, Turkish, Greek and Russian. Then she did the rounds of the music cafés and promoted herself as a singer with an extensive repertoire.

When she returned she made the acquaintance of the Pole, a taciturn, middle-aged man with a fondness for Arabian mocha. Like Laura, he had made it his habit to spend quiet times sitting outside the shop door in the afternoon sun, waiting for customers. Laura pulled up a chair and joined him. In the course of the ensuing hours she discovered that the Pole had made friends with the same local residents as she herself had – the schoolboys and prostitutes, the oyster sellers and the waiters nearby. Laura smoked, drank mocha with the Pole and felt happy to be home again.

Sometimes she went walking round the harbour. The rotten old wooden ships of pre-war days had disappeared; the vessels that now lay alongside the quays were brand-new, gleaming colossi made of steel. The evil old seamen with their clasp-knives and their STDs were also gone, having probably died or returned to their retirement homes. The new steel ships were manned by fresh-faced young sailors in immaculate white uniforms. When they went ashore they roamed the streets in packs, not singly, with nothing more sinister in mind than to spend the night drinking as much and having as much fun as possible.

Every morning after getting up, Laura went down to the mailbox in the hope that it would contain a job offer, but nothing ever came. In the middle of the second week, however, the proprietor of the Chat Noir called and offered her a one-week engagement as a Cossack singer.

Beside the entrance of the Chat Noir was a showcase displaying photographs of the female artistes who appeared there. Because Laura possessed no suitable photographs of herself, the *patron* thrust the Cossack costume and a slip of paper bearing the address of a photographic studio into her hand. When she balked, he told her not to make a fuss; he would pay for the photographs himself. What was more, she could keep the pictures afterwards in case she wanted to go on tour with them – and, now he came to think of it, the old costume as well.

So she slipped into the Cossack costume, threw on her coat over it, and set off. It was warm inside the studio. The photographer took her coat with practised courtesy. He made up her face and fixed her hair, put an operetta sabre into her hand and asked her to lean on it with both hands, like a walking stick, and smile at the camera. Then she had to shoulder the sabre like a rifle, throw back her head and flex her left leg, stand on tiptoe, thrust out her bosom and pull in her stomach, smile, gaze dreamily into space, wedge a long holder plus lighted cigarette between her second and third fingers, lie on her stomach, prop herself up on her elbows and rest her chin on her folded hands.

It was not a disagreeable business and did not take long. The photographer was some distance from her and almost invisible beneath his black cloth. All Laura could hear was his soft, gentle voice giving instructions. Eventually he came out from under his cloth, helped her into her coat and held the door for her. Then she was back outside in the street and on her way home.

For all that, she gave a start when the photos actually appeared in the showcase of the Chat Noir three days later, surmounted by the words 'Anoushka, the Kiev Nightingale' in bold, pseudo-Cyrillic script. Looking at them, Laura couldn't recognise herself. The figure in the Cossack uniform was a stranger, but curiously familiar. It was a moment before she could admit to herself that it was her mother looking at her from out of the photographs. The innocence of the rounded forehead, the unwitting coquetry in the way the shoulders were thrown back, the awkward grace of the trailing leg – she looked like her mother in pictures taken 20 years ago, for her tour of the Near East.

Soon came the night of her first appearance. The Cossack costume trimmed with fake ermine still fitted her like a glove – she had regained her figure after two pregnancies. She suffered worse than ever from stage fright, but when the bar pianist finally gave her the prearranged signal and she emerged from behind the curtain, danced the kozachok and sang a Russian love song, she felt almost happy again. The audience went wild and the young seamen from the shiny steel ships lay at her feet. All was as it used to be – all but the most important thing: her singing had changed.

Listening to herself, Laura was surprised to find that her voice was no longer thin and hoarse but pervaded by a full-blooded emotional intensity that positively embarrassed her. She tried to tone it down and pay attention to her breathing technique, tried to keep time, hit the notes precisely and enunciate all her vowels and consonants cleanly; but hard as she strove to maintain a pianissimo and sing in a well-bred, womanly voice, she sang exclusively fortissimo and missed every note and every beat.

The men in the audience seemed to like it, however, and the bar pianist pounded away at the keys like a man possessed. So she danced until she was almost on her knees and belted out Cossack songs, and when she ended by singing a lullaby and burst into tears, the seamen wept too and joined in a full-throated rendering of *Bayushki Bayu*.

The proprietor of the Chat Noir, who was also pleased, came to Laura's dressing room and brought her a glass of champagne in person. She had made immense strides since the last time, he told her gruffly, and added a couple of notes to her agreed fee. Laura slipped them into her coat pocket, resolving to send them to Bottighofen the very next morning.

At the end of the evening she was met outside the rear entrance by her waiter friend, who fended off some over-enthusiastic admirers and escorted her home as before. They had reached the music shop, and Laura had already opened the door, when she thought of her deserted bedroom upstairs and the sleepless hours that awaited her there. So she pulled the door shut, slipped her arm through the waiter's and drew him closer. If you don't have anything else in mind, she said, let's go for a stroll. It's such a lovely night.

෧

The Palace of King Minos turned Arthur Evans and Émile Gil-liéron into celebrities in the spring of 1900. London, Paris and

Berlin received the long-awaited and gratifying news that, at a time when the ancient Egyptians were already navigating by compass and the Chinese were blowing their noses on paper handkerchiefs, not all Europeans were cave-dwellers attired in bearskins.

Émile and Evans worked round the clock. They spent their days at the excavation site and at night they catalogued finds, made paintings and drawings and wrote articles for archaeological journals. After two months, however, they had to suspend operations because the weather was too hot and over 100 of their labourers were suffering from malaria. On 2 June 1900 Evans left for England to deliver lectures and drum up money for further excavations. The following day Émile took the ferry to Athens, retired to his studio on the top floor of his villa and proceeded to turn out reproductions for the international market.

He made a dry-point etching of the bullfight fresco, dozens of which he sent off to newspapers and periodicals. The camping-stool belles he sent to museums and wealthy private individuals in the form of four-colour silk-screen prints. The saffron picker he painted five times in oils. He presented one copy to the King of Greece, one to the National Museum of Greece and one to Arthur Evans. The fourth he hung in his living room and the last he entrusted to his son, Émile junior, with instructions to make ten more identical copies.

When Émile returned to Crete in February 1901, he took his first-born with him and introduced him to Arthur Evans as his personal assistant on board the ferry. Evans was initially unimpressed by the foppish youngster, who spent their communal lunch gazing pensively out at the grey sea and took absolutely no part in the grown-ups' conversation. Between the soup and the main course, however, Evans noticed despite his short-sightedness that the boy's right hand was perpetually engaged in drawing on the paper tablecloth beside his plate. When he leant forward and screwed up his eyes for a closer look at what Émile junior was up to, the boy sheepishly put his pencil away, laid his napkin down beside his plate, and resumed his melancholy inspection of the sea. So Evans waited for the meal to end and remained seated until the Gilliérons had retired to their cabin and the waiter was clearing away. Then he screwed his monocle into his eye and leant across the table to examine the place where Émile junior's plate had been. He saw that the paper tablecloth was covered with brilliant pencil miniatures of Minoan matadors, snake priestesses and camping-stool belles, all executed with such facility that they might have been the father's work, not that of his 15-year-old son. Evans made his way round the table and sat down in Émile junior's place. He couldn't help smiling: the drawings had been carefully coloured with red wine, spinach, egg yolk, tomato sauce and coffee.

୫ର

The scene that greeted them on their return to Knossos came as a shock. The subtropical winter rains had reduced the archaeological site to one big quagmire. The carefully excavated trenches had fallen in, goats were trampling the precious, age-old detritus beneath their hoofs, and the walls displayed yawning gaps where farmers had come with their teams of oxen and hauled away beautiful limestone ashlars to serve as cornerstones for their goat stables. The alabaster floor of the throne room had ridden up, and the throne of King Minos and Ariadne's bath were smeared with goat dung. The precious remnants of mortar in the ruins had dissolved in the incessant downpour and sunk into the ground, and many of the walls that had been protected for millennia by a layer of earth were now eroded, washed away or demolished.

Arthur Evans and Émile Gilliéron saw their work threatened with destruction. They had to act – to protect the palace with a roof as soon as possible. Evans hurriedly had the charred remains of the 4,000-year-old columns replaced with new columns of timber and plaster and had modern brick corner columns erected on the ancient foundations to support a flat concrete roof. When that had been done, he sent to Heraklion for a metalworker who enclosed the whole site in a wrought-iron grille of the kind that was customarily used in Crete to enclose Muslim shrines.

The throne room was now adequately protected from rain-storms, goats and farmers, but it became hellishly hot under the bare concrete roof in sunny weather. Furthermore, the Palace of King Minos in its renovated form, complete with Muslim grille, brickwork columns and flat roof, did not bear the least resemblance to a Minoan palace as Arthur Evans envisioned it.

In the fourth year, when the bulk of the palace had been excavated, he mitigated the heat by having a considerably larger saddle roof of red tiles and imported steel girders erected above the flat roof. This created, above the throne room, an upper floor that was used during the months when digging was in progress to store new discoveries and to act as a temporary museum. Émile junior set up his drawing table in one corner and provided Arthur Evans with Minoan watercolours and ink drawings based on his father's sketches.

But the saddle roof was reminiscent more of a North European hay barn than a Neolithic Mediterranean royal residence. One can picture Arthur Evans sharing a bottle of wine with the Gilliérons beneath an olive tree one summer evening and staring at the structure with distaste.

I can't see the Palace of Knossos, he said. Can you?

It's right there in front of us, said Émile senior.

But I can't see it, said Evans. All I can see is a tiled roof. Our site is a joke. We've hidden everything Minoan beneath a highly visible roof that has nothing Minoan about it. Why didn't we build a Minoan roof?

Because we've no idea what a Minoan roof looked like, said Émile senior. We've never unearthed a Minoan roof anywhere on the site, nor an upper floor, nor a ground floor. Only foundations.

The foundations are massive, though, said Evans. It's pretty safe to assume that the palace had three or four storeys.

But we don't know what those storeys looked like, said Émile, let alone the roofs. There may have been a roof over a broad flight of steps beside the throne room, the steeply rising foundations indicate as much, but that's all – we can't know anything more.

Émile junior, now 20 years old, was sitting there quietly, listening to his elders. Evans noticed that he was drawing right-handed on the paper tablecloth.

But we aren't entirely at a loss, said Evans. We possess illustrations of Minoan buildings. On frescos. On vases. On coins.

And I have here an American one-dollar bill, Émile senior retorted. Do I have to infer from it that all Americans in the time of Abraham Lincoln lived under colonnaded marble domes?

This tiled roof tells no story, said Evans. Not even the wrong one.

From a scientific point of view, said Gilliéron, telling no story is better than a fabrication.

I take the opposite view, as you know, said Evans. What about the bullfighting fresco?

There's no comparison, said Émile. Playing around a little with a fresco is one thing. It's quite another to drive up with a concrete mixer and use 4,000-year-old walls as the foundations for modern castles in the air.

Architecture is metaphysical too, said Evans. Nothing amounts to anything without metaphysics.

No one can tell whether such a conversation actually took place, nor is there any evidence that Émile junior remained silent the whole time, but we can speculate that the young man passed the time by drawing on the tablecloth with his pencil, and that later that night, when Gilliéron *père* and *fils* had retired to their rooms, Arthur Evans took the tablecloth inside to examine it by the light of a paraffin lamp. If so, that would have been the first time Evans saw the Palace of Knossos in all its splendour, just as he had imagined it for so many years, with its flights of steps and suites of rooms and its characteristic red-and-black columns tapering towards the foot.

What is historically attested, on the other hand, is that in the ensuing years, when Gilliéron senior still ruled the roost and Émile the younger had to toe the line, nothing was erected on the foundations of Knossos save the big flight of steps beside the throne room. It is also true that only six months after the father's sudden and fatal heart attack in an Athenian restaurant, shortly before his 73rd birthday, the concrete mixers converged on Knossos. Finally, it is also true that later on, under the direction of Émile Gilliéron junior, the Palace of Minos was resurrected exactly as Evans had imagined it, complete with flights of steps and suites of rooms and red-and-black columns tapering towards the foot. The old tiled roof over the throne room was replaced with two light and airy upper floors reinforced with columns. In the south was a lofty hall which Evans called the Customs House, in the west a portico whose interior Gilliéron junior adorned with a bull fresco. And a stone's-throw away, to accommodate himself and his guests, Evans built a handsome country house which he christened the Villa Ariadne.

Thus, over the years, Arthur Evans's vision of the Palace of King Minos arose from the plain in steel and concrete, and the higher and more colourful it became, the greater the influx of visitors eager to gain some idea of the cradle of European civilisation.

Today the Palace of Knossos is the second-most-visited archaeological site in the eastern Mediterranean after the Athenian Acropolis. Some visitors are surprised that its frescos are reminiscent of the Art Nouveau of the end of the *belle époque*, whereas the building itself, with its elegant lines and strong colours, could pass for a typical example of the Art Deco of the late 1920s and early 1930s. Many local guides proudly point out that the palace is the earliest ferroconcrete building in Crete.

Time has gnawed away at Arthur Evans's work over the decades. The concrete has cracked in places, exposing rusty girders and steel mesh. Émile Gilliéron's frescos have also suffered from the heat and humidity, and mortar has flaked off the walls in many places. Modern restorers concerned with authenticity are confronted by the dilemma of having to decide whether to stay true to the Neolithic fragments or to Gilliéron's work.

Felix Bloch, now in exile in California, received his first letters from home. He instantly recognised the European envelopes lying amid the scientific journals and newspapers in his mailbox because they differed from the American equivalents in colour and format.

Every three or four days he received a letter from his mother, who found it hard to bear the fact that her only surviving child was so far away. She told him about her tranquil, humdrum existence in Zurich and tactfully avoided any questions about the quality of his accommodation, nutrition and health, and his father usually added a meagre but affectionate salutation below his mother's parting words.

Like all immigrants, Felix chafed at the belatedness of the news he received from home. For instance, if he read in one of his mother's letters that she had cut her finger while chopping onions, he would have liked to hear right away whether the cut had healed; and if his mother's next few letters made no mention of her finger and he had to enquire about it, a month would go by before the information reached him.

Heisenberg wrote once from Leipzig and Niels Bohr once from Copenhagen, but more and more often his letters came from relations who wanted to emigrate to America and sought his advice. His maternal grandmother wrote from Vienna to ask if two 17-year-old girls with no knowledge of English could be sent across the Atlantic on their own. An uncle from Pilsen asked whether honey was produced on a large scale in the plantations of California. A cousin from Erfurt asked Felix to obtain him a job teaching German at a high school. Most of these letters were couched in thoroughly businesslike and cheerful language. In themselves, none of them would have given cause for concern, had not they all struck the same, terrible note of forced irony, flippancy and offhandedness, which sprang from naked fear.

The more often such letters reached Felix, and the higher the pile of them on the little shelf beside the head of his bed, the more strongly he sensed the unspoken fear that emanated from them. It was the fear of crimes already committed or still to come; of uniformed schoolboys marching with impunity through city centres and smashing shop windows with iron bars, of boots tramping and front doors bursting open in the middle of the night; of rifle butts descending on the heads of grandmothers and infants, of looting and typewriters hurled out of windows; of beards torn out and synagogues burning and bills for petrol presented to rabbis by the arsonists; of smashed spectacles and splinters of glass driven deep into eyeballs; and of desperate people poisoning themselves with veronal, throwing themselves out of windows, or walking into electrified barbed-wire fences.

That fear pursued Felix Bloch in his dreams and awaited him at breakfast the next morning, tormenting him all the more because he knew that he himself was safe. He could forget his feeling of dread for the duration of a lecture, but at lunchtime, when he was driving to Berkeley at the wheel of the Chevrolet Sportster with his left arm dangling negligently out of the window, it returned to haunt him. It tormented him most of all when he drove into the mountains at weekends and went walking among the sequoias.

That was when he thought of the unfortunate souls punished for invented crimes by being hung from branches by their manacled wrists, so that their arms were dislocated and they passed out in terrible pain. He thought of those who were suspended from trees upside down until their brains literally burst inside their skulls, and of the days-long cries, audible from far away, of those who were lashed to trees so their toes only just touched the ground. He thought of those who were tied by their wrists to trees in pairs with their arms around the trunk, so that the weakness of one intensified the other's pain, and of those who managed to escape into the woods but were discovered in the undergrowth and mauled by dogs, whereupon uniformed young thugs dragged them back to camp by their legs and threw them into packing cases lined with barbed wire, nailed these down and left them out in the heat of the day and the chill of the night until, after two or three days, their tormented occupants were finally permitted to die.

Most of the trees in Palo Alto Hills were conifers of the genus *Sequoia sempervivens*. Felix got to the stage where he could no longer stand the sight of their rough, reddish-brown bark. He couldn't bring himself to believe that these trees belonged to a different world than the trees of Dachau. The deeper into the forest he went and the longer he spent alone there, the more strongly he sensed the opposite: that everything contemporaneous was as present as the past and the future.

So he steered clear of trees. In order to take his mind off things and avoid being on his own, he spent his weekends on the campus and even joined in the bachelor binges. When solitude was unavoidable, he sat down at his desk and endeavoured to calculate the magnetism of neutrons. But he never forgot that his parents in Zurich, his grandmother in Vienna and the whole of his extended family were in danger, while he, at the safe distance of 5,000 miles, was regaling himself with grapefruit and puffed wheat.

He endured this for 18 months, but in summer 1935, when the long vacation began and the campus became a lonely place because the students had gone home to their parents for three months, Felix too retraced his steps, first by train to New York and then by ship across the Atlantic.

That summer the immigrant ships to America were filled with Jewish refugees. Very few were heading in the opposite direction like Felix. It was the time of the Nuremberg race laws and the National Front initiative with which the fascists aspired to gain power in Switzerland as well; the time, too, when the Gestapo were abducting Jewish refugees from Switzerland back to Germany.

Glorious late summer weather prevailed when Felix arrived in Zurich. Cygnets were cruising on the Limmat and there were sailing boats on the lake. A cattle show was in progress outside the opera house in Bellevueplatz, and the peaks of the Glarner Alps seemed to extend a cordial welcome on the horizon. Felix submitted to hugs from his mother and went for walks beside the lake with his father, and spent hours trying to convince them both that it was high time to quit Europe and accompany him back to America.

Other than that, he resumed the habits of his youth, going to football matches at the Letzigrund and swimming in the lake. At the end of September he visited his grandmother in Vienna and tried to convince her, too, of the need to emigrate without delay. Early in October he travelled to Copenhagen via Antwerp for Niels Bohr's 50th birthday celebrations, to which Heisenberg and von Weizsäcker came from Leipzig and Otto Hahn from Berlin. It was an enjoyable gathering of friends and physicists who once again avoided all talk of politics. Felix described his life in America and, in a quiet moment, told Niels Bohr about his work on the magnetism of the neutron. Bohr urged him to give his brain a rest from theoretical deliberations; he should go back to the laboratory and do experiments. 'If you want to work with neutrons, you need neutrons,' he told him. 'Build a machine that produces neutrons. Then you'll see what can be done with them.'

Felix went home to Zurich when the party was over. His return to California was drawing nearer; his students were waiting for him. Besides, he had plans where the neutron was concerned. Early in 1936 he made a last attempt to convince his parents that Switzerland had ceased to be a safe haven. Then came the day when he walked along the Limmat to the station, carrying his suitcase, and took the train to Antwerp via Basel and Brussels. When his ship was halfway to New York, a Jewish medical student shot the leader of the Swiss Nazis, Wilhelm Gustloff, in Davos.

10

Laura d'Oriano scored a hit with her Cossack number. Sailors from the steel ships poured into the Chat Noir in ever-growing numbers. On the third night it occurred to her to spice up her French announcements with a Russian accent. On the fourth she made up her face with high Slav cheekbones for the first time. The sailors liked her even better that way.

On Saturday afternoon, when her sixth and final performance was imminent, the *patron* suggested she extend her run by a week. On the same day, *Liberté* devoted a two-column report to the Kiev Nightingale and provided her with a biography in which an important role was played by a Ukrainian landed estate and an old, aristocratic family, not to mention a horde of bloodthirsty Red Army soldiers, a massacre in the stable block, and a faithful retainer named Pavlov who had wrapped little Anoushka in a bearskin and conveyed her to safety across the Volga by dog sled.

The result of the press report was that even more customers poured into the Chat Noir during the second week and the *patron* requested another extension; he also upped Laura's fee by 50 per cent without being asked. She greeted her success with a furrowed brow, but also with a shrug; it didn't occur to her to question whether it was merited, she simply needed the money. What her teachers at the École des Beaux-Arts in Paris would have made of her performance and whether her popularity was down to her singing, or her garter, or her mythical CV, was unimportant. The fact was, dozens of sailors burst into tears every night when she sang *Bayushki Bayu* and, when the last notes died away, showered the stage with banknotes which the pianist busily picked up on Laura's behalf.

What about the great, expansive feeling in her breast to which she had long ago dreamed of lending expression? What about the cosmic hum? Well, those had ceased to interest her. Whether she liked it or not, what could now be detected in Laura's singing was quite another sensation. It might not be as great and important as the old one, but it was real. And strong. And it belonged to her alone.

She could not, of course, extend her run at the Chat Noir indefinitely, so it ended after three weeks. After all, she could not afford it to become known that the Kiev Nightingale was really a shopkeeper's daughter from Marseille who had abandoned her own two daughters and was living in her old room at her parents' home in the Vieux-Port. A few months later, however, because the *patron* of the Chat Noir knew some other *patrons* who paid protection money to the same Mafia family as he did, Laura received an invitation to perform in Cannes. After another few months she landed engagements in Sète, Nice and even Barcelona.

Her reputation preceded her, so she had full houses everywhere. Her audiences consisted largely of sailors, and they all burst into tears when she sang *Bayushki Bayu*. Laura had long since grasped that those hard-nosed, hard-working types from the steel ships had in an earlier life been the sons of their mothers, the brothers of their sisters and the grandsons of their grandmothers, and when the lights went up at the end of the night she could see how young they all were – most of them younger than her and many even younger than her brothers Umberto and Vittorio, whom she now saw only at Christmas and Easter.

It sometimes happened that one of the sailors would be waiting for her at the stage door. The brashest of them, who had already ordered a taxi with the engine running, she cold-shouldered; she also ignored the ones who were overly shy and gazed yearningly at her from dark doorways. Now and again, however, there would be one leaning against a lamp-post who had stuffed his sailor's cap in his pocket, was rolling himself a cigarette and paid her a compliment as she passed by. And if he didn't follow her right away but remained beside the lamp-post and waited to see if she would give him a sign, she sometimes turned to take a closer look at him. And if he appealed to her and had a nice smile and well-polished shoes, it could happen – not often, but occasionally, now and then – that she tipped him the wink.

Laura enjoyed those few hours because she knew that sailors had to be back aboard their ships at dawn, so none of them would take it into his head to want to marry her and bear her off to Bottighofen. Nor was she afraid of being alone with them, because she knew that women all over the world most often ran the risk of beatings, rape and murder at home and from members of their own family; in terms of criminal statistics, the girls who led the safest lives were those who steered clear of their fathers, their brothers and their brothers' friends, and who never married but mingled with strangers every evening and chose themselves a one-night lover to whom they said goodbye forever in the morning.

Like human beings in general, the sailors all resembled each other. Their manner towards Laura was a trifle cheeky and a trifle shy, like that of a schoolmate or a big sister's boyfriend, and they were all good-natured and young and healthily redolent of curd soap. True, most were rather clumsy and lacking in the masculine self-confidence with which Emil Fraunholz had made love to her, and only a few of them managed to keep her really warm throughout the night, but they did possess the magic of novelty and the charm of unfamiliarity, and if they were skilful enough or willing enough to be guided, they and Laura usually reached their destination.

Months and years went by in this way. Laura was content with her life. She was far from being the great artist she had aspired to become, and she suffered from pangs of conscience because of her daughters – a remorse she tried to mitigate by sending money to Bottighofen. Nevertheless, she still sang and danced, and her picture was in the papers, and she still turned men's heads at an age when other women were already bowed with care and putting on weight.

But money was often short because several months would elapse between engagements, so she had to live off her parents, who were not well-off themselves. What was more, the Kiev Nightingale had gradually exhausted her job opportunities on the Côte d'Azur and was having to contemplate a final return home to the Ukraine. Laura considered going on tour as 'Agneta, the Copenhagen Lily' or 'Carmen, the Rose of Seville' and later, perhaps, as 'Aisha, Queen of Tripoli'.

At all events, she needed a steady income. Not having received any replies to her original advertisement, she placed some more in which she offered her services variously as a nursemaid, charwoman and waitress. However, it was one of her waiter friends who eventually obtained her a job with his spinster aunt, who ran a ladies' and gentlemen's hat shop on the Avenue du 12 Mars and was looking for a multilingual saleswoman for her international clientele.

Maria Juarez by name, the aunt was a bustling, short-sighted, broad-hipped, middle-aged woman of unmistakably Iberian origin, with black eyes and an olive complexion. The moment Laura entered her shop, Maria Juarez took an instant dislike to this blue-eyed creature who looked blatantly French and probably had no need even to diet to be as unfairly slim as she was. However, because she had long been seeking someone with precisely Laura's attributes – presentable, cosmopolitan, polyglot – she engaged her for a trial period of three months.

The shop was divided from window to sales counter into two halves; the left-hand side was filled with gentlemen's hats, the right-hand with ladies'. A small door behind the counter led to the workroom in which three colourless, ageless drudges – Laura christened them 'the busy bees' – mutely turned out hats from morning to night, were treated with condescension by their employer and responded to all her orders with a *'Oui, Madame'*.

Laura's own workplace was at the left-hand extremity of the counter, as far as possible from the till. It was her job to deal with foreigners. When the shop was patronised by French cus-tomers, who were generally attended to by Madame, she was expected to smile nicely and be as invisible as possible – or, best of all, to disappear into the workroom; but when an American, Italian or Egyptian came in, Madame withdrew into the work-shop and made way for Laura.

Laura was good at her job. She treated every customer with the mixture of courtesy and cordiality she had learnt to adopt in the music shop. From behind the little door, Madame listened to Laura's multilingual sales talk and the customers' grunts and coos of approval when they thought they'd found the right hat. She had every reason to be pleased with her new employee, because few of them left the shop without having purchased at least one hat, but she mistrusted Laura for her very aptitudes. To her, who had seldom left her native city, let alone set foot outside France, the fact that someone could speak five languages was suspect in itself. That might be tolerable, but how was it possible that one and the same person could talk equally knowledgeably about Viennese confectionary, London fogs and rice-growing in the Nile Delta?

At quiet moments, Madame would eye Laura thoughtfully and flair her nostrils like a sleuth-hound, as if she had picked up her scent and guessed that the person behind her counter was not only Laura d'Oriano the gifted linguist, whom she had put on three months' probation, but Anoushka the Kiev Nightingale. And Agneta. And Carmen. And Aisha.

※

At 9:45 pm on Saturday, 26 June 1926, the eastern Mediterranean was shaken by a brief but violent earthquake. A full moon was sailing over the archaeological site of Knossos and the last of the daylight was glimmering above the western skyline. At the Villa Ariadne, Arthur Evans was reading in bed, Émile Gilliéron junior sitting on the veranda with a bottle of Armagnac. At the first sharp shock, the solidly built stone house began to creak and groan, then swayed like a ship on the high seas. Writing in the London *Times* three months later, Evans reported that the motion was so violent, he had felt positively seasick. For the 75 seconds the earthquake lasted, the ground emitted a muffled roar like the bellowing of an infuriated bull. The crash of nearby roofs collapsing mingled with women's screams and the wailing of children. From the city came the sound of bells ringing a kind of inverse peal as the towers of Heraklion Cathedral swayed to and fro and the resonators struck the clappers instead of the other way round. The cloud of dust that arose when the shaking ceased obscured the full moon.

Arthur Evans and Émile Gilliéron spent the remainder of the night in the garden. At dawn, when no further tremors had occurred, they inspected the palace complex. The new ferroconcrete structure over the throne room had withstood the earthquake, likewise the Customs House and the north portico, but 50 large earthenware jars had smashed and two snake goddesses had broken in half. The frescos had also sustained considerable damage. More a figment of Émile Gilliéron senior's imagination than a restoration, the so-called Jewel Fresco in which one Parisienne held another Parisienne's necklace between fingers tipped with lacquered red nails had been pulverised; the reproduction of the saffron-picking Blue Boy, too, had been damaged.

Émile was now faced with the task of restoring the frescos restored by his father. It was 18 months since he had consigned his namesake's ashes to Villeneuve harbour on the Lake of Geneva. He was no longer the junior, but the head and breadwinner of a large and expensive family. He had successively taken over from his father, when the latter's powers began to wane, his professorship of the Royal Academy of Art, his position at the French Archaeological Institute and the artistic direction at Knossos. He had designed a set of new coins for the Greek National Bank bearing the figure of the tutelary goddess Athene, the date 1926, and the words 'Gilliéron fils'. In addition, he was continuing to run his late father's workshop, in which a team of goldsmiths, potters and stonemasons turned out, to order, reproductions of statuettes, vases, jewellery and swords.

He had taken his final step into the world of adulthood by marrying one of his art students. Ernesta Rossi by name, she was the daughter of the king's coach builder and had initially caught his eye because she only ever wanted to paint the Acropolis in oils and showed no interest in anything else he tried to teach in class – neither life drawings in red chalk, nor portraits in charcoal, nor still lifes in watercolour. After they were married she had set up her easel on the roof terrace of the Gilliéron abode and continued to paint the Acropolis in oils – the Acropolis at sunrise and the Acropolis at sunset, the Acropolis at night and in the blazing midday sun, the Acropolis under snow and in the pouring rain – and Émile let her have her way in the knowledge that self-limitation is every artist's greatest defeat but, at the same time, most important virtue.

Émile made an unpleasant discovery after the Knossos earthquake: that the abilities for which he and his father had long been extolled and richly rewarded were less and less in demand. Bold reconstruction and daring embellishment verging on unfettered imagination were no longer valued by a new generation of archaeologists who had received a more scientific than artistic or classically philological training at universities in London, Paris or Berlin. These young fact-mongers worked in a sober, methodical, empirical manner. They were suspicious of Schliemannesque strokes of genius and Evansian daydreams, and took an extremely critical view of Gilliéron senior's prehistoric Parisiennes, with their camping stools and tennis shoes.

Émile registered this development with a shrug; if that was what customers wanted, he was amenable to any form of scientific accuracy. His one regret was that this worthy, methodical drudgery was considerably less well-paid because it required no genius or even talent, just a modicum of conscientious diligence.

But when he set about restoring the Blue Boy fresco in keeping with the latest state of research – not in the form of a boy picking saffron, but as a blue monkey in a flowery meadow – the new version was unanimously rejected, not only by Arthur Evans but by the entire digging crew and every tourist. The Blue Boy was too famous to be done away with; it had become so deeply rooted in the collective consciousness as a valid icon of Minoan art that a likeness of a blue monkey would always be regarded as a fake.

The new desire for authenticity brought about a steady decline in Émile's business. Orders to his workshop dried up because the world's major museums were now headed by academics who felt committed to the fragmentary but authentic rather than the colourfully imaginative and romantic. The British Museum and the Louvre discontinued their orders for Minoan reproductions at the end of the 1920s, and New York's Metropolitan Museum of Fine Arts, which had been one of the Gilliérons' most faithful customers for a quarter of a century, placed its last order in 1931. Gilliéron reproductions had gone out of fashion. Museum curators sheepishly removed them from their showcases and stored them in their basements, whence they never reemerged.

But Émile Gilliéron's workshop remained in production and its stonemasons, goldsmiths and potters still had enough to do. He was sometimes accused of turning out fakes as well as reproductions, but no one could prove this because he carried on his business quite openly and his reproductions could have been described as fakes only if he had passed them off as originals. Which he did not. As long as the good pieces were still in his workshop, they were naturally accounted reproductions and it would never have occurred to anyone to regard them as originals. If they were sold and went out into the wide world, however, and if some middleman somewhere in the convoluted byways of the international trade in antiquities omitted to mention that an object for sale was a faithful copy, not an age-old discovery – if something like that happened in Paris or New York or some other place thousands of miles from Knossos – that deceit lay beyond Gilliéron's sphere of influence and could hardly be laid at his door.

For all that, police searches were occasionally carried out with experts in attendance. We know from their descriptions that the workshop was a fantastic assemblage of prehistoric finds in every stage of manufacture and ageing process. Painted earthenware rubbed shoulders with rough potsherds, rolls of silver wire with completed gold jewellery, soap dishes full of engraved and uncut semiprecious stones with lumps of unfired clay and freshly forged spearheads, double axes and daggers.

For many years, one especially profitable line was the manufacture of female figures holding a snake in each hand and baring their breasts at the beholder. Between 10 and 30 centimetres tall, these so-called snake goddesses or priestesses were regarded by museum curators and private collectors as especially symbolic of Minoan society, which Arthur Evans had always conceived of as matriarchal. Although the first snake goddesses found in 1903, at an early stage in the Knossos excavations, were simple terracotta or alabaster figurines, increasingly elaborate statuettes of gold and ivory appeared during the First

World War, and, despite their obscure provenance, museums paid high prices for them over a period of nearly 20 years.

Émile Gilliéron's workshop contained snake goddesses at every stage of manufacture, from raw ivory to finished and artificially aged figurines. Since the new public taste required it, the freshly carved and gold-embellished figures were endowed with the patina of bygone millennia by being immersed in an acid bath. This dissolved the ivory's softer components and made the snake goddesses look as if they had lain in acid soil since prehistoric times – so much so that not even Arthur Evans could tell the difference between artificially and naturally aged ivory. A simpler and more inexpensive method consisted in burying the snake goddesses at a certain spot in the garden and instructing all the members of the household to urinate there until further notice.

The artificial ageing process was completed by inflicting minor damage on the snake goddesses with blows from a hammer. The usual practice was to knock off an arm or smash a thigh. Blows to the head were avoided because snake goddesses with heads missing or mutilated faces fetched lower prices. If a figure with a mutilated face did appear on the market, on the other hand, experts regarded this as proof positive of its authenticity, because such devaluing damage could hardly be the work of a forger.

The Palace of King Minos remained the world's archaeological Mecca for 20 years. Arthur Evans was knighted in 1911 and Émile Gilliéron made more money out of his illustrations and reproductions than any artist of antiquities before him. When British millionaires' wives, German steel barons or American film stars undertook a Mediterranean cruise, a visit to Knossos was mandatory. They were guided around the palace by Evans and wined and dined on the terrace of the Villa Ariadne, and when dusk descended on the site at the end of a long, hot day, many of them must have felt as if a feather-crowned snake goddess or King Minos himself were about to descend the Grand Staircase. So tempting was this fantasy that the American dancer Isadora Duncan could not resist performing an improvised Minoan-Mycenaean temple dance amid the black and brown columns on the Grand Staircase, barefoot and in flowing drapery.

All this came to an abrupt end when, on 4 November 1922, 1,000 kilometres south of Knossos, the British archaeologist Howard Carter discovered Tutankhamun's tomb in the Valley of the Kings. All at once, millionaires' yachts were making for Egypt, not Crete. Everyone now wanted to see the gold death mask and the eyes rimmed with lapis lazuli, the sarcophagus of solid gold and the numerous gilded shrines, the golden throne and the statues of the two sentinels. All over the world, museums, newspapers and universities succumbed to an Egyptomania that was destined to endure for many years; and the Palace of King Minos lapsed into total oblivion when another Englishman named Leonard Woolley discovered the Biblical city of Ur, which was 1,000 years older than Knossos and strewn with inscribed clay tablets conclusively proving that Sumerian schoolchildren had had to do sums involving square and cube roots.

Arthur Evans, who had always dreamt of finding the grave of King Minos – and even, perhaps, his library – was concerned by this 'downgrading' of his project. He had spent years looking for the king's grave within an ever-greater radius of Knossos, riding back and forth and up and down hills on a wooden-saddled donkey in search of it. In the course of his quest, which had taken him to the southern shores and back, he had crawled into countless caves and visited every islet off the precipitous, rocky coast.

After the major earthquake of 1926, however, these excursions had become infrequent. The burden of the years was beginning to tell on Evans. He more and more rarely undertook the voyage from England to Crete and more and more often spent the whole year at Youlbury, his country house in Oxfordshire. In March 1931, however, or shortly before his 80th birthday, he paid another visit to Knossos to satisfy himself that all was well. While he was there, Nikolaos Polakis, the parish priest of Forteba, offered to sell him a huge, solid gold signet ring that had allegedly been found by a peasant boy named Michael Papadakis while playing in a vineyard. In one version of the story the ring had lain gleaming in the soil, in another it was dangling from a plant that had just sprouted.

Engraved on the ring was a regally erect figure in a boat shaped liked a seahorse and heading between two walls for an olive grove or vineyard surmounted by a building resembling a small temple or tomb. He had been convinced at first glance that the ring was authentic, Evans wrote, because he was familiar with the engraved motifs from the frescos at Knossos. Moreover, its weight, which was a substantial 77 grams, suggested that its wearer must have been of royal blood. The sale did not take place because the priest was asking 20 million drachmas, but he did tell Evans, free of charge, exactly where the ring had been found.

Early in April 1931, Evans and a small team of diggers went to the aforesaid spot in a vineyard three kilometres south of Knossos. He found a small Greek cemetery on the site in question, and beneath it a large, clearly Minoan building. After several days' excavation, this proved to be a colonnaded temple with a paved forecourt and an underlying vault with red walls and a blue ceiling.

Evans was delighted. This tomb was bigger than any he had ever seen in Crete. It did not disturb him that the chamber was unadorned and empty; on the contrary, it reinforced his conviction that he had found King Minos's actual mausoleum. The king was known to have sailed in pursuit of Daedalus to Sicily, where he had been murdered and interred, so his body could not be in Crete. That the tomb was empty proved, or at least indicated, that it really had been built for King Minos.

The gold signet ring that had put Evans on the track of the king's tomb and has since been known in archaeological circles as the ring of King Minos was purchased by Heraklion Museum but later declared a fake and returned to the priest, who allegedly entrusted it to his wife, who allegedly buried it somewhere and then forgot the location – though not before Émile Gilliéron had, for Arthur Evans, photographed, drawn and made a copy of it in his workshop that must have been absolutely identical to the original fake.

Thereafter the ring of King Minos remained shrouded in silence until, 80 years later, the grandson of the priest Polakis presented himself at the archaeological museum in Heraklion and announced that it had reappeared. The director of the museum acquired it for an unknown sum, and it has since 2002 been on permanent display in a prominent position.

৯৯

Back in California, Felix Bloch committed his theory on the magnetism of neutrons to paper within a few days. When his paper appeared in the *Physical Review* in July 1936 (as 'A Letter to the Editor') it caused a stir, and Bohr and Heisenberg both wrote to congratulate him. But Felix himself had lost interest in the magnetism of neutrons – in fact he felt almost surprised that he had beaten his brains about it for so long. Now that he had put it down on paper, the idea struck him as banal and unimportant. All else apart, no one would understand it except a few oddballs like himself.

He had fallen out of love with atomic physics because of the quality for which he had once loved it: its pointlessness. He found it conceited and positively obscene to squander his time on egocentric introspection in view of the catastrophe that threatened to engulf the world. When he lay awake at night in his bachelor bungalow and heard the coyotes howling in the foothills, he felt like a useless outsider for doing nothing meaningful with his life, for having no friends and being unable to support his loved ones back home. His trip to Europe had been merely self-serving – he had been of no assistance to people in need. He felt ashamed of the months he had spent vegetating in his old bed in Zurich and at his mother's kitchen table, and he felt ashamed of the last ten years of his life, which he had wasted without promoting the common good.

However, because he had signed a contract with the university and needed money for food, petrol and rent, he got up every morning, showered, shaved, and made his way to the lecture room of the physics institute to tell his fair-haired, muscular innocents something about the spectral lines of atoms or the structure of the periodic system. He was a good teacher and popular with his students because he took them kindly by the hand and led them across the sea of their ignorance from one ice floe to the next.

But he himself had ceased to be curious. He no longer wished to find out whether electrons performed the long jump or the high jump or some other neat trick, and he now found the not-only-but-also palaver of quantum theory merely quirky. He had stopped going to Oppenheimer's seminars at Berkeley and seldom read any technical journals.

This meant that he had plenty of spare time and too little to occupy his mind. He could have taken to drink, but alcohol didn't deaden his thoughts, it only accelerated them. Besides, he didn't care for watery American beer, and being a tall, strong man, he would have had to imbibe distasteful quantities of it to feel any effect.

And so, one morning in April 1936, Felix drove to Cole Hardware Store in San Francisco, bought himself a set of top-quality spanners and devoted his spare time to renovating the Chevrolet Sportster. He removed the bumpers and immersed them in a chromium bath in the chemical institute's labora-tory. He emery-papered the wings and repainted them fire-engine red. The black roof he painted white to render it less sunlight-absorbent. He reupholstered the worn-out seats, then sanded and repainted the wooden wheel spokes. He removed the cylinder head and, although he could have ordered one from Detroit at very little expense, devoted three days' preci-sion work to cutting a new cylinder-head gasket out of a thin sheet of cork. Then he lubricated all the bearings and replaced the V belt, drilled out the inlet valve and spent days screwing away at the distributor. Last of all, he shortened the exhaust, then lengthened it, then shortened it once more.

When he was through the Chevrolet looked like new and the engine was more efficient than it had been the day it left the factory in Detroit. Felix listened to the purring of the engine and delighted in the beauty inherent in a machine that works. To his surprise, though, it was not the complex electrical components like the dynamo, the distributor or the contact breaker that pleased him most, but simple mechanical parts like the windscreen wiper, with its sluggish pendular motion, or the pretty little Bakelite switches on the dashboard, or the prop shaft that so neatly transmitted the engine's torque to the rear axle.

The manual labour had done him good, but the vehicle would not, with the best will in the world, need any maintenance work for the foreseeable future. So he looked around for another manual task and hit on the idea of building a machine for the production of free neutrons, not bound in atomic nuclei, in the laboratory of the physics institute. He found it tempting to use his own hands to create something that did not exist in nature, and he had never forgotten Niels Bohr's advice: 'If you want to work with neutrons, you need neutrons.' So he would produce some and see what could be done with them.

In the laboratory's store cupboards he found an assortment of physicists' toys such as Crookes tubes and a Leonardo water pump, some spools of copper wire, transformers, all manner of thermodynamic glasswork, a vacuum pump, a few prisms, and, last but far from least, an X-ray tube capable of being fed with a maximal tension of 200,000 volts. Two hundred thousand volts wasn't bad – something could be done with that. For a start, it would produce heavy water to slow the neutrons, and it might be possible to produce a relatively reliable beam with the aid of the X-ray tube. Felix's idea was to polarise the neutron beam by directing it past two powerful electromagnets so as to be able to demonstrate and possibly even measure the neutrons' magnetic charge.

He set to work with great enthusiasm. The prospect of once more reconciling one of his ideas with the real world after such a long time was a great comfort to him. He soldered and screwed away round the clock, just as he had when building his spectrograph in the basement of the ETH in Zurich. Then came the moment when he experimentally placed his radiation source, a mixture of a few milligrams of radium and beryllium, in the interior of the X-ray tube.

Felix Bloch later said of his machine that it had been a source more of inspiration than of neutrons. He did manage now and again, with a little luck, to demonstrate the presence of one free neutron or another for a few seconds before it was trapped by an atomic nucleus, but the output had been far too small and not even a semi-reliable neutron beam had come into being. Moreover, Felix did not have exclusive use of the X-ray tube. He had every few days to lend it to the medics and their students, who used it to irradiate dead sheep or their own hands.

He realised that he needed a bigger machine – a very much bigger machine. There was a substantially bigger one in the laboratory of his friend Robert Oppenheimer – it had been christened the cyclotron and was reputed to be the biggest particle accelerator in the world – but even that produced neutrons very irregularly and unreliably, and it had also to be lent to medical students every few days.

So Felix sat down at his desk, drew a preliminary sketch for a cyclotron of his own and made a rough estimate of the cost of materials. Then he picked up his telephone and proceeded to collect money. The Dean of Stanford informed him that the university had no cash to spare for his seemingly impractical experiment, but that everyone was following his activities with interest and wished him luck. He obtained a donation of 4,000 dollars from the Rockefeller Foundation and one of 1,000 dollars from the Rotary Club of San Francisco, and an additional 500 dollars was contributed by a local wholesale bakery that hoped to supply the university with bread.

But then, out of the blue, came the day that put a stop to all the fun and was to change everything forever – not only in Felix Bloch's life but in the future of humankind and of every living creature on earth.

That day was 26 January 1939.

Felix was listening to the midday news on the radio in 'Pietro's Barber Shop' on Hamilton Avenue, where he was a regular customer. Pietro was a good-looking, taciturn Italian with a predilection for little, home-made electrical gadgets. When you walked down the two steps to his salon and trod on the doormat, the door opened by itself, and when you sat down in the barber's chair, Pietro adjusted its height electrically by pressing a button. To froth the soap he used a home-made electric whisk, and to hone his razors a small machine with contra-rotating whetstones. Pietro had no time for Remington's brand-new electric razors, on the other hand, because he had tested one on himself and come to the prescient conclusion that they would never – not even in a hundred years – give anyone a decent shave.

When it came to cutting hair, however, he relied exclusively on his electrically-powered rotary shears whose bizarre appearance he tried as far as possible to conceal from his customers. When working on the top of the head he operated a machine that differed from the one he used to thin the hair on the temples. He used another to trim nose and ear hair and yet another to clean up the neck, and when he removed snippets of hair from under a customer's collar he employed a miniature vacuum cleaner with a home-made nozzle upholstered in velvet.

Pietro always ended by massaging his customer's temples by hand with Acqua di Parma. Felix closed his eyes and listened to the news from the radio. The newsreader reported that the Supreme Court of the State of California had denied the farmhand Claud David's appeal against his death sentence for murder. General Franco's troops had marched into Barcelona. The fan was humming away on the ceiling, the Coca Cola automat in the corner. The newsreader read out the weather forecast: northern California was in for a cool, cloudy weekend. His voice became suddenly brisker: an important news item had just come in. A rustle of paper could be heard. In Berlin, the German chemist Otto Hahn had succeeded in splitting the nucleus of a uranium atom by bombarding it with neutrons – something hitherto considered physically impossible. The Danish Nobel laureate Niels Bohr had announced this at the opening of the Fifth Washington Conference on Theoretical Physics. The splitting of the uranium nucleus had produced barium and released an immense 200 million electron-volts of energy.

Felix realised at once what this meant. Tearing the cloth from around his neck, he dashed out of the salon, ran to the Chevrolet and drove at top speed to Berkeley. He parked at the foot of the steps leading up to palatial LeConte Hall and raced up the three flights of stairs to Oppenheimer's study, where he breathlessly reported what he had heard on the radio. We can picture Oppenheimer perched on the edge of his desk, saying 'Yes ... yes, yes ... yes ... ' and interrupting Felix at the first opportunity.

What fissile products did Hahn find? he asked.

Barium.

Nothing else?

That's what it said on the radio, but it's impossible, of course. Uranium 92 minus barium 56 equals 36, or krypton. If Hahn found barium, he must also have found krypton.

And free neutrons? Oppenheimer lit another Chesterfield from the butt of its predecessor.

There was no mention of neutrons.

If no neutrons were released, things aren't as bad as all that.

Some will have been, I'm afraid.

One neutron per nuclear fission means the uranium machine, said Oppenheimer. Unlimited energy for the whole of humanity until the end of their days.

But two neutrons mean the bomb, said Bloch. What do we do now?

Oppenheimer shrugged his shoulders. If the bomb is feasible, someone will build it.

Probably.

Most certainly.

The question is, who?

Someone who can, said Oppenheimer. There aren't that many. It's us or the others, isn't it?

Felix nodded.

Where is Hahn at this moment?

Still in Berlin.

And your friend Heisenberg?

Still in Leipzig.

And von Weizsäcker?

Still in Berlin.

11

Émile Gilliéron made his last trip to Knossos at the age of 50, when Arthur Evans was awarded honorary citizenship of Heraklion. Ten thousand people lined the road on 15 June 1935, when the festive procession made its way up from the harbour to the Palace of King Minos. The Deputy Minister of Culture had come especially from Athens to pay tribute to Evans's services in the big square in front of the archaeological site and express the Greek nation's gratitude for his life's work. Speeches from the British Ambassador and the Mayor of Heraklion followed, and the Greek Orthodox Bishop of Crete celebrated Mass when the sun was at its zenith.

After that it fell to Arthur Evans to unveil a bronze statue of himself, complete with marble plinth and memorial plaque. When the applause had died away, he mounted the podium and addressed the gathering – as ever with a strong English accent – in a mixture of ancient and modern Greek which the Greeks understood with difficulty and the non-Greeks not at all. Émile Gilliéron was the only person present who followed the old man's gibberish with ease because his ears had been attuned to it for 30 years.

Evans began by recalling the days when Knossos had still been an olive grove, not a royal palace. Then, with a sweeping gesture, he pointed to his life's work and proclaimed that, although the palace was only the ruin of a ruin, it would remain inspirited for all time by the administrative genius of King Minos and the artistry of Daedalus.

Seated in the second row, Émile watched with a heavy heart as his longtime employer manfully held himself erect despite his 83 years and expatiated on his vision of the Minoan kingdom. None of this was new to Émile, who had heard it all a thousand times before: the pacific maritime power, the dream of a literate matriarchy, the legend of its sudden downfall in the wake of earthquakes and volcanic eruptions. He was wholeheartedly delighted that the old man had received this honour, his sole regret being that, like most honours, it had come two or three decades too late.

If its recipient had been only 50 or 60, he might possibly have abandoned his outmoded visions and entered into a dialogue with his archaeological successors. Now, however, inextricably imprisoned in the obstinacy of old age, he was just a predictable source of annoyance to the young archaeologists who had nonetheless turned up with the firm intention of honouring the famous old man. They stared at their shoes in embarrassment as Evans spoke magniloquently of the abiding spirit of King Minos, and when he had finished they nudged each other and smirked. Looking askance at the palace, they exchanged whispered predictions that the most that would abide under all that ferroconcrete and oil paint was the spirit of Arthur Evans.

Even so, the applause was prolonged and heartfelt. When the ceremony ended, a select number of guests attended a banquet on the terrace of the Villa Ariadne. Late that afternoon they returned to the harbour, where the steamer for Athens was waiting. The farewells were effusive but insincere: for all the esteem accorded to Arthur Evans, who had devoted all his vital energies and his personal fortune to Knossos, the archaeological community of Crete was glad to be permanently rid of the old man, who was merely getting in the way of his successors. And when the passengers had gone aboard and the seamen had cast off the hawsers, Émile Gilliéron knew that his time in Crete had also run out.

When the ship had left harbour and all the waving and shouting was over, the two travelling companions had tea in the small saloon.

Do you remember our first voyage together 30 years ago? Evans asked. The time you drew on the tablecloth?

I was 15, Émile said apologetically. My father made fun of me for weeks after that.

Ah, your father, said Evans. How long is it since he left us?

Eleven years. He died four days before my son's fourth birthday.

Then young Alfred must be 15 himself by now. Has he inherited your talent – does he draw on tablecloths?

Not that I'm aware, Émile said tersely.

After a while, Evans cleared his throat and looked around as though in search of something.

Tell me, Gilliéron, isn't this the ship we made the crossing in 30 years ago? Isn't this the very same table whose cloth you drew on?

Afraid not, sir. I happen to know that that ship was wrecked many years ago.

Are you sure?

Positive.

What a shame, said Evans, running both hands caressingly over the edge of the table. I could have sworn … He looked round, embarrassed and confused.

Émile felt sorry for the old man.

It may not be the same ship, he said, but I quite agree with you. This ship bears a strong resemblance to that one.

Really?

An amazing resemblance. Like two peas in a pod.

It does, doesn't it? Evans gave a contented nod. All ships bear a strong resemblance to each other, don't they?

Absolutely, said Émile, looking out across the grey sea. A ship is a ship, that's for sure.

Conversation lapsed. Evans contemplated the tablecloth with raised eyebrows and Émile was annoyed with himself for feeling sorry for him.

It had been a tiring day, so they retired to bed early. When they said goodbye in Piraeus harbour the next day, they shook hands and promised to meet again soon, both knowing that they would never see each other again in this life. It is quite possible that Émile shed a tear on the way from Piraeus to Athens, because he was taking leave not only of Arthur Evans and his era but also of his father's era and, possibly, of his own.

For that day, for the first time in 30 years, he was returning home from Crete bereft of professional success – without the smallest commission or invitation. This was no coincidence and would not remain exceptional. Émile Gilliéron had no illusions. At yesterday's festivity the young fact-mongers had, with unspoken contempt, sent into retirement not only Arthur Evans but himself as well. This was quite in order and consistent with the way of the world. Émile felt no bitterness because he did not regard the fact-mongers as victorious and himself as vanquished; it was just a changing of the guard. The youngsters would now have to show what their scientific dogmatism was worth.

Arthur Evans and Émile Gilliéron had, after all, resurrected the palace of King Minos. What did the fact-mongers have to set against that? A few scientifically accurate heaps of stone. One of them languished in solitude on the outskirts of Palekastro and another just inland from the beach at Kato Zakros. The Italians had made a few finds at Phaistos and the French had unearthed a heap of stones in Malia, and it had all been conscientiously surveyed, archived and catalogued. But what did these ruins convey to anyone? Did they tell even the ghost of a story? And who would want to see them after seeing the magnificent palace of Knossos?

Arthur Evans and Émile Gilliéron were the creators of the palace at Knossos, nothing could change that. It would still be so in a century's time, when the youthful purists and archaeological pedagogues and their bookkeepers were lying in their graves, long since decayed and forgotten, in company with the museum curators and civil servants and all the other frigid, bloodless bean-counters, pedants and parasites whose lives had been devoid of passion, who had preened themselves at public expense and never spent a drachma of their own on anything but their own bellies. Even a century hence, of this Émile Gilliéron was convinced, the collective memory of mankind would remember the early history of Crete as he and Arthur Evans had created it, complete with its throne rooms, flights of steps and reddish-brown columns tapering towards the foot, its camping-stool belles, its saffron-pickers and snake-priestesses.

In decades of work he and his father had created an oeuvre which, irrespective of its historical authenticity, had earned a place in the great museums of the world. Émile Gilliéron realised that he would never be awarded an honorary degree, never be knighted or receive the honorary citizenship of anywhere, and that he should, on the contrary, count himself lucky not to have ended up behind bars for fraud or forgery. But even if the world had failed to acknowledge his artistic achievements, he could nonetheless claim to be the greatest forger of all time. He hadn't simply copied a few oil paintings, ivory figurines or banknotes; he had done nothing less than invent the outward appearance of Europe's earliest advanced civilisation – with all its playful *joie de vivre* and its penchant for Art Nouveau and Art Deco.

The only fly in the ointment was that he wasn't 83 years old, like Evans, and he needed to go on earning money for quite a while yet. His business affairs were in no better state in Athens than in Crete. Major museums and institutions had stopped buying from him. The previous year he had managed to win a last battle against the young archaeologists and install a whole roomful of Minoica from his own workshop in the National Archaeological Museum, but that was that. There were no new commissions in prospect.

The road from Piraeus to Athens had been asphalted and a tramway laid along it. Horse-drawn vehicles and donkey-carts were now a rarity; the city had been full of motorcars for some years, and dense clouds of exhaust fumes hung over the streets during the summer months. Most of the tram conductors could speak French, most of the waiters German. No longer in a goat pasture, the Gilliérons' family home now stood in the midst of a noisy, rapidly growing city.

For over half a century, Gilliéron *père* and *fils* had between them traversed every stage in the development of archaeology. They had roamed the Aegean with Schliemann like archaeological hunter-gatherers, then settled in Knossos with Evans like agriculturalists. When the fields they had cultivated became unproductive, they switched to specialised arts and crafts for a wealthy upper crust, and when this small, exclusive market collapsed they explored a wider range of purchasers by setting up a factory and reducing unit costs. They had taken the final step towards industrialisation by getting their reproductions mechanically mass-produced by a factory in southern Germany.

Employing a galvanoplastic or electrotyping process, the Württembergische Metallwarenfabrik of Geislingen turned out any desired number of replicas of Gilliéron's Minoan bulls' heads and Mycenaean gold and silver drinking cups, as well as all manner of vases, oil lamps and goblets, swords and daggers, coins and death masks, and gold rings like the ring of King Minos, which had led Arthur Evans to the temple and tomb. The lavishly illustrated catalogue listed 144 different items. Orders were to be addressed to Émile Gilliéron, 43 Rue Skoufa, Athens. Professor Paul Volters of Munich pointed out in the introduction that the artefacts had not been left in their bent and broken condition, but restored to their original shape.

The Minoica from Geislingen, which were inexpensive and sold well, had provided Émile Gilliéron with a secure livelihood. Gradually, however, demand for them dwindled and the market seemed glutted. Besides, the WMF was receiving more and more orders from Germany's resurgent armed forces and seldom found the time to meet Émile Gilliéron's special requirements.

To prevent this source of income, too, from drying up, he was obliged to make continual additions to his range. Twice a year – usually in spring and autumn – he travelled to Geislingen to deliver new artefacts and issue instructions on their reproduction. He would then remain at the factory for a few days, supervising the manufacture of the moulds and inspecting the preliminary copies, before travelling back to Athens.

He was finding these trips by sea and rail increasingly burdensome and looked around for some way of offloading them. His son Alfred would take over the job at some stage, but he was still a few years from adulthood.

On the morning of 2 September 1939, when Émile was about to set off on his usual autumn trip, he read in the newspaper at breakfast that a war had broken out between Germany and Poland. He put down his coffee cup, called Lloyd Triestino and postponed his voyage to Trieste by four weeks. The war would be over by then, so it said in the paper, because Poland wouldn't last a month.

A month went by, and Émile prepared to leave once more. The night before, he and his wife Ernesta dined on octopus on the terrace of his house. It was a warm night in late summer, and the moon was rising above the resplendent Acropolis in the south. After coffee, Ernesta placed a lamp beside her easel and continued to work on her latest oil painting: a view of the Acropolis by the light of the full moon. She made sketches of the shadows the moon cast as it rose and had to decide which position was the most effective.

Émile watched her at work as he sipped his Armagnac. He had been married to her for 20 years and had watched her painting for 21. He admired her pictures for their craftsman-like technique, but they were uninspired and lacked artistic courage. There was an element of tragedy in the fact that Ernesta's Acropolis paintings were too good to be hawked to tourists and too banal to attract the attention of gallery owners and collectors. Any hack, bungler or genius could find purchasers on the insatiable Athenian art market; Ernesta's works alone remained unsellable, stacked up by the hundred in the Gilliérons' house. It was only every few months that one dusty example found its way out into the world, to end up on permanent loan in the drawing room of some friend or acquaintance.

The moon detached itself from the horizon with surprising speed, as it always did. When it neared its zenith and the Acropolis was casting hardly any shadows, Ernesta put her painting things away and retired to bed. Émile poured himself a last Armagnac. His suitcase was already packed. This time he would have to go, even though the war wasn't over yet; his stock of merchandise was running low.

He was dreading the journey. The customs checks would be more irksome than usual, the train journeys longer and the arrival times more uncertain. Under present circumstances it was inadvisable for his luggage to contain Menelaus's battleaxe or Theseus's broadsword. This time he was taking only Minoan gold rings and Mycenaean coins to Germany and leaving the other things at home.

When the bottle was empty he went into the house and washed his face and hands, then undressed and set the alarm clock for half past six. It was shortly after midnight; 30 September 1939 had just begun. He slipped into bed beside his wife and fell asleep with his usual speed. There had been scarcely a night in his 54 years of life when he hadn't got off to sleep easily and quickly.

Two hours later, however, his wife woke up because he had stopped snoring. He was already cold when she shook him.

Laura d'Oriano often reflected that it was her duty to return to Bottighofen and Emil Fraunholz and her daughters. Particularly during long afternoons behind the counter, when few customers entered the shop and her hours amid ladies' and gentlemen's hats were crawling by, she occasionally had the sneaking sensation that she was awaking from a deep sleep to find herself unaccountably in the wrong place at the wrong time in the company of strangers with whom she had no business. She was sometimes on the verge of snatching up her handbag and coat and walking out without a word of farewell, but because she didn't know where to go, she never did.

One thing Laura knew for sure: it would do no one any good if she returned to Bottighofen. Certainly not her daughters, who were growing up beside tranquil Lake Constance into well-fed, good-natured, hard-working peasant girls in their grandmother's care; nor her husband, who would get over his jealousy and the pain of separation all the quicker the less he saw of her; nor herself, because she would never bring herself to spend her days among apple trees and clothes lines as a clogs-wearing Thurgovian housewife.

And she had realised something else: that she hadn't left Bottighofen because she wanted to sing. It was the other way round: she wanted to sing in order to keep away from places like Bottighofen. It was far from true that she had pursued a grand objective in life. She had always known what she did *not* want, that was all. She had never aspired to be an obedient child, or an attractive teenager, or a desirable girlfriend, or a dependable spouse, or a prudent housewife, or a loving mother. That was why she had always sat on steps and sung.

She had declined all the puppet roles the world had offered her. In that respect she had been inflexible and strong, but as soon as she was expected to write herself a part that suited her, she was as much at a loss as most people and surrendered to force of circumstance by making the best of things from day to day.

So Laura stayed on at Maria Juarez's hat shop for year after year, selling hats to foreigners, and every few months she sang in a music café in the guise of Agneta, Carmen or Aisha. Although this was a defeat compared to the ambitions of her youth, it was an elegant one; after all, she was answerable to no one for the colour of her underclothes and was free to go whenever and wherever she wanted. She had no ties – no one was gagging or binding her, though she ought really to have counted herself lucky she wasn't sent packing, because times were hard. The music cafés had few paying customers and Maria Juarez's hat shop was doing less and less business.

This changed almost overnight in the summer of 1940, when the city was suddenly inundated with people from all over Europe. After the German army descended on northern France, millions of French people fled into the so-called free zone, together with several hundred thousand refugees from the Nazis who had previously taken refuge in northern France and now thronged southwards in search of a ship that would take them overseas and out of the clutches of their would-be murderers.

Every train from the north that pulled into Saint-Charles Station sent another batch of new arrivals streaming down the big flight of steps and into the Canebière. A few of them were smartly dressed and employed uniformed porters to carry their bags to the taxis, but most were down-at-heel and carried battered cardboard suitcases tied up with string. Fear, deprivation and exhaustion were written on their faces, and rich and poor alike were consumed by the question of how long the nest egg concealed somewhere about their person would last.

Overall, however, the new arrivals brought money into the city. Every incoming train increased the demand for food, accommodation and articles in daily use, and because supplies were short, prices went sky-high. Maria Juarez's hat shop benefited from the fact that many refugees, having lost their hats en route, took advantage of their temporary breather to look around for replacements that would make them feel relatively human again. The bell over the shop door never stopped ringing. Business was booming, so the busy bees in the workroom turned out ladies' and gentlemen's headwear from morning to night. And because most of the customers were foreigners who spoke little French, Laura d'Oriano was more indispensable than ever.

What was more, the music cafés were crowded again. Laura got as many engagements as she wanted – in fact there were nights when she appeared on-stage in three different establishments and in three different guises: Agneta the Copenhagen Lily, Carmen the Rose of Seville and Aisha the Queen of Tripoli.

The money she earned seemed to evaporate. Life in Marseille had become expensive and anything she could spare she sent, as usual, to Bottighofen. Since Emil refused to accept her remittances, she addressed them to her mother-in-law, who reciprocated every few months by sending her, without comment, photographs of her two daughters in which they beamed at the camera and showed off their chubby cheeks and blond plaits. Laura appreciated this unspoken gesture of feminine solidarity, but she also interpreted it as an indication that the girls were doing well and that she shouldn't take it into her head to reappear in Bottighofen.

Laura turned 29 in the summer of 1940. She celebrated her birthday alone in her old room in the Vieux-Port. Her father, who had aged somewhat, let her have her own way in every respect save one – she wasn't allowed to bring any gentlemen visitors home – and her mother had also come to terms with her refusal to be a puppet. Unless, of course, it was puppet-like to be gradually turning into an old maid who still lived with her parents, had affairs that would never lead anywhere and had for years been doing a job originally meant to be a temporary solution.

Laura did not feel uncomfortable in this role, and it is quite conceivable that she would have continued to play it for a long time to come, had not Italy declared war on France and Mussolini ordered his compatriots home to the fatherland. Laura's parents packed their bags and summoned their four youngest children to join them, then sold their apartment and took the ferry to Rome – not in obedience to Mussolini but to avoid detention by the French police, who were no longer issuing residents' permits to Italian citizens.

Laura remained behind on her own. She was not expecting any immediate trouble with the authorities, being Swiss by marriage, but she had to move out of the Vieux-Port apartment and find somewhere else to live. This proved difficult because all the hotels and boarding houses were booked solid and the rents of even the draughtiest bedsits had risen to absurd heights.

Out on the street one Sunday morning in July 1940, Laura went off to work with all her worldly possessions in her shabby but expensive old suitcase. Madame looked stern and the busy bees whispered together. When Madame took the day's takings to the bank shortly before closing time, one of the busy bees darted out of the workroom, thrust a slip of paper into Laura's hand and whispered that she would be welcome to share her attic until further notice – there was a place for her to sleep there.

Laura gratefully accepted the offer. The attic room was situated on the sixth floor of a house in the Rue du Tapis Vert, and her sleeping place was a decrepit old Empire sofa beside a draughty window. In the middle of the room was a screen with the busy bee's bed behind it. The two women went to bed early. Then they lay in the dark, shielded from one another's gaze, and talked for a long time, woman to woman. They did so the following night, and it wasn't long before they became friends of whom each knew everything about the other. When the next week's rent fell due, Laura paid half.

Six months went by in this way.

On the afternoon of 10 January 1941, the hat shop received a visit from a rotund little man whose quiff was only one of his resemblances to Napoleon Bonaparte. When Madame welcomed him to her establishment he answered curtly in Italian and looked around for help, so she indicated Laura with a sweeping gesture of her plump arm and withdrew to the workroom.

Laura had detected from the first words the little man uttered that he spoke Italian with a French accent, but she played along and asked him in Italian what he wanted.

I need a black felt hat for the winter months, said the little man. Size 54, please.

Laura took an assortment of felt hats from the shelf, put them down on the counter and explained their special features while the little man tried on one after another.

I'll take this one, he said eventually. Please don't wrap it, I'll wear it right away. You speak very good Italian, by the way.

My parents are Italian, said Laura.

Then you're bound to have noticed that I myself come from Corsica, said the little man.

Laura nodded.

My Italian is terrible, but you seem to have a talent for languages. I'm told you speak Greek, Turkish and Russian. Is that true?

It is.

What about German?

Laura did not reply. She eyed the man with heightened attention.

What about German, signora?

Sorry, I don't speak German.

It doesn't matter, said the little man. I have to speak with you, signora. It's extremely important.

I'm listening.

Not here. I'll expect you in the bar of the Hotel Select at seven o'clock this evening.

What do you take me for, monsieur? said Laura. Nobody orders me to meet them in a hotel bar, least of all …

Not so loud, said the little man.

… least of all a fake Italian who won't tell me his name.

I strongly advise you to come to the Select this evening, signora. Your resident's permit runs out soon, did you know that?

Laura nodded.

You shouldn't let that happen, you could be arrested in the street for no reason. Incidentally, you've yet to notify the Swiss consulate of your new address – better remedy that deficiency. Do you have a licence to appear on the stage?

What sort of licence?

For public, commercial appearances on-stage. Decree dated 12 November of last year.

I didn't know about that.

You should get your papers in order quickly and be very careful in the meantime, signora. Come to the Select at seven. I can help you.

I still don't know who you are.

It's better for you not to know my name.

I don't make appointments with unknown men.

Signora …

I insist.

My name is Simon Cotoni, I'm an inspector with the Directorate of Territorial Surveillance in Nice. Tell no one of my visit and never mention my name. What do I owe you for the hat?

That'll be 14 francs 50 centimes, monsieur.

The little man put 15 francs on the counter.

Seven this evening, he said. Be on time.

When Laura pushed the receipt and the change across the counter, he deposited a sheaf of banknotes beside them.

Those are for you, to cover your immediate expenses. Take them, quickly. Your rent in the Rue du Tapis Vert is due again. Send something more to Switzerland, if you like. And not a word about my visit, not to anyone. Understand?

Laura counted the money after the little man had gone. It was 300 francs. Enough for a week.

Then came the year when Felix Bloch attended a conference at the Massachusetts Institute of Technology in Boston and met a young physicist named Lore Misch, who had gained her doctorate at Göttingen with a thesis on X-rays and had fled to

America in 1938. They got married on 14 March 1940. Having initially lived in Felix's bachelor bungalow on the campus, they then moved to a pretty little house on Emerson Road in Palo Alto. On 16 January of the following year their twins George and Daniel were born. Looking after two new-borns in the first year was hard on their young mother, who was soon in urgent need of a rest. Felix had already made preparations to spend summer 1942 with his family at Carpinteria Beach, south of Santa Barbara, when Robert Oppenheimer called and asked him to participate in his summer seminar at Berkeley.

Not this time, said Felix.

It's important, said Oppenheimer.

I'm sorry, said Felix. We've already packed the bathing costumes and the nappies – and paid a deposit on the beach house.

Then unpack the nappies and the bathing costumes, said Oppenheimer, and don't worry about the deposit. Give my regards to Lore and tell her I'll make it up to her.

I can't do that. We've had a tough winter.

I'm sorry. It's about neutrons, Bloch. I need you at that seminar. Participation is compulsory. I can't say more on the phone.

What are you getting at?

Listen, the seminar will take place whether we like it or not. If we don't do it, the others will. It's us or them, Bloch, get my meaning? The others are probably hard at it. There's no time to lose.

I understand.

It's President Roosevelt's personal wish that you attend. We start at the beginning of July. A few of our old friends from Copenhagen days will also be there.

Who?

Hans Bethe and Edward Teller. Van Fleck. My assistant Robert Serber. And a few of my doctoral candidates. Didn't Teller take his PhD under you in Leipzig?

No, under Heisenberg. On ionised hydrogen molecules. With me he only made tea. In the ping pong cellar.

And that was how it came about that Felix Bloch spent the summer of 1942 on the top floor of LeConte Hall in Berkeley, not on the beach at Santa Barbara. The seminar was a brainstorming session aimed at discovering, purely hypothetically, whether it was possible in principle to manufacture weapons of immense destructive power by releasing binding energy in the interior of atoms.

The nine men who took part in the seminar were the leading scientists in this field. The meetings were secret and took place in a top-floor room to which only Oppenheimer possessed a key. Two french windows led out on to a balcony screened off with wire mesh for security reasons.

On the morning of the first day, Robert Oppenheimer set the stage by describing the hitherto biggest and most disastrous explosion ever attributable to human agency, which had occurred on 6 December 1917 in the port of Halifax, Nova Scotia. The detonation of 5,000 tons of TNT aboard a French munitions ship had resulted in a gigantic fireball and a pressure wave that flattened an urban area of two-and-a-half square miles and killed 2,000 people. When silence descended on Halifax once more, a mushroom-shaped cloud of smoke rose into the sky.

The destructive power of the explosion had been immense, but a uranium bomb – of this the scientists attending the seminar were convinced from the very first day – would be ten times as powerful. The mushroom cloud would rise ten times as high and the fireball would be ten times bigger, and the energy released would be sufficient to wipe out a big city like Berlin or Hamburg or Rome, not just a small one like Halifax. And it would not kill 2,000 people, but 20,000 or 200,000.

The participants in the seminar quickly realised that it would be a technological challenge to make the bomb small and manageable enough for a B29 bomber to transport it to its destination over a long distance, but it did seem fundamentally practicable. In a preliminary memorandum, Oppenheimer stated that a container with a diameter of 20 centimetres filled with uranium 235 would be sufficient for a rapid chain reaction, although the detonating mechanism and casing would naturally be many times greater in volume and weight.

The nine men on the top floor of LeConte Hall spent the whole summer making calculations and planning their hypothetical bomb. It was essential that they decide on the minimum amount of uranium 235 needed to initiate a reliable chain reaction. One problem was the firing mechanism, which had to be constructed in such a way that the mass would become critical as fast as possible and the chain reaction would run its course completely without being interrupted by a premature detonation.

Felix Bloch's special task was to investigate the problem of neutron diffusion; he had to determine the behaviour of fast neutrons in a chain reaction. Some questions he was able to settle, many remained open, but no fundamental difficulties of a theoretical or technological nature arose during the seminar. The bomb was achievable; all the participants agreed on that.

Doubts were expressed on only one occasion. That was one morning in July, when Edward Teller limped into the conference room, asked Oppenheimer if he might have the floor, and disclosed his fear that the heat of an atomic explosion could ignite the whole of the earth's atmosphere, a conflagration that would spread to the water in the oceans and extinguish all life on the planet.

This announcement came as a shock. Oppenheimer, Bloch and Bethe temporarily abandoned their calculations and pored over the new problem. It was a known fact that hydrogen became unstable at high temperatures, as did nitrogen, which constitutes 78 per cent of our atmosphere. The question was, what temperature would have to be generated by a chain reaction to set the earth on fire?

Edward Teller was the first person to entertain this idea, to which no one knew the answer. Oppenheimer deputed Bethe to check Teller's calculations. A few days later, Bethe sounded the all clear: the possibility of a global conflagration of air and water was next to non-existent. No such chain reaction could be set off, even by an extreme initial temperature, because the atomic nuclei in air and water were too far apart and the loss of energy would thus be far too great.

Bethe could offer no guarantee, however, and one or two of the scientists continued to harbour doubts. Robert Oppenheimer himself breathed a sigh of relief, because recent events had more than ever convinced him that the bomb was essential in order to bring Hitler to his knees. In Russia a few days previously, German troops had attacked Stalingrad on their way to the oilfields of the Caucasus, and in the Atlantic the U-boat U201 had sunk the unarmed British passenger steamer Avila Star.

The seminar resumed and everyone went on with their work.

Summer drew to a close. The seminar was enjoyable, and the debates continued to be lively. Late one afternoon in August, when the setting sun was shining into the room through the french windows, there occurred an incident which Oppenheimer's assistant Robert Serber would remember for the rest of his days. Oppenheimer broke in on the discussion.

Jesus, he said, look at that.

The entire room was steeped in shadows cast by the steel netting suspended over the balcony to screen its occupants from view. Walls and desks, chairs and stacks of paper – even the atomic physicists' hands and faces – were tattooed with the netting's dark, diamond-shaped pattern.

12

On the afternoon of 7 June 1941, Laura d'Oriano was sitting in the cross-country bus from Toulouse to Mont-de-Marsan. It was a hot day, and the bus was heading through vineyards and fields of grain towards the sun, which was already low in the western sky. All the vehicle's sliding windows were open and the curtains fluttered in the breeze. Laura, wearing a headscarf, was reading a book. In the luggage net above her was a small travelling bag; she had left her handsome but conspicuous old suitcase in Marseille.

The driver eyed her in his rear-view mirror. He may well have taken her for a war widow from Toulouse going to see her husband's family about his will, or a primary schoolteacher visiting her parents in the country and passing the time with some Verlaine or Stendhal.

If policemen had boarded the bus and conducted a spot check, Laura would have produced her new identity card from her handbag and identified herself as Louise Fremont, French citizen resident in Paris, born Marseille, 27 September 1912. Marital status: single. Height: 5 ft 3 ins. Occupation: singer and dancer. Meanwhile, she would have studiously avoided looking at her travelling bag, sewn into the lining of which were 7,000 francs in small notes and an assortment of ration cards.

The bus, which was quite full when it left Toulouse, had gradually emptied; now that it was nearing the restricted coastal zone, Laura was the only remaining passenger. The driver, having formed his own picture of her, had ceased to take any notice of her. At the last stop but two before the demarcation line, a wine-growing village named Aire-sur-l'Adour, she got out and found herself in a narrow main street lined with closed shops between which small side streets led off to right and left. Further on, church bells were ringing for Mass. The cobblestones were still warm from the afternoon sun.

When the bus drove off, a gaunt old peasant with a red nose and a chin frosted with grey stubble waved to her from the other side of the street. He hailed her loudly and delightedly as 'ma petite Louise', as if she were his favourite niece or a granddaughter, then crossed the street, gripped Laura by the shoulders and kissed her firmly on both cheeks. Taking her bag, he put an arm round her and quickly shepherded her down a side street that terminated in a farm track leading out into a vineyard.

Parked in the vineyard was a red tractor. The peasant settled himself behind the wheel and Laura scrambled on to the small seat over the right rear wheel. They drove to the far side of the vineyard, whence another farm track led to another vineyard, and another, and another. Laura and the peasant spent two hours lurching and juddering westwards across the vineyards of Aquitaine until they had crossed the demarcation line and disappeared into a sparse pine forest that extended for dozens of sandy, marshy kilometres to the Atlantic Ocean and up to the Gironde.

The following afternoon, with hair tousled and shoes badly scuffed, Laura turned up in Bordeaux on her own. She went for a preliminary walk in the city centre, bought herself some new shoes and had her hair done, then drank a coffee in a pavement café. When evening came she made her way to Madame Blanc's boarding house at No. 4 Rue du Quai Bourgeois, the address of which she had noted on a slip of paper. This establishment was situated on the banks of the Garonne, not far from the harbour. Some rooms were still vacant and the prices were low. There were a lot of vacant rooms in Bordeaux now that the refugees had fled from the advancing Wehrmacht.

Laura gave her first performance at a café called Le Singe Dansant the following Saturday. She wore her old Cossack costume, showed her garter and sang *Bayushki Bayu*, and the sailors in the audience duly burst into tears. The only difference between this and earlier performances was that the sailors wore Italian naval uniform because they belonged to the crews of the 32 submarines based under German command in Bordeaux harbour, which were preparing to take part in the Battle of the Atlantic. They had to be back on board their submarines by midnight, so none of them was waiting for Laura when she left the café by the back door and emerged into the street at half past twelve.

For all that, her task proved to be simple – pure puppetry. It was so easy, it would have saddened Laura if she hadn't felt so relieved about it. All she had to do the next day was give herself a hint of Slav cheekbones in her make-up mirror and drape the Cossack jacket around her shoulders, and the Italian sailors recognised her as she strolled past the harbour entrance on her Sunday walk.

She didn't even have to sway her hips to turn the youngsters' heads. It was quite enough for her to pause on the Quai du Sénégal and put a cigarette between her lips. When she felt in her handbag for some matches, a whole bevy of them dashed over to light it for her and show off in various ways, and when she thanked them in flawless Italian, wiggled her fingers at them over her shoulder as she walked on, said a casual *arrivederci* and flashed her white teeth, their delight knew no bounds.

It was all so predictable: a game as old as time, but Laura played it because it suited her purpose. From that Sunday onwards she was treated as a celebrity by the Italian submariners. If she ordered a Martini in a pavement café, it was automatically paid for. If she was carrying shopping bags, an admirer always volunteered to carry them back to the Rue du Quai Bourgeois for her. And if she sat down on a park bench in the Botanical Gardens with her Stendhal or Verlaine, someone always asked if he might join her for a moment.

So Laura got into conversation with the submariners. Again and again she had to admit that she wasn't a genuine Cossack in real life, but a respectable schoolmaster's daughter from Marseille, and that her name wasn't really Anoushka but Louise – Loulou to her friends – and that she spoke such good Italian because her mother was Italian. And when she abruptly changed the subject and asked the submariners whether life underwater was hard, they would all draw a deep breath and start talking.

They told her of the heat on board, and the stale air, and the ominous silence when the submarine turned off its electric motors and lay on the seabed amid centuries-old wrecks, compelled to lie doggo for days in order to elude the enemy hydrophone operators. They told her of the unspeakable bliss of surfacing, when they could once more stand on deck in the fresh air, faces spattered with spray, and of their malign jubilation when they landed a direct hit and 10,000 tons of enemy shipping went down with all hands.

It was all very simple. The sailors ran off at the mouth all by themselves, and it would never have occurred to any of them that Laura had been interrogating them. The fact was, she seldom if ever asked a question, merely encouraged her companions to go on by uttering sporadic exclamations of surprise and admiration – against which, like all men, they were defenceless. So they talked and talked. They told Laura how one got a submarine to submerge and surface, and where the air to breathe came from, and where the bunks for the crew were situated. They told her how many submarines were lying in the harbour basin – only 32 at present, but not all in a combat-ready condition, and Italian boats only, no German – and they told her the names of the boats in which they had already served.

On a few occasions it so happened that a submarine would be entering or leaving harbour while Laura and a male companion were sitting near the harbour entrance. Then she would get him to point out the conning tower and entry hatch, take note of the ballast tanks along the sides and the retractable anti-aircraft gun on the deck, memorise its calibre and greet all she was told with a polite nod of interest. But when she suggested a tour of the closely guarded submarine base, her companions regretfully shook their heads and begged her pardon in phrases learnt by heart. Top secret. Walls have ears. A submarine's most potent and important weapon is its invisibility. A submarine whose location or course the enemy knows in advance is as good as lost.

Laura memorised everything, and in the evening she made notes in her room. Two or three times a week she wrote letters to a friend in Toulouse whom she had never met. That was the extent of her duties. On Saturday nights she sang her Cossack songs at the Singe Dansant, and on Sundays she took a bus to the sea, to Lacanau or Cap Ferret, and went for long, lonely walks across the dunes. That summer in Aquitaine was long and peaceful. The war was far away and the weather fine, and a cool sea breeze was always blowing inland. When a sailor recognised Laura at the bus stop on her way back to Bordeaux, she sometimes accepted his invitation to a plate of *moules frites*.

But out at sea the war still raged. Whole fleets of vessels were sunk and tens of thousands of young sailors sent to a watery grave. It is conceivable that some of the latter had been companions of Laura's, for an exceptionally large number of Bordeaux-based Italian submarines failed to return from patrol that summer of 1941.

The *Glauco* sailed for the Mediterranean on 24 June, was attacked in the Strait of Gibraltar three days later and sank west of Tangier. Out of a crew of 50, 8 were drowned and 42 taken prisoner.

On 4 July the *Michaele Bianchi* set off on a mission, objective unknown, but was sunk in the Gironde estuary with all 60 men on board.

The *Maggiore Baracca* was sunk off Gibraltar on 8 September. Of her crew, 28 drowned and 32 were taken prisoner.

The *Guglielmo Marconi* sailed early in October 1941. For unknown reasons she sank off the coast of Portugal with all 60 crew members on board.

In October, Aquitaine was suddenly assailed by autumnal storms and weeks of rain. Laura quit her engagement at the Singe Dansant and took leave of her landlady. Then, carrying her suitcase, she made her way southwards into the great pine forest. The peasant was doubtless waiting for her on the other side next day, complete with red tractor.

Although the Italian submarine flotilla based at Bordeaux continued to go out on as many patrols as before, it sustained no more losses in the months that followed.

ॐ

Having been built in theory, the atom bomb had now to be built in practice.

Felix Bloch had had no contact with his physicist friends in Germany since the beginning of the war, but he had undoubtedly read in the paper that Heisenberg and von Weizsäcker were working on a uranium machine in Berlin. He may also have learnt that, during their last visit to Niels Bohr in Copenhagen, they had spoken of the imminence of victory and the biological necessity for war. He may furthermore have known that von Weizsäcker had filed a patent for a plutonium bomb in Berlin, and that the German armed forces were amassing as much uranium as possible during their depredations in Europe. At latest since Pearl Harbor and at the very latest since Stalingrad, it had been obvious to any rational person that Germany resembled a chess player with two rooks fewer on the board than their opponent; but it was equally clear that an atom bomb would bring the two rooks back into play. And possibly a queen as well.

Such was the situation when, on a spring day in 1943, Robert Oppenheimer came to Palo Alto and asked Felix Bloch to dispense with a summer vacation on the beach and accompany him into the New Mexico desert, there to work on building an atom bomb at a secret location not marked on any map. Not just for the summer but for the rest of the year and an indefinite period thereafter.

We do not know what Bloch's immediate response was, nor whether Oppenheimer made his request at the university or at home on Emerson Road, nor whether the meeting took place in the morning, afternoon or evening. We do not know if Bloch's wife Lore was present, or whether the twins were already asleep or still awake. We do not know if the conversation took place on the veranda or inside the house, or if they went for a walk to avoid unwelcome eavesdroppers.

We do not know, either, if it was a short or a long conversation, a brief man-to-man dialogue or a passionate debate between two scholars arguing about the root purpose of their science. We know nothing about this conversation, which must have been the weightiest and most momentous in Felix's life because it required him to find an answer – yes or no? – to the question of whether his conscience would permit him, in the service of liberty, humanity and world peace, not only to reflect on the most terrible killing machine in human history but actually to build it; and whether – yes or no? – a European Jew like himself was entitled or even obliged to combat the Nazis' genocide by all available means including the manufacture of a weapon of mass destruction whose egalitarian efficiency would surpass that of Fritz Haber's poison gas many times over.

We know nothing about this question of conscience because Felix Bloch devoted not a word to it anywhere in his writings, which comprise many thousands of pages. None of his carefully filed essays, letters and memoranda, which he bequeathed to Stanford Library for the benefit of posterity, contains a word about the atom bomb. The subject is so thoroughly avoided – one is tempted to assume that every relevant scrap of paper was carefully removed – that there is no mention even of

Oppenheimer's name, although 'Oppie' was for ten years his closest friend and scientific confidant.

What mattered most about their conversation can, for all that, be definitely ascertained: first, that it actually took place, and, second, that Felix Bloch answered both questions of conscience in the affirmative. If he wondered aloud whether three centuries of research into physics were really to culminate in the building of an atomic bomb, Oppenheimer would have dismissed his misgivings by remarking that, setting aside any philosophical arguments, all that mattered in the current geostrategic situation was who got the bomb first: Hitler or the United States.

This conversation, or something like it, must have taken place, because early in summer 1943 – possibly at the end of June, when the summer vacation began – Lore and Felix Bloch packed their bags and set off for the New Mexico desert with their twin daughters, who were then two-and-a-half years old.

For security reasons, Oppenheimer had instructed Bloch not to buy tickets all the way through to Santa Fe, but to change at Bakersfield, Albuquerque and Lamy and buy new tickets there en route. The journey took 44 hours in all, and it was not until late on the morning of the third day that Felix Bloch and his family arrived in the old capital of New Mexico.

At that time Santa Fe was still a peaceful little Spanish town from way back. In the main square, old trees shaded cast-iron park benches on which men of all ages took their siesta at all times of the day. Little groups of dark-haired young women with crimson lips and colourful dresses paraded around the obelisk in the middle of the park, shyly on the lookout for potential admirers. Cars were a rarity, and horses and mules were tethered outside the La Fonda Hotel. Children played on the steps of St

Francis Cathedral, and Indian women seated on the veranda of the governor's palace with gaudy shawls swathing the babies on their backs offered pottery and jewellery for sale.

In summer 1943 the sleepy town was invaded by an unusual number of strangers. Mostly pale-faced urbanites from the north, few of them could speak Spanish and many spoke English with European accents. Many came on their own but some were couples with children, and they brought with them, in addition to their suitcases, curious items such as brooms, buckets, mirrors, pot plants and baby buggies.

Waiting for these newcomers every morning on East Palace Avenue was an old school bus inscribed 'US Army' in bright red lettering. A brawny GI helped the ladies to load their household goods and amiably permitted them to order him around. When everything had been safely stowed on board, he heaved himself in behind the wheel, secured the door handle to the dashboard with a length of string, engaged first gear and drove off.

The bus was reserved for Robert Oppenheimer's guests, over 1,000 of whom made the two-hour trip to Los Alamos in the early summer of 1943. Most of them were physicists and their families, but there were also chemists, explosives and ballistics experts, biologists, precision engineers, electrical engineers and metallurgists. The red dirt road ran north-west, past lilac rocks and ochre crags, to the former boarding school for boys at Los Alamos, which stood on the lip of a huge, extinct volcano 2,300 metres above sea level. Visible in the distance were the southernmost foothills of the Sangre de Cristo Range and, nearer at hand, the ominous black basalt shape of the Black Mesa table mountain. There were Indian pueblos among the rocks. Many were ruined and deserted, others still inhabited.

Here and there, red peppers were suspended from the mud walls to dry, and yellow, blue, white and black maize cobs lay in the sun-baked yards.

The road crossed a narrow timber bridge spanning the red waters of the Rio Grande before climbing steeply past flowering cacti and rattlesnakes that wriggled off into the desert sagebrush. Coming suddenly into view around a bend, huge, roaring US Army bulldozers shrouded in clouds of dust gnawed away at the lilac rocks and ochre crags to level the road for heavy traffic.

The bus toiled uphill for an eternity. When it reached the lip of the crater, the road led straight on to Los Alamos, which had within a few weeks lost all resemblance to a boys' boarding school and grown into a small, hutted town housing 1,000 inhabitants and enclosed within a radius of six kilometres by a continuous barbed-wire fence. There were two gates, one in the east and one in the west, each forming a roadblock manned by military policemen armed with submachine guns. They checked the passengers and peered silently into the bus. Then a sergeant gave the signal to drive on.

Oppenheimer was waiting to welcome the new arrivals when the bus pulled up outside the former school. He slapped the men on the back and asked their wives how the journey had gone, said 'Yes ... yes, yes ... yes ... ' and lit cigarettes all round, then beckoned to some soldiers, who picked up the newcomers' luggage and allocated them their accommodation.

Felix and Lore Bloch were housed not far from the water tower in Apartment House T124, a rapidly erected timber building painted lime-green and containing four flats. The kitchens were equipped with soot-stained wood-burning stoves from army stocks, the bedrooms with camp beds. The coverlets and sheets were emblazoned in black with the acronym 'USED', which stood for 'United States Engineer Detachment'.

The Blochs were not lonely in Los Alamos. The walls were thin and their neighbours were old friends. Living next door to them on the ground floor was Edward Teller, Felix's erstwhile tea-maker in the Leipzig ping pong cellar, who had alarmed the secret summer seminar at Berkeley with his vision of a global conflagration. Billetted upstairs was Robert Brode, whom Felix had got to know as a student in Göttingen and later as a member of the 'Monday Evening Journal Club' at Berkeley. Living nearby were Robert Oppenheimer and Hans Bethe, and, somewhat further away, the Zurich physicist Hans Staub and the mathematician John von Neumann, with whom Felix had studied at the ETH.

Most of them were accompanied by their wives, many by their children, and they all realised that by working in Los Alamos they had become privy to a state secret of the first order and would have to remain so until the war ended. Their average age was 29. Hardly any of them were over 40, and the birthrate at Los Alamos was far above the national average throughout the war years. Oppenheimer, Bloch, Serber and Bethe were among the oldest, at least until the arrival of Enrico Fermi and Niels Bohr.

They had all come to work; Los Alamos had no pensioners or invalids, idlers, artists or speculators, ne'er-do-wells, parasites or pickpockets, malingerers, legacy hunters or shirkers. When the sirens wailed at seven am, the men hurried to the laboratories situated in closely guarded areas on the outskirts of the settlement. The children went to school or were taken to a crèche, the women worked in administrative offices, canteens, libraries or schools. A summer camp atmosphere prevailed.

More experts arrived daily, as did army trucks transporting heavy equipment from the furthest corners of the United States. In July 1943 alone, the four biggest and most efficient particle accelerators in the world arrived in Los Alamos and were installed in specially-built huts on concrete foundations laid for the purpose.

Felix Bloch was working with Edward Teller and John von Neumann on a detonating mechanism in which the radioactive isotope was shaped like a hollow sphere and compressed very quickly by implosion so as to attain the critical mass required to trigger a complete chain reaction without premature detonation. Their task was to theoretically ascertain and experimentally prove that this was possible. Calculating the pressure waves travelling inwards from all directions proved to be extremely difficult, mathematically speaking. In the absence of electronic calculators, it took several weeks.

Once the calculations had been completed, the experimental proof followed. Felix and his friends made small bombs out of hollow metal spheres surrounded by explosives, took them down into a steep-sided canyon and placed them on a thick, ferroconcrete slab. They then withdrew to a specially constructed gun emplacement and put their fingers in their ears.

When the thunderous echoes had died away and the smoke had cleared, they emerged and gathered up the fragments of the metal spheres. The earliest experiments were discouraging. The spheres had not been evenly compressed but reduced to fragments of the most unpredictable shape.

So the men returned to their laboratory, laid aside the spheres and designed tubular bombs in the hope that this would reduce the countervailing pressure waves by one dimension.

At six pm the sirens signalled knocking-off time and everyone went home. In the evenings the inhabitants of Los Alamos met for cocktails in the former boys' school. Being academics, they were accustomed to social life in university cities. There were few forms of entertainment in the New Mexico desert, so they organised an endless succession of concerts, film shows, amateur dramatics and dances. Dances were sometimes performed for the scientists by Indians who worked for them by day as furnacemen, manual labourers or domestic servants. On one occasion a group of theatre-mad physicists staged *Arsenic and Old Lace* with Oppenheimer playing the first corpse in the window seat and Edward Teller the second. At midnight everyone made their way home along the gloomy, unlit dirt roads. When the moon was shining, the pines cast dark shadows.

Silence reigned at night in Los Alamos, whose residents slept protected by the barbed-wire fence surrounding the settlement. Soldiers noiselessly patrolled the perimeter and coyotes howled in the distance. From time to time a shot would ring out. On nights like this Felix Bloch lay awake for a long time, wondering how he had found himself letting off miniature bombs in remote ravines, like a schoolboy. It astonished him that he, who had once aspired to do something peaceful and militarily useless in life, should have wound up behind barbed wire. He sometimes wondered what the barbed wire was protecting, Los Alamos from the world or the world from Los Alamos.

His neighbour Edward Teller, too, was often awake until late at night. It was his habit to spend the small hours playing the Steinway grand his wife had bought at a hotel auction in Chicago and somehow contrived to transport to Los Alamos. A brilliant and enthusiastic pianist, Teller was forever playing Franz Liszt's Hungarian Rhapsody No. 12 in the autumn of 1943. Its strains must have penetrated the thin walls of

Apartment House T124 and emerged into the nocturnal hush of the surrounding plateau, audible as far away as the hills and the dark canyons in which the Indians' deserted old pueblos slept their millennial sleep.

13

When Laura d'Oriano returned to the unoccupied zone on 12 October 1941, she went straight to Nice and called on Inspector Cotoni at his office, which was situated opposite the railway station on Avenue Georges Clemenceau. To her surprise, the little Corsican not only stood up and saluted when she came in, but clapped her on the back like someone congratulating a soldier who has distinguished himself in battle.

The Directorate of Territorial Surveillance is extremely satisfied with your work, he said, handing her an envelope containing 7,000 francs. General de Gaulle has asked us to express his personal thanks.

Thank you, said Laura, pocketing the envelope.

May I request you not to leave town in the immediate future? We may soon have another assignment for you.

She nodded and turned to go, but Cotoni caught her by the elbow.

Tell me, Laura, are you feeling all right?

Yes, thanks for asking.

You'll think I'm being indiscreet, he said, but there's a look on your face I know from my wife.

Very observant of you, said Laura.

Yes, said Cotoni, except that my wife only has that look

once a month. You, on the other hand, had it the last time we met. And the time before that, if I remember rightly.

Can't be helped. It's a woman's lot.

How long has it been?

A year, maybe 18 months. Laura shrugged her shoulders. It varies in intensity.

Then take off your coat and sit down, said Cotoni, picking up the phone. This needs to be dealt with. I can't use you in this condition.

On 19 October he drove Laura in his official car to the Hospital of the Holy Virgin, where she underwent surgery the next day. The exact nature of her trouble cannot be ascertained, but she stated under interrogation a few weeks later that, because the surgeon had already opened her up, he removed her uterus as well. This had seemed to cure her symptoms.

Inspector Cotoni settled the hospital bill for 7,000 francs. Laura spent 11 days recovering in the hospital after the operation, then continued her convalescence in a hotel room. Cotoni looked in on her daily, bringing her fruit and fresh milk. He sometimes took her out for a meal and insisted on her ordering a big steak.

Meat and milk were scarce at this time because the majority of agricultural produce went to the German forces of occupation. However, October 1941 was also the time when German tanks first became bogged down in Russian mud. In the Mediterranean, Churchill was making preparations for a campaign against Italy, and in the Atlantic, President Roosevelt's US Navy warships received orders to fire on any German or Italian vessels without warning if found in waters 'deemed necessary for national defence'.

When Laura had recovered her strength, Inspector Cotoni

summoned her to his office and gave her the details of her next assignment. She was to travel to Italy under a false name and visit the naval bases at Genoa and Naples. In Genoa she was to undertake only a brief reconnaissance, but she would spend six weeks in Naples and submit regular reports of what ships came and went.

On 6 December 1941, Cotoni took Laura to meet a go-between named Ćosić. The latter drove her in a silver-grey Panhard to Briançon, the highest town in the far east of the French Alps, only 10 kilometres and a 500-metre climb from the Italian frontier.

There they took two adjacent rooms in the Auberge de la Paix and lived like tourists. They went for walks in the snowy woods and strolled through the old quarter of the town. Ćosić bought Laura a Norwegian sweater, woollen skiing trousers and a pair of climbing boots. They bought picture postcards from kiosks and drank coffee on sunlit terraces. In the evenings they dined on steak in the hotel restaurant and shared a bottle of good wine.

Five days went by in this way. On the second of these, great excitement reigned in the little town because the Japanese attack on Pearl Harbor had been reported on the radio. There was more excitement on the fifth day because Germany had declared war on the United States.

That night, 11 December 1941, Laura spent a long time looking down into the street from her window. She was wearing her new Norwegian sweater and her woollen skiing trousers. She had already said goodbye to Ćosić, who had given her a forged Italian identity card in the name of Laura Fantini, a forged driver's licence, a membership card for the National Federation of Fascist House-Owners' Associations and a bulging envelope containing 9,000 Italian lire, together with a warning to spend them sparingly so as not to arouse unnecessary attention.

Shortly before midnight, a young man wearing a red bobble hat appeared in the street. He loitered beneath Laura's window, rubbing his hands together as if cold. This was the signal. Laura laced up her climbing boots and clumped downstairs, waving to the night porter on the way out as if she were going for a nocturnal sleigh ride or a curling contest. She had no luggage with her.

The young man in the bobble hat neither introduced himself nor asked her name, but led her silently across town to the road leading to the Montgenèvre Pass, where he produced two pairs of snowshoes and two alpenstocks from behind a mound of snow. He showed Laura how to strap on the snowshoes and how to save energy when wading through deep snow. Then he led the way up to the pass, which had been closed for the winter two months previously.

This nocturnal trek across the precipitous pass in deep snow must have taken them between seven and nine hours and been extremely strenuous for Laura, who had seen little snow and few mountains in her life. According to information from the French Meteorological Institute, the night of 11/12 December 1941 was not exceptionally cold, but a strong north-west wind was blowing and some 30 centimetres of snow fell at altitudes of around 1,800 metres.

It must have been at about daybreak when Laura and her mountain guide reached the top of the pass and crossed the border in driving snow before making their way down to the frontier village of Cesana. There they were awaited at the Pensione Croce Bianca by a landlady who didn't ask too many questions and gave Laura a room in which she could rest for a few hours. She entrusted the Norwegian sweater, skiing trousers and climbing boots to her guide, who was to keep them for her until she returned six weeks later and crossed the pass in the opposite direction.

The snowshoes she left behind at the *pensione* as if she had forgotten them. At midday she went to the road leading into town and at 12.20 pm boarded the bus that would transport her out of the mountains and down to Turin's central station in the plain below. There she took the next express to Genoa, and when the Mediterranean came into view and the train pulled into the ancient seaport's Piazza Principe station, she must have felt almost at home once more.

Ćosić had given her a letter of recommendation to a woman named Maria Talia, who ran a small boarding house at No. 2, Via San Donato, on the edge of the old quarter and not far from the harbour. When Laura got there, two men were standing beside a car parked nearby, smoking cigarettes and gesticulating as they talked about football. She paid them no attention.

As Laura would learn two weeks later, the men were members of the Italian secret police. They had been waiting in Via San Donato all day long, having been informed by a counter-espionage agent from Nice that on Friday, 12 December 1941, a female French spy belonging to a certain Ćosić's network would arrive at Maria Talia's boarding house. Once Laura had disappeared inside, they got into the car and kept watch on the entrance. There was no back door – they had checked that afternoon. They had dinner at the restaurant on the corner and maintained surveillance on the street through the window. Then they got back in their car and smoked cigarettes. They were relieved at midnight.

Laura did not reappear until just before nine the next morning. She walked down the Via San Donato, past the Architectural Faculty and the National Theatre, to the street that ran along the waterfront, where she ordered a coffee and a brioche in a bar called the Santa Lucia. She surveyed the harbour basin through the window with noticeable frequency but did not make contact with anyone and spoke only briefly to the waiter.

After that she went back into the city and, patiently shadowed by the two secret policemen, embarked on a lengthy shopping trip. Starting at 9:30, it took in a wide variety of shops and did not end until 12:30, when they closed for the midday break. The first thing she bought, after thoroughly examining various models, was a light 'Il Ponte' holdall. She then acquired an assortment of women's clothes and toilet articles, all of the best quality, and stowed them in her new bag. She made no contact with anyone during these three hours and exchanged only the usual pleasantries with the shop assistants.

On her way back to Via San Donato she stopped at a bakery to buy a *panino al prosciutto crudo*, which she ate in her room. The wrapping paper and the ham rind were retrieved from the wastepaper basket after her departure. She spent Saturday afternoon and evening on the premises. She received no visitors, according to Maria Talia, nor did she make contact with any other resident.

At 9:53 on Sunday morning, 14 December 1941, Laura left the boarding house just as the bells of San Donato were ringing for Mass. She entered the church and sat down in the third to last pew on the left. No one else joined her. She took an active part in the service, apparently being familiar with the hymns and prayers in Italian, and went up to the altar to receive Holy

Communion with other members of the congregation.

After Mass she went down to the harbour, just as she had the previous day, and ordered a coffee and a brioche in the Santa Lucia. Thereafter she went for a walk to the gates of the naval dockyard. The barrier was guarded by two sentries. She spoke to them, but they refused her admittance.

She then returned to the boarding house. Nothing more happened until the evening. At 10:18 pm she emerged, this time carrying her new holdall, and went straight to Piazza Principe station, where she bought a second-class ticket for the night train to Naples. Shortly before the train left she posted a letter in the concourse, whereupon the secret policemen split up. One of them followed her on to the platform and sat down in her compartment when the train pulled out at 11:14 pm; the other opened the mailbox and took possession of the letter. It was in a pink envelope and addressed to Emilio Brayda in Turin.

My dearest,
I'm waiting impatiently for news of you. Please let me hear from you really soon. Knowing me, you'll know that I'll be unhappy otherwise, and I always fear the worst. If you only knew how apprehensive I am! Please write and tell me that all is well, and that you haven't forgotten me. I pray for us every day to the Holy Mother of God and fervently hope that she will hear my prayers.

I kiss and kiss and kiss you,

Your Antonia

The secret policeman took this letter to headquarters and pressed it with a flat iron lying ready for the purpose until the notepaper began to go brown and a second, hitherto invisible message emerged from between lines in pale lettering. Written in a saline solution, it can still be seen in the Italian State Archives.

Genoa Harbour STOP
4 torpedo boats STOP
Cruiser Roma converted into aircraft carrier STOP
Everything very hard to make out STOP
Moving on to Naples FINAL STOP

The overnight train journey to Naples passed off without incident and the train pulled into Napoli Centrale at 10:30 am on Monday, 15 December 1941. As Laura was looking around for a taxi in the station forecourt, a soldier accosted her and invited her to have coffee with him. She declined with thanks, but asked him if the harbour was accessible to civilians. When he was unable to give her any information on the subject, she hailed a cab and got in.

The soldier was subsequently detained and taken to the station's police post for questioning. There he credibly stated that he did not know the woman and had accosted her only because his eye had been caught by her blonde hair and expensive clothes.

The taxi drove straight to the Lombardi, a boarding house in Via Angiporto, where Laura took a room for an indefinite period and paid a month's rent in advance. She spent the ensuing two days strolling through the old quarter of the city and along the waterfront, without contacting anyone.

On the evening of 16 December, Laura went to the cinema and got into conversation with a non-commissioned officer in uniform. He also insisted, when questioned by the police, that he had never seen her before and had not spoken to her of military matters.

After leaving the cinema, Laura went straight back to the boarding house on her own. No further incidents were recorded for the rest of the night.

Early on the morning of 17 December she unexpectedly left the boarding house before daybreak, made her way to the central station and bought a ticket for the 7:30 am express to Rome. Shortly before leaving she posted another letter.

Dear Cousin,

Just a few lines to let you know that my wife is better. We were terribly alarmed by this illness, which is now – thank God – a thing of the past, hopefully for good. Mamma is particularly glad not to have to be so afraid any more.

We hope to see you soon, then I'll tell you everything in greater detail. And how are you? Well, I hope. Do drop us a line, we're always so happy to get your news. A hug from Papa, affectionate regards from everyone in the house, and a cordial handshake from me.

See you soon!

Bartoly

This letter, too, was heated with an iron. Written between the lines were the words:

———

Naples Harbour STOP
1 destroyer, two hospital ships STOP
Immense difficulties, little to be seen STOP
Have to visit my mother FINAL STOP

The train journey from Naples to Rome took three hours six minutes. Not that she knew it, Laura d'Oriano spent the whole journey sitting opposite a secret policeman who handed over to a Roman colleague on arrival at Roma Termini station. The latter tailed her to her parents' apartment at No. 83, Largo Brancaccio. The building remained under surveillance throughout Laura's ten-day visit, but because she seldom went out, received no visitors and wrote no letters, the police reports were meagre and uninformative. We shall never know what went on during this period.

It may be assumed that mother and daughter were over-joyed to see each other again when, after 18 months' separa-tion, Laura rang the doorbell unannounced, and that they hugged and kissed on the threshold and may also have shed a tear or two. It can likewise be assumed that Laura's mother led her into the *salotto*, sat her down on the sofa and plied her with tea or advocaat and biscuits. Doubtless surprised to find her mother all alone in the big apartment, Laura would then have learnt that she had been deserted by one member of the family after another.

Laura's brothers had become ardent fascists overnight during the voyage from Marseille to Rome. Immediately on landing at Ostia they had dashed off to the nearest recruiting office and got themselves assigned to an infantry regiment that was shortly afterwards deployed to East Africa. Since then their mother had received a few invariably uninformative letters in almost identical handwriting from Massawa, Addis Ababa and Adwa.

Once in Rome, the two girls had abandoned their dreams of Russian princes and developed a predilection for smart young Blackshirts in glossy jackboots. One of them had married an accountant in the Ministry of Finance and moved to Palermo, the other had gone off to Greece and become an auxiliary nurse on a hospital ship.

Finally, Laura's father had left for Albania on business a few months earlier, hoping to resuscitate the family finances. He had invested the last of his money in a printing works in Tirana that specialised in banknotes and produced paper money of the highest quality at unbeatable prices – or could have done so it if it had not run out of paper and printer's ink in December 1939 because no suppliers could be found on the war-shattered world market.

The mother may have taken several hours to pass on all this news, and Laura may have asked her to repeat many items twice or more to be sure of having hoisted them in. It is also possible that mother and daughter went to the kitchen together to prepare a meal, possibly a *parmigiana* or a *spaghetti aglio e olio*, and that they entertained one another with family anecdotes until bedtime. They may even, after drinking an advocaat or two, have sung a few songs before going to bed. We can picture them resuming their conversation over breakfast coffee next morning, then doing the housework, playing cards, doing each other's hair, or looking at photos from days gone by.

We can imagine all these things, but we cannot know them for sure because the policemen outside in the street seldom set eyes on Laura for the next ten days. Mother and daughter bought their groceries from the shop on the corner every morning, then disappeared into the flat again. They never went out and received no visitors, not even on Christmas Eve, Christmas Day or Boxing Day.

After ten days the detectives became convinced that the spy Laura d'Oriano would engage in no espionage and visit no contacts in Rome, but had come to the capital for family reasons only.

To eliminate all doubt, however, they did not arrest her on the morning of 27 December 1941, when she returned to the central station with her bag and bought a second-class ticket to Naples. She did not post a letter this time, so the two secret policemen did not split up but sat together in her compartment, just in case she did, after all, meet a contact on the train.

But Laura was still alone when the train left at half past ten, and she remained alone throughout the half-hour it took to get to Littoria, the first intermediate stop. When the train came to a halt she looked out of the window at the passengers alighting. There were an unusually large number of Carabinieri on the platform, all with their submachine guns pointing at the train. Two men in black leather overcoats strode swiftly past them and climbed aboard.

A few seconds later they entered Laura's compartment. They saluted, introduced themselves as Maresciallo Riccardo Pasta and Maresciallo Giovanni Spano and asked her for her papers. Then they arrested her on suspicion of military espionage against the Kingdom of Italy.

Laura was handcuffed, taken back to Rome by the next train and consigned to Regina Coeli, a damp old prison in a 17th-century convent. One wing was reserved for the Ovra, Mussolini's secret police, who kept political prisoners in solitary confinement and interrogated them there.

14

Time went by. In Los Alamos, Felix Bloch and his family lived for days, weeks and months in a town that did not officially exist and was not marked on any map. It had no postal code, no telephone prefix and no sports clubs, and its residents were disenfranchised because they appeared on no electoral roll. They possessed no telephone number and had to submit any letters they wrote to military censorship before sending them off.

Felix tried to regard it as part of a big game of Boy Scouts, having day after day to show his identity card at the same old checkpoint although the same old sentries had known him for ages and greeted him by name. He tried to ignore the fact that, when his wife went shopping in Santa Fe, she was shadowed by secret servicemen recognisable as such from afar in their dark suits, dark hats and grey ties, and their white, always freshly-pressed shirts. He tried to laugh at the fact that he couldn't speak Swiss German with his sons because adolescent military policemen from Oklahoma mistook his Zurich dialect for Hungarian or Esperanto or some other secret language. And at night, when he laid his children down on their camp beds and tucked them up in bedclothes marked 'USED' in black, he called himself to order and sternly reminded himself that it was all in a great and worthy cause.

His experiments with tubular bombs in remote ravines had made progress. The implosion method of detonation had now been perfected. It was complicated but extremely reliable. Oppenheimer was satisfied when Felix Bloch, Edward Teller and John von Neumann presented him with their results at the end of October 1943.

The final problem consisted in getting hold of the 20 to 30 kilograms of uranium 235 that would be needed for the manufacture of an atomic bomb. No such quantity of the artificial isotope yet existed anywhere in the world because of the immense expenditure of energy, raw material and manpower required to isolate it from natural uranium. However, the War Department had conjured up huge factories in widely separated parts of America and employed 150,000 workers to produce uranium 235 and plutonium without the faintest idea of their intended purpose.

In only one year, Robert Oppenheimer's bomb project had developed from a theoretical brainstorming session between close friends into the most expensive scientific venture in human history. There were no obstacles left, the major technical problems had all been solved. At the same time, the technical solutions had also provided answers to the big ethical questions – or at least made them seem redundant. For example, the first question of conscience – whether it was right to build an atom bomb just because one could – had become superfluous now that whole towns had been conjured up for that purpose, billions of dollars budgeted and 150,000 people recruited. Abandoning the project was no longer feasible, if only for financial reasons.

Although the second question of conscience – whether one should detonate an atom bomb just because one could

– had yet to be debated, Felix Bloch suspected that it, too, had already been answered. Preventing its detonation was no longer in his power, nor in that of Robert Oppenheimer, and not even the combined efforts of all the scientists in Los Alamos could now have prevailed against it. The bomb would probably still have been built even if, by some historic miracle, Roosevelt, Churchill, Hitler, Stalin and Hirohito had attended a peace conference together and jointly and sincerely sworn to renounce the bomb for evermore.

The question that did present itself anew, however, was who would be the target of America's new weapon? Until recently, every resident of Los Alamos had considered it axiomatic that a B29 bomber would drop it on Germany to terminate the Holocaust and end World War Two, but this was no longer self-evident. It had become ever clearer that the Allies would win the war with or without the atom bomb. American and British troops had landed in Sicily, Mussolini had been deposed and the Japanese Navy had been on the retreat since the Battle of Midway. Allied bombers had ignited a firestorm in Hamburg and Soviet troops were driving the Wehrmacht westwards.

Hitler's chessboard now lacked not only two rooks but both bishops as well, and he had no hope of bringing an atomic queen into play. Although Heisenberg, von Weizsäcker and Hahn were continuing to work on a uranium machine in Berlin, it was now obvious that war-weary Germany would never muster the requisite energy, manpower and raw materials to produce sufficient plutonium or uranium 235 before the war ended.

Such was the situation when Felix Bloch completed his work on the implosion detonator for which Oppenheimer had brought him to Los Alamos. Everyone else was continuing to work at top speed. Felix should now have taken on another job, for there were still a lot of minor problems to solve, but they were calculations any physics student could tackle, and Oppenheimer did not need him for that.

It became more and more probable with every passing day that the war would be over before the bomb was ready to be deployed. On Sundays, Felix and Lore went out into the wilds in search of silence and a respite from the clamour of the world. They left the twins in the care of neighbours and borrowed a car from the Tellers. Snow had already fallen in the mountains, so they left by the west gate and drove 18 kilometres along the Valle Grande, the bottom of an old volcano thickly carpeted with grass. At the entrance to Frijoles Canyon they parked the car and walked along the river bed between yellow pine, blue spruce and trembling aspen trees, where squirrels, raccoons and skunks still had no fear of humankind and the ponderosa pines grew higher than elsewhere in search of light.

Visible here and there in the perpendicular walls of the canyon were deserted, centuries-old cave dwellings dug out of the soft tuff by long extinct Indian tribes. Felix and Lore were now alone. The secret servicemen did not follow them here because contact with the outside world would have been a physical impossibility in the canyon.

When they paused to rest in silence, they could hear the rustle of autumnally weary rattlesnakes seeking a place to hibernate, and when they got to the end of the canyon, where the Frijoles joined the Rio Grande, they came to a halt and gazed in awe at the red river and the white sandbanks and the still-flowering cacti.

It must have been one day early in November 1943 when Felix called on Robert Oppenheimer at his office and requested permission to leave Los Alamos. We know nothing of the content of this conversation because Felix maintained a life-long silence about his time in Los Alamos, perhaps on account of the secrecy to which the military had pledged him, even after the war ended. There is only one reference to Los Alamos in the whole of his surviving correspondence: a telegram from the military commander, General Leslie Groves, expressly warning Felix that the end of the war had not annulled his vow of secrecy. This may be why he remained tight-lipped in the family circle as well. His children and grandchildren could not remember him ever speaking about Los Alamos, and as far as is known he only once referred to it in public.

He had gone to Los Alamos for one reason only, he told the historian of science Charles Weiner on 15 August 1968 in his office at the Institute of Physics at Stanford University, and that was because he feared the Germans would develop the bomb first. When it turned out that this was very unlikely, he had taken his leave – a step that rather annoyed some of his friends, and Oppenheimer in particular.

The day Felix and Lore Bloch were leaving, General Groves called on them at Apartment House T124 and reminded them of their obligation to maintain secrecy. Their neighbour Edward Teller had offered to drive them down to Lamy station in his own car. There was no sign of Oppenheimer when the time came for them to leave – when their luggage was already stowed in the boot of Teller's car and the twins were sitting in the back. Felix went to look for him, but he was nowhere to be found.

The drive to Lamy took two-and-a-half hours. Conversation touched on horsemeat, Orson Welles and Hungarian red wine. Other than that, there was nothing to discuss. Their goodbyes at the station were brief. The train would soon be leaving and Teller had a long drive back ahead of him. He had a date to play poker with Oppenheimer that evening.

❧

On the day after her arrest Laura d'Oriano was interrogated by officers from the Ovra. According to the record, she at first denied all active involvement in espionage and claimed to have come to Italy purely in order to visit her mother in Rome, not having seen her for years. She had made her clandestine crossing via the Col de Montgenèvre under a false name because the Italian authorities had refused her an entry visa.

The policemen then produced the letters in her handwriting, which, when ironed, had revealed secret messages. Laura thereupon made a full confession.

At the beginning of April 1942 she was transferred to the judicial prison in Turin and questioned again there. In December she was brought back to Rome. In all, she spent a year and three weeks in detention. The Axis powers were coming under ever-increasing pressure at this time, and the fascist regime felt it necessary to display internal strength.

Laura d'Oriano's trial opened at 8:30 am on Sunday, 15 January 1943. Judge Antonino Tringali Casanuova pronounced the guilty verdict the same day. The sentence was death by firing squad.

Immediately after being sentenced she was conveyed by prison van to the fortress of Bravetta on the western outskirts of Rome. At 6:15 the next morning a priest came to her cell and heard her confession. A warder brought her some breakfast – coffee and a brioche, which she had ordered the night before. Laura was then escorted to the parade ground and the commander of the firing squad read the sentence aloud. It was carried out at 07:07.

$$\mathscr{Po}$$

Émile Gilliéron's unexpected death left his family in dire financial straits. The aunts and sisters-in-law moved out, the younger children were taken in by godparents. The only people left in Rue Skoufa were his first-born son Alfred and his widow Ernesta, who continued to paint pictures of the Acropolis and endeavour to sell them. At the end of October 1940, when Italian troops invaded northern Greece, Ernesta, being Italian by birth, had to leave Athens. She and Alfred went to Italy and were initially put up in Naples by relatives. They then moved on to Rome, where Alfred became an apprentice stonemason and sculptor. It seems unlikely but cannot be entirely discounted that he unwittingly crossed Laura d'Oriano's path when she was visiting her mother in Rome at Christmas in 1941.

In 1945, when Ernesta and Alfred Gilliéron returned to Athens, they found their house in Rue Skoufa densely populated by displaced persons from all over Europe and had to reconquer it gradually, room by room. After the war Alfred carried on the family tradition and produced Minoan reproductions for well-heeled tourists. He did not, however, manage to resurrect his father's business relationship with the Württembergische Metallwarenfabrik because the firm had lost all its moulds during the war. In 1956 Alfred married a Latvian woman with the surname Rosentreter. Their only son, who was born on New Year's Day 1959, he named Émile in honour of his father and grandfather. In the mid-1960s Rue Skoufa sprouted some tall ferroconcrete buildings that soon obscured the Gilliérons' fine view of the Acropolis, so Alfred had the old villa demolished and built a modern six-storey apartment house whose top two floors he occupied with his family. His son Émile III, who studied chemistry, still lives in Rue Skoufa with his mother. The duplex is lavishly adorned with works by his father, grandfather and great-grandfather, and hanging in the drawing room is a nice oil painting by Grandmother Ernesta. It depicts the Acropolis at sunset.

After leaving Los Alamos, Felix Bloch joined Harvard University's radar project, which made an important contribution to the Allied defeat of the Axis powers. In 1945 he returned to Stanford University and resumed teaching. In research he continued to concentrate on the magnetism of the neutron. In 1952 he won the Nobel Prize for Physics for his discovery of nuclear induction, a novel method of measuring the magnetic momentum of atomic nuclei. In 1954/5 he was Director-General of CERN, the European nuclear research centre in Geneva.

Nuclear induction led straight to magnetic resonance imaging, which revolutionised medical diagnostics in the latter decades of the 20th century. It can thus be said, without exaggeration, that Felix Bloch's life work has saved many more human beings than the atom bomb destroyed.

Laura d'Oriano was the only woman in the history of the Kingdom of Italy to be condemned to death and executed. She was buried in an unmarked grave which her father, Policarpo d'Oriano, located after the war. He had her reinterred in the Campo Verano, a Roman cemetery that also houses the remains of Giusepe Garibaldi, Natalia Ginzburg and Sergio Leone. When Policarpo himself died on 8 June 1962, he was laid to rest beside her.

Until his death on 20 January 1989, Emil Fraunholz never uttered a word about the wife from whom he was never officially divorced. The girls were not allowed to mention her name. Anna, the younger of the two, performed as a singer in the 1950s, using the forename Laura, without knowing that her mother and grandmother had also sung. In 1960, however, she ran her grandfather Policarpo to earth in Rome, and it was from him she learnt that her mother had been a spy.

THE END